The traffic showed no sign of letting up, so she turned to walk the block to the main pedestrian crosswalk.

She stepped back onto the curb, but she found herself blindsided as a rush of warm, stinky liquid assaulted her. She tried to get out from under the stream and inadvertently stepped off the curb. Phoebe heard the oncoming traffic and felt paralyzed on the spot.

"Look out!"

"Skye!"

Several people cried out over the sounds of squealing breaks and car horns. Phoebe's voice joined them as her ankle cruelly twisted in the high heels, forcing her first to her knees and then hands as she landed on the asphalt. Directly perpendicular to the traffic, she didn't see but felt a car bumper hit her shoulder. Knocked on her side, she curled into a fetal position to save herself from the inevitable.

She was about to be run over.

* * *

The Coltons of Roaring Springs: Family and true love are under siege

* * *

If you're on Twitter, tell us what you think of Harlequin Romantic Suspense! #harlequinromsuspense

Dear Reader,

It was a great surprise and honor to be asked to write Phoebe and Prescott's story, *Colton's Mistaken Identity*. The Coltons of Roaring Springs, Colorado, are an enigmatic and dynamic family, with scary twists and turns around the always-sizzling chemistry each couple shares. I'm so excited to share this story with you! It was especially fun to write about a movie star and the beautiful setting of the Rocky Mountains.

I love to hear from you. Please visit my website, gerikrotow.com, sign up for my site news and newsletter, and immerse yourself in the world of Silver Valley P.D. and the Coltons that I've written for Harlequin Romantic Suspense. You can also join me on Facebook, Instagram and Pinterest.

Enjoy the read!

Peace,

Geri

COLTON'S MISTAKEN IDENTITY

Geri Krotow

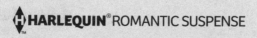

HARLEQUIN® ROMANTIC SUSPENSE

Special thanks and acknowledgment are given to Geri Krotow for her contribution to The Coltons of Roaring Springs miniseries.

Recycling programs for this product may not exist in your area.

ISBN-13: 978-1-335-66205-7

Colton's Mistaken Identity

Copyright © 2019 by Harlequin Books S.A.

This edition published by arrangement with Harlequin Books S.A.

For questions and comments about the quality of this book, please contact us at CustomerService@Harlequin.com.

www.Harlequin.com

Printed in U.S.A.

Former naval intelligence officer and US Naval Academy graduate **Geri Krotow** draws inspiration from the global situations she's experienced. Geri loves to hear from her readers. You can email her via her website and blog, gerikrotow.com.

Books by Geri Krotow

Harlequin Romantic Suspense

The Coltons of Roaring Springs

Colton's Mistaken Identity

Silver Valley P.D.

Her Christmas Protector
Wedding Takedown
Her Secret Christmas Agent
Secret Agent Under Fire
The Fugitive's Secret Child
Reunion Under Fire
Snowbound with the Secret Agent

The Coltons of Red Ridge

The Pregnant Colton Witness

The Coltons of Shadow Creek

The Billionaire's Colton Threat

Visit the Author Profile page at Harlequin.com for more titles.

To Patti McNulty,
who has never doubted my dreams.

Chapter 1

The mountains began to glow with the sunrise, and the sky's violet streaks yielded to a deeper summer blue as Phoebe Colton ran along the resort's jogging path. The Chateau stood two miles behind her, on the other side of the copse of aspen birch trees ubiquitous to Colorado.

Phoebe loved her work at The Chateau but also needed her morning run to escape the constant whirlwind that was Roaring Springs, Colorado, during its annual film festival. Her dawn workouts soothed her soul. Roaring Springs and these mountains were as much a part of her as her red hair and dimples—features she shared with her identical twin, Skye.

Why did you take off now, sister?

At the reminder that she had no freaking idea where

Skye was assaulted her, her breath broke from the easy rhythm she'd enjoyed the past hour. She slowed to a walk and forced herself to calm down.

It didn't make sense to be concerned, not to someone who didn't know Skye. Skye's jerk of a boyfriend had up and married another woman with zero warning to her, leaving Phoebe's sibling devastated. In a move so typical of her more impulsive twin, Skye had taken off with no word of where she was going.

While Phoebe totally understood Skye's need to be alone, she didn't understand why her sister had left so close to the beginning of the Roaring Springs Film Festival. The weeklong event kicked off tonight with the first red carpet event—The Chateau's welcome gala, held in The Chateau's grand ballroom, the showpiece of the Colton empire. The following days would be a blur of activity until the end of the week, when their grand ballroom would again be the venue for the star-studded award ceremony that officially closed the Roaring Springs film fest.

Skye was needed for each and every event this week, as she was the public face of the Colton empire's resort. Phoebe had to admit that Skye had created quite the social media stir, with hundreds of thousands of followers across several platforms, and she'd recently garnered a few top-earning videos featuring sponsored content. Not bad for her twenty-five-year-old sister, or for their hotel business. Even their father, Russ, normally more detached from the twins, had expressed keen enthusiasm at the power of "millennial marketing." Their mother, Mara, was more about making sure the girls—and all of her five biological children—appreciated what they'd been brought up with and did their parts to give back to the Colton efforts. Her two older cousins that Mara and Russ had raised, Fox and Sloane, were also part of the family.

Phoebe leaned against a tree and gave herself a minute to go over what was bothering her, underneath her jangling nerves about her sister being off-site. A sinister cloud of fear had lingered over Roaring Springs ever since the discovery of several murdered bodies at the base of the town's mountain. The saddest part was that one of the Avalanche Killer's victims had turned out to be their cousin, Sabrina.

Phoebe and Skye had regrouped and decided they needed to be the energy behind keeping things positive for the film festival. Skye had been so excited about making this festival work no matter the odds, especially after she learned that the online Hollywood entertainment magazine *In Film Today* was in place at The Chateau and broadcasting Skye's two red carpet events live.

Their father had certainly been pleased. Anything that spelled more money for the resort empire he'd built from the ground up thrilled the chronic workaholic.

"Give your father a break." Her mother's admonishment taunted Phoebe as she tried to not stress about her sister. It was only natural she'd blame her father for not worrying about Skye's emotional state, instead of the always-present Mara. Whereas Russ tended to be emotionally unavailable, Mara made up for it in spades. Not in the motherly attention they'd enjoyed as kids

but in her focus on keeping The Chateau the premier private resort spa in North America.

As the two youngest of five biological Colton siblings, Phoebe and Skye had been born years after their three older brothers and almost a decade after the two cousins her parents had raised as their own. Phoebe and her sister had learned to cling to one another through the thick tension that often existed between Russ and Mara, and through what often felt like strained ties with their immediate family.

Phoebe knew she could always count on Skye, one hundred and ten percent. Which was why she had to fight from allowing her concern over Skye to blossom into all-out panic. Skye was more outgoing, more engaging than Phoebe, and Phoebe liked it that way. It kept the social pressure off her. But it made a logical explanation of Skye's disappearance challenging, if not downright scary.

She rubbed her sternum through her thin running shirt. Whenever Skye hurt, she hurt. And right now her entire body was humming with worry over her sister. It wasn't the first time her "twin radar" had issued warning alerts about Skye. There was the time Skye had fallen out of a tree when they were six and Phoebe had convinced her mother that Skye's sore leg was indeed broken. And when they were seventeen, Phoebe had somehow known that Skye's homecoming date was going sour on their basement sofa and she had burst in upon her sister and that louse of a football quarterback who wasn't taking no for an answer. Despite herself, Phoebe let an evil smile flicker across her lips for a second. It had been such a sister moment to face down their high school idol–turned–potential rapist by kicking him in the privates, tying him up with zip ties from their father's work bench and then reporting him to the police. By coming forward and with Skye's brave testimony, they'd helped half a dozen other young women the athlete had threatened find justice.

But they weren't in high school anymore, and they had phones, the ability to text. Skye always texted her at least three times a day, if not more often. And she hadn't heard a thing since that last message when Skye told her she needed space to work things out. Phoebe didn't blame her sister, as she'd been almost as upset as Skye when they'd found out that Skye's serious boyfriend, a successful music producer, had gone and married the rock star whose album he'd produced. They'd married in Las Vegas and had sold exclusive rights to a celebrity magazine, which meant the photographic proof of the infidelity was unavoidable. Skye's broken heart was the topic of many gossip rags and social media posts.

Phoebe tried to distract herself from her worry by staring at the gurgling brook, where deer and birds hung out to get a sip to ease July's heat. It led to the area exclusive to the resort that housed the refurbished thermal springs spa and sauna from the 1920s. Her muscles craved a soak in the mineral baths—she'd not visited her favorite respite in far too long.

She'd lost the ability to focus on anything but her own grief the past several weeks. Ever since Sabrina had been found, brutally murdered. It was one thing to host the premiere of a violent movie that portrayed a serial killer and his victims; it was devastating for it to become real life as unspeakable violence struck her own town, her family.

The sound of broken twigs, followed by a sudden silence, sent a jolt of fear spiraling through her. Phoebe stood straighter and took stock of her surroundings, swinging her gaze over the running water, the wet stones, the woods beyond. Since she'd found out a murderer was on the loose, she hadn't felt safe. It galled her, losing the security this land had always given her. The mountain was a constant source of reliability in her life. Now its serenity was tainted by an evil serial killer.

Nothing seemed out of order as she scanned the running path, the birch and pine trees that made up the woods, the flowing brook. When a buck's hooves sounded on the forest floor, she caught sight of the animal as it sprinted not more than ten feet in front of her, fleeing an unseen predator.

Phoebe let out a shaky sigh.

It's just nature, nothing more.

She suspected the culprit for the deer's run was a fox or even a stray dog, nothing that threatened her. Midsummer wasn't hunting season, nor was it a time to worry about grizzly bears, which were busy enjoying the plentiful berries and smaller wildlife. They'd had occasional grizzly sightings over the years, but nothing too close. The bears liked to wander the mountains that surrounded their valley but rarely ventured anywhere near the Roaring Springs population.

When she'd first heard of the Avalanche Killer's activity, Phoebe had wanted to believe it was a grizzly attack. It might explain the gruesome nature of the killings, and it allowed her to deny that such a brutal murderer lived among them in their close-knit town. The killer was most likely someone they all knew, which made it so much more personal to Phoebe and her family. It also increased her constant stress, as the fear of being the killer's next victim was relentless.

Phoebe put herself under enough pressure—the last thing she needed this week was more from a lethal predator. While Skye grasped the concept of joie de vivre, Phoebe was the more sensible and grounded of the two. She rarely admitted it to Skye, but Phoebe liked the role she played in their twinship. Sure, sometimes she took herself too seriously, and wished like heck that her sister would do the same, but Phoebe never saw herself being able to behave so lightheartedly as Skye. That was why Phoebe had earned her college degree in finance in under three years, while Skye still had some courses to complete for her bachelor's.

She shuddered in the warming air, and it wasn't from her perspiration's cooling effect. She'd text Skye as soon as she got back. Once again, her twin radar was going off like fireworks. Phoebe had purposefully left her phone in her room, wanting the freedom from the constant intrusion of texts and emails about the Roaring Springs Film Festival. But now she wished she'd kept it with her.

Since the film festival was upon them, it was by far the busiest time of year for The Chateau. That said a lot, considering Roaring Springs was nestled in the heart of ski country. A film event second only to Sundance and maybe the Toronto Film Festival, the Roaring Springs Film Festival was also an important source of income for The Chateau. The resort her mother had started from the ground up years ago had turned into a literal gold mine. Until this year.

Normally they'd be sold out for almost a year in advance. But reservations had dropped since the discovery of bodies on the property, on its most striking feature, the mountain that overshadowed the beautiful valley where The Chateau was nestled.

Her parents had informed her last night that the national news outlets were about to carry the story of the Avalanche Killer, and it was stressing her out. Having the criminal reports shared word-of-mouth locally had cut into their bookings, and they'd dropped off more when the local television station reported them. The chance that their film festival earnings would tank was high.

Phoebe offered a last glance at the brook, the surrounding peace of the forest, and sent up a little prayer that there would be a text from Skye when she returned to her room. Her sister most likely wanted to talk to Phoebe about her boyfriend's unforgivable betrayal. Phoebe had never been a fan of Brock, the overly flashy record producer. Skye's relationship with him had been constant trauma-drama and now it was clear why—Brock had been lying to Skye about loving her.

As painful as life was for Skye, and as hard as the drop in reservations and thus cash flow was for The Chateau, the film festival would go on. Phoebe's days would be filled with taking care of the guests who showed up. And fortunately, the movie companies were still showing off their best and most promising works, regardless of the Avalanche Killer. That meant that the actors and actresses would appear, and along with them, their fans. Maybe the rooms weren't all filled yet, but Phoebe sent up an affirmation that they would be, soon.

She squared her shoulders and began to run back to The Chateau. To her work, her family, her life.

Prescott Reynolds saw the lithe woman with striking, flame-red hair as she ran up to the edge of the brook. Her ponytail reached between her shoulder blades, which meant her unbound hair would be at her waist. An image of scarlet waves flowing over her creamy naked shoulders struck him, and he mentally batted it aside. This wasn't a time to entertain his libido, not with a probable crazed fan on his tail. He mentally caught himself up short. He assumed this was a fan, he was so used to his struggle to get solitude. Maybe the redhead was just another nature lover.

"Don't ever let your guard down." His security detail's implicit instructions reminded him that he'd not alerted them that he was coming out here this morning, alone.

The redhead's footsteps had alerted him that he wasn't alone on his hike, setting off his anger.

He was upstream of the attractive redhead, on the other side of the creek, by at least twenty yards. It was twenty yards too close, though. She stood stock-still, as if she'd seen a ghost, but he didn't trust her, didn't trust any other human being who "happened" to show up when he was trying to live a normal, private life.

He'd come out for an early-morning hike to escape the cacophony of the Roaring Springs Film Festival. From the first ping of his phone at dawn until he excused himself from the last social event of the evening, he was never alone. Usually he rolled with PR junkets like the professional he'd become, but in the midst of healing his sore heart, he despised the promotional part of his job.

What he really resented, though, was his privacy being invaded, especially by an innocent-looking woman. He'd been burned enough times to know better. There were no coincidences when you were one of Hollywood's highest-paid actors.

He stood behind the nearest tree and decided to wait for the redhead to make her move. Maybe he'd play naive for a bit before he told her in no uncertain terms that not only was he not interested, but his security detail would be happy to provide her name and contact information to the local sheriff.

It's your nerves.

True, he'd been on edge since thinking his ex might be stalking him, but it wasn't as if his concern wasn't justified. A young woman was literally yards from him, and he'd heard her nearby footsteps as she approached, running, then slowed to a walk more in rhythm with his stride.

Maybe you're being paranoid.

Anger swelled at the constant need for vigilance.

He'd known PR and media attention was all a part of pursuing his life's passion, but there were days he had to ask himself if it was all worth it.

Take a breather.

Prescott wasn't unmoved by the beauty around him, and as he waited for this possible latest superfan to try her hand at charming him, he distracted himself with a family of woodpeckers. As he watched, two large black-and-white birds with red crowns pecked voraciously at various tree trunks, then flew to a hidden nest in a nearby tree. He heard the peeps of the woodpecker chicks, and if he hadn't been intent on confronting the interloper, he would have taken the time to try to snap some photos with his phone.

After twenty minutes, the woman finally moved from where she'd stood practically motionless, as if meditating. He wasn't fooled and braced himself for the confrontation. He was tired of running from life and from his haters. This overzealous fan had picked the wrong day to mess with him.

Before he had a chance to look into the woman's eyes, she turned and ran. Not toward him, but in the opposite direction. As if she'd never seen him. As if he, Prescott Reynolds, weren't her obsession. As if she'd just been someone out for a morning workout and had taken a break by the running water. Hadn't he done the same?

The chuckle started deep in his gut, so rare since his abominable breakup with Ariella Forsythe last year. At first he wondered if he was losing it. But as he laughed at himself, admitted to himself that he wasn't the center of everyone's universe, he felt the tightness in his chest ease up. Hadn't his mother always told him he took himself too seriously?

The unexpected relief that rushed through him was as cool and calming as the mountain stream. It'd been too long since he'd simply relaxed, stopped thinking about disastrous breakups or crazed fans. It was time he let go and enjoyed being plain old Prescott, the Iowa farm boy who was lucky to have had a big Hollywood break.

He ran his fingers over the smooth white aspen bark. Maybe this film festival wouldn't be so bad. There was the problem of the Avalanche Killer making national headlines, but he faced more danger walking down a busy street in LA. At least in Roaring Springs he had his security detail with him, and the opportunity to draw on the beauty of the stunning valley surrounded by such powerful mountains. He needed all the peace and tranquility he could get.

Ariella adjusted the climbing belt and dug her spikes into the tree trunk. Thank goodness for the free-climbing and rappelling classes she'd taken at REI; they'd enabled her to keep tabs on Prescott no matter where he went.

He'd almost caught her, thanks to the stupid bitch who'd been running on the same trail he hiked. Another woman hoping to get into Prescott's bed and have him declare how much he needed her, she was certain.

Her cheeks pulled tight as her lip curled. Prescott had been so gulliblc. He'd truly believed that she'd loved him. And she supposed that she had, as much as she could feel for anyone. When he'd told her he loved her, though, she knew he meant it. Unlike her, Prescott was able to give a damn about other people.

All she cared about was winning what she wanted. And what Ariella *really* coveted was Prescott's pull and influence in the entertainment industry. His salaries had gone up by the millions for each film, along with his clout. Exactly what a girl like her needed to get her career going in the right direction.

Poor Prescott had been so righteously angry when she'd admitted she'd been screwing Donald Channing, another actor on their film set over a year ago. He'd left in a huff and then stopped taking her calls and texts. Said he was done with her.

But she wasn't done with him, and Ariella was certain that once she presented Prescott with her plan, he'd agree to again partner with her. That had been her one mistake—she hadn't let him in on her career plans right from the start.

He wasn't going to come easily, though. It'd be impossible to get him to meet with her and have a calm adult discussion. Ariella knew it would be risky, but she was determined to win Prescott back, even if it meant officially kidnapping him to get him in the same room as her.

And getting rid of women like the redhead who were in her way.

Chapter 2

"Have you heard from Skye this morning, sweetheart?" Mara Colton was already dressed in her work clothes, which meant she looked like she'd just stepped out of a boardroom. Her navy suit was official looking enough to give her mom the impression of measured control over what they both knew could erupt into total chaos with one wrong decision. They planned all year for the Roaring Springs Film Festival and worked well together, but this year felt different. Between Skye's failed romance, the Avalanche Killer, and the loss of revenue due to the latter, nothing was going as usual.

"No, not since she told me she needed some space." Phoebe wiped her brow with the bottom edge of her running shirt. "Don't worry, Mom. She's had a rough breakup, and you know how she takes them."

"'Space' is not an option, with the press arriving today. What on earth are we going to do if she's not here to handle tonight's event?"

Mara's concern made the tiny lines around her mouth deepen, and Phoebe hated that her twin was putting her mother through this. It was one thing to go all trauma-drama when you were a teenager, or even in college, but at twenty-five it seemed a little excessive.

Not that Phoebe could relate. Skye had always enjoyed a healthy dating life, her outgoing nature attracting men like adrenaline junkies to the high mountains that surrounded The Chateau. As the quieter twin, Phoebe normally didn't have a problem with her more introverted personality, but she was starting to wonder when she'd have more than the more casual relationships with men she'd enjoyed so far. She wasn't sexually inexperienced, but it'd be nice to have a man who wanted something more. Something lasting.

While she tried to think of how to answer her mother, a skinny boy of thirteen came barreling around the corner, followed by a rosy-faced toddler.

"Hey, Phoebe!" Joshua pulled up short and looked over his shoulder to make sure the little girl was with him. "Come on, Chloe."

"Good morning, you two." Phoebe gave Josh a quick hug and then bent down to lift Chloe into her arms. She buried her nose into the baby curls, savoring the sweet scent.

"Grandma, can me and Chloe go to the playground? I'll make sure she doesn't climb too high." Josh was Phoebe's nephew and the son of her brother Blaine, who'd just returned from his military stint. They'd all only met recently, as no one had known that Joshua's mother, Tilda, gave birth to Blaine's son back in high school. Russ and Mara were proving much warmer grandparents than they had been parents, and immediately wrapped Joshua in unconditional love. Still, it was disconcerting to hear him call Mara "grandma." Phoebe smiled and poked at Chloe's stomach. "Who has a cute tummy?"

Chloe's squeal of delight warmed Phoebe and chased away her worries about Skye. Chloe was the daughter of her cousin Sloane, the woman Russ and Mara had raised as their own. Both children were the first grandkids for Russ and Mara, and it showed in how very spoiled they were whenever they came to the resort.

"Phoebe. We need to settle how we're going to fix this." Mara hugged Joshua to her as she spoke, her eyes softening for the young teen.

Chloe started to squirm, her legs kicking like all getout, and Phoebe reluctantly set her back down.

"You two go on ahead, I'll have Lania meet you there." Mara spoke to Joshua, referring to the nanny she'd hired to help during festival week.

"Thanks, Grandma! See you, Aunt Phoebe!" Joshua and Chloe sped off, the toddler's legs furiously pedaling to keep up with her older cousin. Mara placed a quick call on her cell. She instructed the nanny to text the minute she arrived at the playground. With the Avalanche Killer on the loose, there was no such thing as being too careful.

When Mara turned to face Phoebe, she was ready with the best answer to ward off her mother's inevitable freak-out.

"Skye will be back in time, Mom. I'll text her in a bit and see where she's at."

"You remember that I still need you in the ballroom by nine this morning, right?"

Phoebe looked at her watch. "Yes, and that leaves me another two hours to shower, eat and show up."

"And I thought we agreed you weren't going to go running by yourself until everything gets cleared up?" Mara reminded her.

Great. Now her mother was turning her angst on the nearest target—Phoebe.

"Mom. There's no safer place on the planet, second only to maybe downtown Roaring Springs. I never went off the main path, and it was light by the time I took off." She opted to not mention the creepy feeling she had of being watched, nor the sounds of breaking twigs that she'd been afraid might have been some unseen trespasser. Her imagination had always been on hyperdrive, a byproduct of having her nose in a book since she was a kid. Her reading tastes ran the gamut of genres, but her favorites remained thriller and horror.

"Sabrina thought it was a safe place, too." Mara's mention of her niece and Phoebe's cousin hit Phoebe square in the heart. She winced, wishing the pain would somehow ease and then immediately felt guilty. Sabrina Gilford hadn't been given a chance to escape the pain and suffering of her murder. What right did

Phoebe have to even consider complaining about her own life?

"I'm not going to win this conversation, Mom. Let me get something to eat and I'll see you in the ballroom later."

"Wait a minute, sweetheart." Mara's normal businesslike tone was tinged with concern.

"Yes, Mom?"

"You need to be prepared. If this is one of Skye's more prolonged relationship-grieving periods, she might not be back in time for tonight. I'll need you to step up." Mara's words made Phoebe's heart stutter. Skye wouldn't leave them in the lurch, not with the opening gala tonight, would she?

Her clenched jaw told her the truth. Skye could take breakup misery to a whole new level, and there was a good possibility she'd back out of tonight if she truly didn't feel up to the task. But it wasn't something Phoebe wanted to reveal to her mother, who always bore the brunt of the festival's pressure each year. She forced a smile, made her stance more relaxed and put a hand on her mother's shoulder.

"Mom, we've been through this. Skye is the face of The Chateau's marketing. She's a natural at dealing with the public and especially the press. I'm the depth of our team. Like when I ran cross country in high school and college. I never was the fastest, but Coach could always count on me." And she never wanted to be in front of a television camera, not willingly. The thought of having to stand in front of the gauntlet of reporters, all craving the latest and greatest gossip on the featured actors, was more frightening than the scariest novel she'd ever read. "Trust me, Mom. You don't want me doing one bit of her job."

"Coltons don't quit, Phoebe." Mara clearly had her teeth sunk into the idea that Phoebe could instantaneously replace Skye, and she balked.

"Wait a minute—I'm not the one who took off with a broken heart. I'm right here, Mom, standing in front of you. Please don't put this on me. If on the very *tiny* chance Skye isn't here in time, we can ask one of the hotel management interns to step in. It'd be the best training for them, and we can let the press know we're giving an intern from another part of the country a great opportunity."

Mara's mouth gaped. "You've had your nose buried in our financial books far too long, Phoebe. There is no way on earth I'd allow an intern to do Skye's job. Not during the festival, anyhow. It's too risky, even if we'd taken the last month to train them."

"Mom, we're wasting time here. Skye will be back on time—we can count on her for professional commitments." And they could. Skye never missed a work appointment.

"Let's hope you're right and she shows up in time to get ready for the red carpet. For now, I'd feel much better if you'd plan on handling the press briefing at three. If Skye is back by then, great, no problem. If not, however, you'll be ready to go."

Mara wasn't budging, and Phoebe couldn't really blame her. More like her mother when it came to planning, Phoebe preferred a sense of direction and purpose. With no surprises. Once again, her heart cracked a little, seeing her mother's anxiety during what was normally a time of year they all looked forward to.

"Fine." She blew a long breath out of her mouth. "I'll look over her notes after my shower. Just in case."

"Thank you, sweetheart." Mara turned and walked away, and Phoebe wished for once she was the more outgoing sister. The one who'd tell their mom that no way in heck was she going to talk to the press or corral the VIPs into the ballroom. She'd honestly be content to play the shadow sister for the rest of her life. It might mean she didn't get the accolades that Skye enjoyed, but she'd have peace of mind.

Are you sure? Maybe this is a chance to show your mettle.

"Whatever." Phoebe grumbled to herself as she went to her apartment, a collection of rooms in a private residential wing of the hotel. Skye had better show up sooner than later. Otherwise Phoebe was going to be pretending to be her sister, something she hadn't done since high school, when Skye skipped two classes to go skiing with her boyfriend of the week. Because, ultimately, she knew that she'd never be able to stop her mother from getting what she wanted. Mara Colton was a force of nature all to herself.

Before she stepped into the shower, Phoebe sent off a quick text to Skye. She'd give her sister until noon to get it together and come back to work. Skye knew how important the next several days were, and no matter how shattered her heart was, she'd never put the Colton family in a rough position.

Unless something really wrong was going on. Phoebe's twin radar wasn't firing off as it had earlier, but it wasn't giving her any warm fuzzies, either.

It's because Skye's upset over being dumped.

"Well, two can play at this game." Phoebe spoke to herself as she got under the hot stream of water. Closing her eyes, she focused on her gut and envisioned the invisible cord that connected her to her twin. Once she had a solid mental image of the thread, she yanked on it, as if this would alert Skye to the fact that her twin needed her. "It's your turn to feel my pain, Skye. Get back here now."

Skye did feel Phoebe's mental nudge, Phoebe assumed, because when she got out of the shower, her twin's response was on her phone.

Sorry but still can't come back. Need more time. Thanks for handling it all for me. Xx

Phoebe's wet hair dripped water onto her phone as she fired a quick text.

No choice—we need you. Be here by noon, no later!

Her finger wavered over the emoji keyboard, wondering if their tried and true symbol would work its magic this time. She hadn't used it since freshman year in college, when she'd found out her roommate was sleeping with the boy she'd hoped to spend the weekend with. Phoebe looked at herself in the steamy mirror and realized that Mara would have to take her from her current nondescript style to Skye's over-the-top motif. That would mean cutting at least nine inches off her hair and wearing tons of sparkling makeup and equally glittery clothing. *No, thanks.* Without further hesitation, Phoebe texted back, Get back here or Mara's going to be the end of me.

She added the barfing emoji symbol and pressed the send arrow. Skye would know how stressed Phoebe was because she'd referred to Mom by her first name, something they never did to her face.

Prescott had to admit that if he had to deal with his business manager's constant pressure to make it appear that he was leading the life expected of a successful actor, it was best done from the balcony of his VIP suite. The warm air was dry and the colors of the mountain sharp.

As was his tone with Jon, his manager, but he was determined to be himself as much as possible, without falling prey to the trappings of celebrity.

"I'm here to promote the premiere of the film we've worked so hard on." Prescott didn't want to add the implied period at the end of his statement. Jon knew the deal.

"We're only saying that it's been a year since your big breakup with Ariella, and it would be nice if your fans saw that you'd moved on. Plus it will underscore who was the villain in that relationship." By *we*, Jon meant not only Prescott's agent and the business staff but also the director of the film being showcased in the festival.

"I don't give a—" He stopped himself. Regrouped. Made his mind go back to this morning's hike. The aspens, the breeze, the cute redhead… "You know I'm going to do the best job I can while I'm out here. You also know that press junkets aren't my forte, but I'm not the worst. As for my ex, she's not stopped bashing me every chance she gets. I think her reputation speaks for itself."

"Just make sure you keep up with your security detail." Jon's reminder was warranted—some strange things had happened over the past several months, from weird packages being mailed to his home to random scathing voice mails from Ariella herself. But Prescott still didn't like to dwell on it.

"The team's here, and we're talking. I won't go anywhere without them, save for my room." Which, as it was located in The Chateau, was surrounded by the top security in the business. "I am grateful to stay here this year, away from the throngs. Thanks for setting it up for me."

"You've earned it, and it's a nice break from being in downtown Roaring Springs. As small as that town is, it explodes into a mini–New York City for the film festival."

Prescott agreed. "Jon, I'm sorry if I'm coming off like a dick. I'd hoped that Ariella and our breakup would be far behind me by now."

"Sometimes the media can't let go of it, Prescott.

Either way, anything you can do to be seen with other single women this week would be a plus."

Prescott ended the call and any thoughts of finding another actress to connect with. He'd carefully avoided any romantic commitments this entire year, keeping dates to one-night events and eschewing the Hollywood social scene. His ex had done the exact opposite, including getting herself kicked out of bars and fired from her last film set. No wonder she'd amped up her attempts to get his attention—he'd only ever been a celebrity ticket to her.

If he were to ever get involved with another woman again, as more than a sexual interest, it wouldn't be with a celebrity.

That had to be why the image of the redheaded runner kept flitting through his mind. She'd been attractive, mysterious, and he hadn't recognized her as anyone involved in the industry.

Prescott didn't believe in fate.

He looked around the view of the resort property from his balcony and absorbed as much of the good nature vibes as he could. A small movement in one of the trees caught his eye and he set his mug down, intent to spy a bear or large raptor. It was impossible to tell what he'd noticed from this far away, though, as the tree line began a full half mile from the The Chateau.

Who was he kidding? The tight knot of apprehension in his gut hadn't loosened since Ariella had begun her constant attempts to reconnect with him. Now he was getting paranoid, feeling as though she was around every corner, in each dark shadow that crossed his path. She didn't have the money to travel here, much less stay in Roaring Springs during the film festival.

No matter how much he tried to approach his anxiety with logic, it never left. Ariella had done more than scar his heart—she'd taught him that you never really knew a person even after you'd lived with them.

Chapter 3

The rest of Phoebe's morning went as planned, with several short meetings with the event staff and regular team to ensure everyone knew what was expected of them. She'd gotten through the ballroom meeting with Mara and told her mother that Skye had texted her back. But she didn't tell her mother exactly what her twin had said, hoping to delay Mara's descent into festival madness.

At ten minutes past noon, however, there was no more stalling. Skye still hadn't answered back and was nowhere in sight. So she'd been forced to spill the beans to her mom.

Phoebe gritted her teeth. She was going to make Skye pay the next time she saw her. Maybe for that nice pair of leather-strap sandals she'd been eyeing in The Chateau's boutique. They were still expensive with their employee discount, but since Skye's departure at the worst time for the festival meant maximum distress for Phoebe, she figured it was the least her sister could do.

However, for now, she had to survive her mother's attempts at making her look like her twin.

"Hold still." Mara waved a pair of very sharp shears too close to Phoebe's eyes.

"Please, Mom, let Amber do it." They were in The Chateau's spa, and Mara had actually canceled a regular client's standing appointment so that Amber could fit Phoebe in. Mara's dismissal of a client's needs underscored the absolute necessity for the festival to go off without a hitch.

"I've got it." Amber, the spa's most congenial employee, took the scissors from Mara and motioned for Mara to stand back. She smiled at Phoebe, her white teeth stunning against her dark skin. "We'll have you Skye-a-fied in no time." They'd let Amber in on what had to happen. It would be bad PR for word to get out that Skye was out of the area for any reason, and most importantly, Mara didn't want it to be discovered that Skye had been dumped in such a shoddy manner. To avoid in-depth explanations, it was easiest to let Phoebe play Skye for the immediate future. With so little time and such huge stakes at hand, there was no choice. Although Phoebe would have preferred to keep Mara's shenanigans on the covert side. If she was going to commit a huge deception, she didn't want everyone to know about it.

"This is crazy. It'll never work. And Skye's going to show up at any minute." Her voice sounded a lot more confident than she felt.

"We can't count on that, Phoebe." Mara spoke as Amber snipped away at her crimson locks, the same shade as her twin's but much longer and straighter. Phoebe wore her hair long and sleek and couldn't be bothered to blow-dry and curl it for the time it took Skye to get her perfectly natural-looking hairdo to fan perfectly around her face and shoulders. She watched her sodden locks drop onto the protective salon cape that draped from her shoulders and she wanted to scream.

"It's official. I'm going to kill my sister."

"This isn't the time to talk like that." Mara's quick admonishment made Phoebe cringe. Her mother had been through enough and had the weight of the festival launch event on her shoulders. "It's only the first day of the festival, and after you cover the press conference and gala red carpet, Skye will no doubt come waltzing in and take over the rest of the week."

"You're right. I'm sorry, Mom. Ow!" Sharp pains ran from her skull to her nape as Amber used a wide-tooth comb on the back of her hair.

"Sorry, hon, but you've got a snag back here."

"Don't worry about it. Just cut away. As long as we got the long ponytail in one piece to donate for children's wigs, I don't care what you have to do now." Phoebe had been meaning to cut her hair for the last several months and she'd found a charity that accepted long lengths to make wigs that helped out kids going through chemo treatments.

"You're a champ for doing this for us on such short notice, Amber." Mara at least had the decency to look apologetic to the hairstylist. As if reading Phoebe's thoughts, she turned her gaze back to her in the mirror. "You, too, sweetheart. I know you're already swamped with all the extra business this month."

"You're the one who trained me, Mom. Stepping up is what a Colton does." Besides, most of what she did was via financial software. Once she set up an event, the invoices usually tracked pretty seamlessly. Automatically. Unlike today, so far.

"We can't afford to make a public mistake. Not with the reservations down and the bad news trying to stomp out the good PR we planned for the festival."

"I understand, I really do. It'll work out, Mom. It always does." Phoebe tried to reconcile the image that emerged with each cut of Amber's shears to her response. Skye was naturally upbeat and would have sat here laughing at their mom's concerns, cheering her up in a flash, unlike Phoebe, who considered herself more like a quiet strength in the family.

Maybe being Skye for a bit wouldn't be so bad. It might break her out of the social and dating rut she'd been in over the past few months.

"Are the biggest actors here yet?" Phoebe didn't think she'd be able to pull a real Skye move and personally introduce herself to the key players ahead of the gala, but she did want to be prepared.

"Not officially." Mara watched as Phoebe transformed into Skye. Amber had started to blow-dry her hair using a ridiculously huge round brush, and both Mara and Phoebe were shouting over the dryer's roar.

"But?"

Mara shrugged as she watched Amber brush out a long length of hair close to Phoebe's temple and curl it backward, aiming the dryer nozzle to set the curl. "Several have checked in under their assumed names."

"Do we have Mr. Sherlock Holmes or Ms. Elizabeth Bennett here?"

"No, nothing that obvious."

"Mom? Who is it?" It wasn't like Mara to be cagey or without information she could trust Phoebe with.

"The lead."

"Prescott Reynolds?" Immediately the image of two aquamarine-blue eyes flashed in front of her mind's eye. They drew her attention every time she saw a photo of the actor, or caught one of his movies. Tall, with dark hair and a cut body that he'd partially bared in more than one romantic scene, he fit the description of "tall, dark and handsome" but she sensed something else there, maybe true depth to his personality that so far, many of the men she'd dated had lacked. Not that she'd ever admit it to anyone. Phoebe wasn't one for celebrity culture and gossip—that was more Skye's department. But he had starred in several historical dramas that she'd adored, not only for the beautiful settings and superb cinematography.

"Yummy." Amber didn't hide her opinion of the Oscar-nominated star.

"Yes." Mara spoke so quietly it was only the movement of her lips that conveyed her response over the hair dryer's noise. She looked at her with the same eyes Phoebe and Skye had. "Prescott is here already, but I haven't seen him."

"Well, we'll meet him tonight." Which was soon enough for her. Skye was going to show up, wasn't she?

Not if Phoebe went by her twin's last text.

Amber clicked off the dryer. "Okay, close your eyes while I spray."

She closed her eyes and tried to relax as Amber doled out what felt like half a container of hairspray onto her "Skye" coif. After she was done, her mother and Amber fussed over her makeup application, matching her style exactly to Skye's. While they were indeed identical twins, their personalities reflected in clothing styles as well as hair and makeup preferences. Skye loved more sparkling shades of eye shadow and lipstick, while Phoebe gravitated toward a more natural, polished look. And while Phoebe had intended to cut her hair after the festival, her cut would have been a fun chin-length bob, not the longish layers that required hot rollers and half a paycheck's worth of hairspray.

It didn't matter, though, as she'd peeked at the finished style and figured cutting off several more inches to attain the bob wouldn't be a problem. She'd just have to wait until either Skye returned or the festival ended.

Annoyance flashed in her gut. Why was she so agreeable all the time?

"Here, let's use Skye's favorite perfume on you." Her mother plucked a round glass bottle from the spa's vanity.

Phoebe held up her hands, causing Amber to freeze midair with the mascara wand. "No. I am not going to smell like Skye. Look like her, act like her, fine. Please hand me the clear bottle, that one." She pointed at her favorite scent, a very light floral with tones of linen. Skye's signature scent was musky and overtly sensual. Phoebe liked it, too—on Skye.

For the next hour Phoebe could pretend that the worst thing facing The Chateau and the Coltons was her having to pose as her twin. It was impossible to forget the ever-present fear that smothered her positive ideas whenever she wondered why Skye hadn't texted back again. Her thoughts kept jumping to the horrible conclusion that the Avalanche Killer had somehow found Skye and harmed her.

Stop it. She texted back, she's fine.

Yeah, staying present by helping Mara and Amber pick out the makeup Skye would wear was a *much* better place to stay in.

Prescott liked his private time but could only stay in his hotel room for so long. He'd checked in to The Chateau last night under an assumed name, as he didn't want the staff fussing over him before the big premiere. The staff knew their jobs well and never blinked when he'd presented his credit card. He'd noticed a few extra glances here and there, but no one had approached him for a selfie, and no camera phones had been aimed at him. None that he could see, anyway.

The hotel was remarkable. Unlike so many high-end places he'd stayed in around the world, The Chateau wasn't just a catchy name. The entire building was styled like a French countryside manor, only larger. The huge fieldstone hearth in the entrance lobby looked like the perfect place to relax après ski, and it proved a good space to hunker down on an overstuffed leather chair, his baseball cap pulled low to hide his face. The coffee was excellent, and he'd enjoyed an espresso this morning but now was sipping a freshly made iced tea. He'd have to go upstairs to his room in a few minutes and get ready for the gala tonight, but right now he was enjoying people watching.

Prescott liked people, and he gained tremendous satisfaction from playing different characters on film and stage. His film career had soared over the past five years, but given his druthers he'd take a stage production any day.

The dream he'd nurtured for the past year or so was to open a summer theater back in his Iowa hometown. A place for young kids like he'd been to go and find themselves amid the rich stories playwrights provided, from Greek tragedy to contemporary, avant-garde works.

A flash of red, the distinct shade he'd first laid eyes on this morning in the copse of aspen trees, caught his attention. The same woman he'd seen on the trail walked past him and began to climb the stairs to the grand ballroom. He knew where the impressive stairs led, as he'd already memorized the layout of the hotel. His privacy had necessitated he know every nook and cranny to escape to if the paparazzi became rabid.

She wasn't in running clothes any longer, and her

hair was styled to show off the unique hue. From her profile he saw that she was wearing makeup, a little much for his taste, but he was used to being around women who enjoyed dolling themselves up. It was all part of being an actor.

This woman intrigued him when she shouldn't. And yet as she'd walked by, oblivious to him, he'd caught a whiff of floral perfume that captured him like a trout in a net. The sight of her profile again, this time with makeup on and offset by the backdrop of the luxurious resort, struck a chord deep inside him. Prescott wasn't a stranger to immediate attraction but this took it to a new place for him. Besides the obvious physical pull of her beauty, he sensed the potential for something deeper, more meaningful, between them.

What the heck was going on with him?

She wasn't wearing anything exciting, and her business suit didn't show off her curves as well as her workout clothing had. Still, in the view he had of her backside, there was no denying her very feminine shape under the jacket and dress pants. Insta-lust made him pause, not wanting to get an erection in public.

You've been alone too long.

After what he'd been through with his ex, he knew better than to even look twice at this stunning woman. But he couldn't help himself. Truth be told, he hadn't been able to stop thinking about her. Nor how relieved he'd felt when he'd realized she wasn't trailing him. It was always in the back of his mind that Ariella could show up again, and her penchant for ugliness wasn't something he relished. He'd been drawn to Ariella's intelligence and quick wit. And it had worked for a while, until her true nature of career-climbing at the expense of the men in her life reappeared. Or maybe he'd simply come out of his denial about her dark side. Either way, it had been a rough go of it for his dating life ever since.

But the redhead… His gut told him to go after her.

He didn't entertain the rational side of his brain that told him he was out of his league. That not everyone was impressed by actors, not that he ever consciously used his job or status to seduce a woman. He believed more in allowing an attraction to grow organically.

This inexplicable urge to talk to the stranger, the only redhead he'd seen at The Chateau, was definitely organic on his part. But would she think he was odd?

What if she wasn't available? Preston stopped midway up the staircase. He hadn't even considered that she might be with someone already. Hell, she could even be married.

Chill, dude.

Prescott hadn't had to go after a woman in years. And he missed it. The constant attention from the opposite sex had been heady when he'd arrived in Hollywood and been cast in his first roles ten, twelve years ago. But it quickly grew old, and he didn't want to spend time with someone who only saw him as an actor. The redhead clearly worked here or had a role to play in the film fest, so she was probably used to celebrities. Would she see past the Caribbean-blue eyes that had become his trademark? Not that he'd ever expected to be known for his eyes. His dream wasn't even so much to be recognized for his acting as to be give the opportunities to bring meaningful roles to life. He wasn't a fan of the celebrity culture that came with it but he understood it was all part of the gig. Except when he wanted a woman to see him as more than a contender for a tabloid's annual sexiest man.

He walked through open, massive carved oak doors and into the hotel's pièce de résistance—the grand ballroom. The floor was entirely parquet but covered with a huge red carpet that ran into its center, where the area delineated for dancing remained clear. Hundreds if not a full thousand round tables framed the open area, the crystal chandeliers catching the fading sunlight, their bulbs still dim. Soon they'd be bright and the room a cacophony of press, actors, studio executives and the teams of people it took to make it all happen.

It was that rare quiet moment before a major event launched. Right now it was hushed as workers rapidly set tables and moved last-minute lighting equipment into place. A DJ set up in a far corner of the room, her control panel as large as any he'd ever seen in a concert. But in another hour and a half, it would burst to life with an entirely different personality.

Prescott liked the quiet anticipation before an event. As much as he enjoyed the slow build of desire as he met and wooed a woman into his bed.

The redhead stood alone in the middle of the room, silently moving her lips as she read from her phone. Her running clothes were gone but she hadn't upgraded her look that much, wearing easy black pants and a simple pale pink silk shell. Her skin was dewy, and as he'd already noticed she liked her makeup heavy, but on her stunning features it only emphasized her beauty.

His running shoes, silent on the plush carpet, hit the parquet floor, and a loud squeak sounded. The woman gasped as she startled and dropped her phone onto the carpet. Her caramel-brown eyes lasered in on him, and he knew how a bug felt under a magnifying glass. But it was more like an ant under a sunbeam as heat immediately flared in his chest, rushing toward his groin. The woman was so damned beautiful, from her glorious red hair to her full lush lips, down to her full breasts and hips. He couldn't remember the last time he'd been so smitten, from the get-go.

Because you never have been.

He held up his hands. "I'm sorry. I didn't mean to scare you." He bent down and retrieved her phone, on which he saw notes displayed before he handed it back to her.

"I-I'm not…scared." She cleared her throat, and he had to consciously force his gaze from the creamy skin of her neck to her eyes. He swore he already knew what she'd taste like, how her soft skin would give under the pressure of his lips.

"What can I do for you?" She'd been surprised by his appearance but recovered quickly. The immediate shock in her brown eyes was already replaced by cool assessment. Yup, definitely someone used to working with celebrities. And not easily impressed, he'd guess.

"I'm Prescott —"

"I know who you are, Mr. Reynolds. Is there something you need before tonight's premiere?" Her tone burst with brusque efficiency, but all he could see was the way her pink-glossed lips formed the words.

"You didn't notice, but this morning we were both on the hiking trail."

"You mean the running path?" She bit her lower lip, and her cheeks flushed under the makeup. Why did she have an expression of guilt on her feminine features? "Sorry, but I'm not a runner. You must have seen my twin sister, Phoebe. She, ah, goes for a few miles every morning. I'm more of a night owl. Did you enjoy your time on the property?"

"Yes, of course." He waved his hand around, motioning at the room. "This entire place is amazing. It's easy to feel like I'm in the middle of Normandy or Burgundy while I'm here." Too late he realized what a snob he sounded like. His global travel was a direct privilege of his celebrity status, and the Iowa farm boy inside him cringed at his careless mention of a destination so few ever afforded.

"Thank you. I'll pass that on to my parents. Is there something else?" There was an air of impatience, no, make that *desperation* about her as she repeated her question. Maybe she had to practice red carpet introductions, or there had been some last-minute disruptions to the festival's launch gala.

"Actually, it's me who'd like to do something for you. What did you say your name was?"

Most women were impressed enough by this point to at least show a spark of appreciation in their gaze. But not this woman. She actually hesitated before she answered, as if reluctant to let him know anything so personal. Talk about the tables being turned.

The warmth in his center from her nearness exploded into something he hadn't felt in a long while. Joy.

Prescott realized that he'd sorely missed having a woman turn him on his head. Maybe this film festival wasn't going to be the laborious weeklong junket that he'd resigned himself to.

"I'm Skye Colton, the resort's marketing director." She held out a slim hand, and he took it. As they shook he was again distracted, this time by the silky softness of her skin that contrasted sharply with the firmness of her grip. "Pleased to meet you."

"Not as pleased as I am. Call me Prescott, please." He loved how she grasped his hand like a boss. She'd be incredible in bed, he instinctively knew. But what stunned him was that he wasn't interested in that, not right now. Well, maybe he was completely enthralled by how seductive her mere presence was, but he was feeling something very different from first-meet attraction. Something more palpable.

All Prescott wanted was to get to know Skye Colton better. Suddenly his seven-day junket in Roaring Springs felt as if it was already half over. There would never be enough time to know this woman the way he wanted to.

But damned if he wouldn't give it his best shot.

Phoebe knew she gripped Prescott's hand too tightly, but to his credit the man didn't even wince. She'd had no choice, as there was no other way to hide her nervousness. Thank goodness she'd wiped her palm on her pants before she'd shaken his. Otherwise he'd have known how rattled she was.

The photos and films didn't do this man justice. Not even close. She'd never had a *zing* of awareness when she'd seen him on the big screen, nor had she grown wet with pure feminine need as she'd watched his performances. Standing so near to him, it was a shock to her that his star status wasn't at play. She felt as she would with a non-celebrity man she was attracted to. Except her reaction was so far over the top. Between his deep voice, his words that made her feel like she was the only woman in the room, and the confidence in his posture and body language that hinted at his athleticism, her knees felt like her mother's pepper jelly. All wobbly but with heat washing over her skin, making her want to run away before she did what her hormones were begging for: to kiss Prescott Reynolds right here in the ballroom and tell him to follow her to her room.

This must be what groupies feel like, and why they go after movie and rock stars.

This had to be some kind of sexual overreaction due to the morning's upheaval caused by Skye's disappearance.

Prescott flashed his familiar white-toothed I-leave-hearts-crushed-with-every-footstep grin that she recognized from his film promos and it snapped it out of her sexual trance.

It was nothing like the smile she'd witnessed in her favorite work of his —an historical period piece where he'd played a struggling artist amid the French Revolution. While his smile was part of his trademark good looks, as he looked at her, she was aware that there was more to this man than his celebrity. And he knew how to turn it on and off, not a virtue of many people she'd met who lived in the spotlight.

"Okay, then. Nice to meet you, Prescott."

"Nice to meet you, too, Skye." Phoebe didn't like lying, *ever*, yet as she stood in the middle of the grand ballroom, her hair and makeup perfectly done in Skye's signature style, it was surprisingly easy to fall into the role. Save for Skye's effervescent presence. And extreme comfort around attractive, powerful men.

"You must be very excited for tonight. I'll be announcing each of you, I mean the VIPs, as you arrive." She'd watched from the sidelines as her twin had handled actors over the past three years since they'd both left college. Skye made it look so easy, but Phoebe was drained at the mere thought of having to play "happy to meet you" with countless actors.

He shrugged, his tall, muscular frame formidable in measure but his energy anything but. He made her feel as though she were the only person he wanted to be with. No doubt all part of his practiced Hollywood charm.

"It's a thrill to know the world's going to finally see something I worked so hard on, but to be frank, I left this film's set almost a year ago. My mind is on other…projects."

She couldn't help but laugh, his flirting was so obvious. "I'll bet it is." It seemed silly, but she went ahead and batted her eyes anyway. And immediately felt like Skye. She wanted to tell him that she wasn't really her twin, please forgive her, and would he call her Phoebe?

But she couldn't. So she smiled, content to soak up his aura of good cheer as pseudo-Skye.

He smiled back, but it wasn't the predatory grin of a man on the prowl. She'd watched plenty of actors behave poorly over the years, and this wasn't it. Prescott seemed relaxed, and there was a special light in his eyes that she couldn't attribute to the chandeliers, as they weren't fully lit yet. She didn't know the man, but if she had to name it, she'd say he was happy. A man in his element. Exactly where he wanted to be.

And oddly enough, he appeared a little…nervous?

"Please, Mr.—ah, Prescott, let me know if there's anything you need while you're our guest. The Chateau aims to please, and we want to make sure your every need is met to your specifications." The Chateau's mission statement rolled off her tongue, and she had to refrain from biting it.

He shook his head, looked away, as if gathering courage. Courage, to speak to her? No, wait—he thought he was talking to Skye. And she looked like Skye. A sad spurt of disappointment blossomed. He'd never know her as herself. Of course, he'd never be interested in Phoebe Colton, so she'd best count her blessings where she could.

"I, ah, know that you're in the middle of the event planning, but is there any chance you'd have some time for me over the next several days?"

Crap. Playing her sister Skye was one thing, and

Skye would definitely jump at the chance to get to know Prescott Reynolds better. But she wasn't Skye, she was Phoebe and she didn't want to add guilt to the list of emotions she was dealing with.

Where are you, Skye?

She smiled at Prescott. "Are you in need of a companion for any of the events?" Maybe that's what he'd meant. The Chateau didn't usually provide dates for their guests, but she supposed she could take a request for an escort to Mara and have her to worry about it.

"No, no. Nothing at all like that." He shook it off dismissively. "I'm asking you if you'd like to go on a date with me. Although, in this environment, privacy is hard to come by. I can't expect you to want to jump into the midst of a horde of paparazzi, and I don't want that anyhow." He sighed. "I'm screwing this up so badly. I'm not seeing anyone at the moment, and I was wondering, if you're also single, if you'd like to at least have a cup of coffee together?"

Phoebe couldn't speak for a full moment. Prescott Reynolds, movie star extraordinaire, was behaving like a sixteen-year-old asking a date to prom. And coffee… he wasn't trying to impress her with expensive wine or a fancy meal, as she'd watched wealthy men do with Skye. He was asking her to see him as any other guy who'd ask her out.

Which, whether she was Skye or Phoebe, was impossible. There was no question she needed to decline his endearing request.

"Of course. I'd love to spend time with you." As

soon as she spoke, she bit her tongue, hard. This was so not the time for her girl parts to begin calling the shots.

Prescott's entire countenance lifted.

"Really? That's great. Really, really great. Want to meet for a walk tomorrow morning? To be honest, I'm glad it was your sister who's the runner. I'm a hiker. Running is something my knees gave up after I stopped playing rugby in college."

What had she done? Nerves assaulted her, and she wished she could take her words back. This man thought she was Skye, and he wanted to get to know her. It would mean more than a walk through the woods if Prescott's tabloid reports were any indication. This would be difficult enough if she were able to be herself, and not have to put on the exuberant act, but considering the circumstances...

It's only for a week.

And what did Mara say? *Coltons do whatever it takes to get the job done.* The leading male actor in the film festival wanted to have coffee with her, to go on a hike, maybe more. In less than a week he'd be gone, and she'd be just another woman he'd been with to help while away the time. How much damage could it do to go along with it?

"I'll meet you in front of the gym's outside doors at six tomorrow morning." Her mouth moved of its own volition, and Phoebe could hardly believe what she'd just agreed to.

Was she *insane*?

He lifted his arms as if he was going to embrace her, and then stopped, his expression unreadable.

"Make it five thirty, if that's okay. And thank you, Skye." He tipped his ball cap to her and left the ballroom, his footsteps silent once he stepped onto the plush red carpet.

Unlike her heartbeat, which clanged in her ears.

Chapter 4

"Skye, how do you plan to make up for the minimal attendance at this year's film festival due to the Avalanche Killer?" One of Roaring Springs' most intrepid reporters spoke over the national news outlet that had asked a much easier question about the opening gala's menu.

Phoebe fought for breath in the tight-fitting, couture suit that Skye had laid out for this year's festival. Tried to remind herself that any hope of keeping the serial killer out of the national news cycle had always been futile. And she especially ignored the sting of tears behind her eyes at the reminder of her cousin Sabrina's awful death. She thanked the makeup gods for waterproof mascara.

"We're going to have a moment of silence for the

victims, of course. I'm sure you've noted that our flags are at half-mast. The Chateau and Roaring Springs Film Festival share the grief of the families and friends affected. And we have every confidence that the sheriff's department will find and apprehend the murderer imminently. We've upped our security profile, and I can personally assure each and every guest and festival attendee that their safety is our utmost priority." She paused for effect, just as she'd witnessed Skye do countless times. When the reporters appeared as though they were ready to ask another question, she nodded. "And as much as we're all hurting right now, the festival will go on, because it's more important than ever that we celebrate life and all of its joys. I know you all agree that the best revenge is a life well lived."

Murmurs and several nods gave her the first bit of relief from her nerves over posing as Skye since she'd first looked into the mirror after Amber had finished her makeup. The bronze foundation and colorful eye shadow, along with blush and lipstick, didn't faze her. But the false eyelashes really took getting used to. They'd made looking at Prescott Reynolds without continually blinking a bit of a challenge.

"Call me Prescott." She, Phoebe Colton, had been asked out by Hollywood hunk Prescott Reynolds and was going on a walk with him in the morning.

As Skye. He thinks you're Skye.

The reporters fired more questions at her, and she had no time to revel in the soft glow that Prescott's presence in the Chateau and subsequent request to spend time with her had ignited earlier today. Which was a shame, because it truly was a lovely way to move through the day. As she answered the more rudimentary festival questions, a separate part of her mind realized her sister must have this kind of feeling all the time. That a man she was attracted to was truly interested in her and wanted to get to know her better. Phoebe could certainly get used to it.

Once she wrapped up the press conference, she took a few minutes to stop in Skye's room to find costume jewelry, accessories and maybe some clothes that were definitely more Skye than Phoebe. She had half an hour before the red carpet event.

The red carpet scene would be tougher for her than the press conference. Answering questions for which she usually prepped the answers for Skye had been doable, even if she was nervous about behaving like her twin. However, facing international celebrities and engaging them with small talk was Phoebe's idea of a fiery hell.

Stop.

It was downright childish and self-serving to be so dramatic over all of this. The Chateau needed her; the Colton empire needed all hands on deck. Skye had pulled an ugly stunt by not returning in time for the gala, but at least Phoebe and their mother knew she was okay. Skye wouldn't lie in a text to her twin, would she?

A prickle of warning skittered over her nape as she stood at Skye's vanity and chose one of her sister's more glittery sets. Not full-on twin warning radar, but the feeling she was being watched. She looked over her shoulder toward the open cathedral window that was her favorite part about their in-resort apartments. Both she and Skye had matching apartment suites, but they'd decorated them quite differently. Skye had gone for a very upscale, gilded, Louis XIV look, while Phoebe's apartment was more relaxed with modern touches. "Colorado chic" was what she liked to call it. Skye referred to it as "something our grandmother would love." Phoebe missed Skye's constant teasing. It was how they often showed their deep affection for one another. She could use some sisterly love to help her get through the next several hours, possibly the next week.

Of course, if Skye were here, Phoebe would be happily engrossed with the production and guest services end of the festival. It wouldn't matter what shade of lip gloss or eye shadow she wore.

The view of the mountains was unsurpassed even by the extensive terraces that surrounded the majestic Chateau. A summer breeze puffed the sheers that hung from the rods with French provincial finials, bringing the scent of Skye's potted jasmine into the room. The French doors onto her small but well-used terrace were closed. Walking to the door to open it, Phoebe chided herself for being so edgy. It had to be a combination of playing her role as Skye and the scary murders that had tragically touched her family with Sabrina's death.

But when she reached to unhitch the hook at the top of the door, it was already unfastened. Phoebe pushed open the door and stepped in bare feet onto the stone-paved terrace, checking to see if Skye's chaise, small side table and several potted plants were as she'd last seen them this afternoon, when she'd been here to pick out some clothes and jewelry.

When she saw Skye's potted jasmine was crushed on one side, and a smear of dirt drawn on the mortar railing, a cold rush of fear ran over her scalp and down to her toes.

Taking the few steps forward, she saw the imprint of feet on the soft lawn not more than six feet below. Someone had been in Skye's room and exited via the terrace, but why? And who? And had they been in her apartment, too?

It could be Skye.

Skye was pulling a doozy on Phoebe and Mara, but if she was back in Roaring Springs she'd help with the festival, wouldn't she?

Phoebe checked the terrace more thoroughly before she returned inside and shut the door. She'd have to ask about getting a dead bolt—on both of their patio doors. In all the years her family had lived in The Chateau, she'd never felt the least bit afraid for her safety. Mara had been vigilant, though, and always kept Phoebe and Skye away from the public and guest eyes as needed.

She walked into her sister's closet, a luxurious feature they both relished, and stepped out of Skye's dressy business suit that she'd borrowed earlier and dressed in the T-shirt and drawstring shorts she'd left behind on a small dressing bench. Wearing Skye's business clothing helped her play the part to a T in front of the press, but she wasn't going to trade out her own evening wear, which was cut to fit her shape and more comfortable. Even though she was an avid runner, Phoebe's curves were slightly fuller than her twin's, and she'd always worn dresses that flattered her bust and hips. Skye's clothes tended to flatten out her curvier features, plus the waists were a tad tight.

Phoebe reached up to take a sparkly wrap from the hangar on the back of the closet door and stopped when she saw a large sheet of cardboard, one of The Chateau's desk blotters that was in each and every guest room, hanging by a thread over the gossamer shawl. In matte, bloodred lettering, a shade creepily similar to Skye's lipstick, Stay Away from Him! was lettered in slanted print. The sign definitely hadn't been here earlier when Phoebe had raided the closet for the suit.

"Stay away from whom?" She wanted to believe the scary message was some kind of prank that her sister had done, but Skye wasn't here and had no idea that Prescott had asked her out. And while Skye was the definite extrovert and prankster between the two of them, she'd never done anything this frightening.

Besides, Skye would never waste a good lipstick on something so childish.

Someone else clearly had seen Phoebe with Prescott and wasn't happy about it. But who could it be?

She gingerly unhooked the warning, and when she lowered the cardboard to the floor, she noticed a lipstick case, open, the stick of makeup ground into the carpet. Sure enough, it was one of Skye's designer shades. Phoebe wasn't a cop, but she knew she needed to call the head of hotel security. If it needed to be reported to the police or sheriff, they could pass it on.

Grabbing all that she needed from Skye's room,

Phoebe check to make sure no one was in the corridor that linked the residential apartments before she scurried to her room, careful to keep the cardboard message facing away from her so it wouldn't smear. Once in her room, she placed the warning sign on her dining table and went through to her bedroom and into her closet to change.

Call Security now.

But if she called the security officer, he'd tell her parents, then Mara would find out and have a freak-out, the last thing they needed as the festival launched. She'd have to speak directly with security, They'd handle it discreetly and have dead bolts placed on their terrace French doors.

Melancholy gripped her as she fumbled to zip her halter-style sparkly pink gown. In such a short time, her happy, secure life The Chateau in Roaring Springs had taken a serious nosedive. All because of a cold-blooded murderer who'd snuffed out Sabrina's life so horrifically.

Her first instinct was to find Skye and talk out her feelings. While Phoebe always had a sense of being in Skye's public shadow, she could trust her twin with her life and heart. Sadness slammed the thought back as she remembered Skye wasn't here.

"You'd better get back here, Skye." She spoke to the empty room as she added more powder to her face and made certain the false eyelashes weren't going to fall off in the middle of her red carpet interviews.

Prescott Reynolds was going to be there, in a tuxedo and smiling his killer trademark grin. And instead of being behind the backdrop with an earpiece and clip-board, making sure it all flowed perfectly, she'd be the one interviewing him.

Playing her twin sister had its perks.

It was as if a dozen separate orbs of sunlight edged the red carpet that ran across The Chateau's circular drive, up the stone stairs to the expansive landing and circled to the front entrance doors. The bright lights that were brought in by an event production tech group from Denver each year were the definition of blinding.

Phoebe longed for the familiarity of the smart tablet she usually carried, and her running shoes, which allowed her to work the entire red carpet behind the scenes. She'd done it for three years and was proud of how she'd streamlined the process, which had been pretty messy when Mara ran it. Her mother was more about keeping guests comfortable and well fed, while Phoebe was far more interested in the operational part of a business. The rest of the year she did the books, but during film fest week she liked to think of herself as a producer.

Not tonight.

Her legs quavered like a brook's water trickling over craggy rocks as she approached the spot where she'd stand on the landing, microphone in hand, to greet each actor, film VIP and celebrity. Skye had worked out a deal with a major network last year, and the produc-ers had spoken to Phoebe after the press conference. They'd gone over each part of the red carpet, including the opening ceremony, which would include the moment of silence she'd already briefed the press about.

"Hey, Skye." Remy Colton, Phoebe's cousin and the Colton empire's public relations director, stood in front of her. The tall man exuded confidence and calm amid the chaos of pre-event preparation. Next to him was his maternal half-brother, Seth Harris, who had similar hazel-green eyes and brown-blond hair but whose temperament Phoebe had never synced with. Still, they worked well enough together during festival week.

"Hi yourself, Remy. Seth." She gave Seth a bare glance, opting to keep their interaction minimal, and silently cursed Skye, who was so much friendlier with their extended family.

"Seth's helping out with the production tonight." Remy must have seen the question in her eyes. He held her gaze a beat too long and panic swelled in her chest.

"Have you seen Phoebe? I haven't been able to reach her." Remy's concern paralyzed Phoebe, and she wondered if this was Remy's idea of calling her bluff. Did he know she wasn't Skye? But after another moment, she decided his concern was genuine.

"Uh, I'm sure she's around, and her phone battery has been acting up. We had a lot of last-minute reservations, so she's probably helping my mother in reception." Lying for her sister was one thing, but now she was defending her own reputation. A swirl of nausea swarmed inside her belly. Phoebe counted integrity as one of her most important values. Having to skirt it was the pits. Skye couldn't get back soon enough.

Seth nodded knowingly. "Phoebe's always hiding.

She's shy." Phoebe fought back a defensive retort, but Remy handled it with aplomb.

Just as Phoebe thought she'd have to literally turn and walk away to avoid either man from figuring out that she wasn't Skye, a young man with a headset touched her forearm.

"Ready to get wired up?" The tech assistant handed Phoebe a large gold microphone with a rhinestone-studded handle, and an earpiece. "Give me a test, gorgeous."

She blinked, not used to being spoken to with such familiarity. Her sister was as much a feminist as she was, but Phoebe didn't encourage the sexy banter that Skye did, and this put her at a disadvantage. A disadvantage she was going to have to conquer right here, right now, in front of her two cousins.

"Um, please call me Ms. Colton, okay? Just to keep it professional!" Grinning like Skye would and batting her eyes at the man, she tapped the top of the mic. "One, two, three." Nothing.

"Good one, Skye. Now try turning it on and do it again." Seth's tone matched his smirk. Heat rushed into her cheeks. Way to toe the professional line when she didn't even bother to see if the mic was on.

She found the switch on the bottom of the wireless mic and pressed. "Is this better?" She spoke into it, and the techie pressed his hand to his earpiece, listened, then nodded and gave her a thumbs-up before he jogged away.

"Looks like you've got this, Skye. Let me know if you need anything else." Remy turned to walk away and Seth lingered a brief moment, waiting for her to meet his eyes.

"See you, Seth." She kept it light and kind, as Skye would do.

"Yeah, you too, Skye. Break a leg!" As he walked away, she felt a pang of guilt. Seth wasn't a bad guy, he'd just had it tough, as Remy's half sibling, and he'd most likely had always felt like an outsider to the huge, extended Colton family.

Phoebe sucked in a deep breath and pasted a large, wide smile on her face. Tonight she had one job: to play the role of Skye.

Scores of people stood on either side of the red carpet, and the bleachers erected on the south side of the drive were full of fans. They'd all won a ticket lottery, so that they could be prescreened for security. It was a festival standing practice since tonight's gala was on private property and meant to be a safe haven for the VIPs before the onslaught of premieres and press interviews that made up much of the week, culminating with the huge awards ceremony. But this year it felt more necessary than ever, after word of the Avalanche Killer got out.

And, on top of that, someone in their midst was threatening Phoebe, or Skye, for being around Prescott. At least that's what both she and the security team had agreed was the motive for the harassing note in her closet. They had assured her he'd have the dead bolt in place before she returned to her room tonight, and that he'd inform the local police. Mara wouldn't find out until Phoebe planned to tell her about it, tomorrow morning after her run.

Er, after her *hike* with Prescott.

She had to remember she was Skye, and Skye not only didn't run, she detested working out unless it was in a yoga studio with the perfect temperature and high-end workout gear that left little to the imagination. Phoebe bit her lower lip, tasting the heavy lip gloss her sister wore. How did Skye deal with all the layers of makeup every day?

At least she only had to do it for tonight, hopefully. At most, a week. Then she could return to her regular ol' life.

"Skye, the first set of limos are pulling up." The voice of the television network's producer filled her ear, and she looked down the steps and out toward the main road. Sure enough, the dozens, if not hundreds, of gala goers were arriving. Reminding herself that she was only interviewing the key actors and VIPs, she straightened her back, squared her shoulders and plastered a wide smile on her Skye-lipsticked mouth. When the first set of actors and actresses climbed up the stairs, and the producer's voice rang out "Action!" over the wireless sound system, she planted her feet in the thick carpet. Action, indeed.

Prescott felt the tightening in his stomach that anticipation triggered as the limo approached The Chateau's red carpet. He thought it was silly to have to arrive in a fancy car when he was staying here, but the cocktail reception his film production company threw had been in downtown Roaring Springs, so he needed a ride back, anyhow.

Focus on the film.

He let a long breath out, remembering how much he'd enjoyed shooting the action drama, and how eager he was for the audience to see the story of a single dad who worked as an FBI agent play out. Prescott had bonded with the five-year-old who'd played his son, and thought the film did a great job of showing how torn his character was between his duty as a parent and his career.

The young actor who'd played his son had tonsillitis and was missing the premier. That left Prescott as the main attraction for the media and fans.

"You ready for the onslaught of babes, Prescott?" Brian Gordon, the film's director, sat directly across from him in the spacious automobile.

"Not interested."

"You're not still letting Ariella bother you, are you? She's treated every other guy on set the same, trust me. I've watched her bad behavior through three of my films." Brian spoke, but his eyes were on his phone. "Hey, look what my kid just did." He held up the screen to show a picture of toddler completely covered in something purple.

"What is that stuff all over him?"

Brian grinned with pride. "Shower soap, grape scented for kids. My wife says he grabbed the bottle out of her hand and poured it all over himself."

"I hope it's the kind that won't make his eyes hurt." Prescott kept Brian talking. He knew the director was anxious to be back home with his family, as his wife was due with their third child at any moment.

Brian laughed and wiped his eyes. "You know I used to dream about this level of success for so many years. But other than being able to bring stories to life and work with great actors like yourself, what makes my life worth it each morning is my family. My wife, these incredible kids. How I got to be so damned lucky I'll never know."

"It's nice to hear that." Prescott meant it. Too many people in his industry were all about the material and didn't stop long enough not only to enjoy what mattered, but to share it with others.

Brian's gaze rested on him. They couldn't be more than five or six years apart, but the director often filled the role of mentor for Prescott since he'd cast him in his very first film twelve years ago. "You deserve the same, buddy. I know that Iowa calls to you, and I think it's great that you want to build yourself a place back there. But nothing will protect you and keep you sane from the Hollywood crazies as much as the love of a family."

"I hear you. Unfortunately the love gods don't agree." His mind went back to the ballroom, and Skye Colton. He'd not been enchanted by a woman in so long—even Ariella had been straight, no-holds-barred sexual attraction from the get-go. And while he was incredibly attracted to Skye, there was something more about her. As if she had a special secret she'd only share with him.

"You don't believe that, man." The limo halted, and

Brian leaned over and affectionately slapped Prescott on the shoulder. "Just look at all the women who are here to meet the award-winning actor."

Prescott opened his mouth to tell Brian that he wasn't interested in any of the adulation that fans so generously gave, but the driver had opened their door and the roar of the small crowd drowned out any opportunity to reply.

He stepped onto the red carpet and nodded at his security guards, who waited just feet away. They'd shadow him most of the evening unless he asked them to leave him alone. He noticed a lot more RSPD officers than he had last year. Security was definitely a top priority of The Chateau.

He admired the red carpet's setting. The Chateau earned its name as it stood in the middle of the valley with all the mountains around it, and tonight with the red carpet, twinkling fairy lights and bright camera illumination, it looked otherworldly. He appreciated the immense amount of work that went into such a show and made a mental note to personally thank the hotel staff.

But the only staff member he was truly interested in stood at the top of the grand outdoor staircase landing. He spotted her immediately. Skye Colton was a blaze of pink glamour as she held out the mic to his costar. The cameras made it hard to keep his gaze on her for long, but only encouraged him to get to his spot so that she could interview him sooner than later. At least that way he'd be next to her again.

Five thirty tomorrow morning seemed too far off.

With a desire that was surprising even to him, he wanted to be alone with Skye tonight, to find out what ticked behind those enchanting whiskey eyes.

Prescott wasn't a stranger to industry events and did his part to grip and grin, making eye contact and sincere small talk with each person who approached him. What kept him going tonight with a bounce in his step and positive attitude was the beacon of Skye at the top of the landing.

Finally it was his turn to be interviewed by the experienced hostess. He'd heard from several other colleagues that Skye had a knack for bringing out the best in each actor, and she never tried to dig out personal information that other entertainment reporters prided themselves on. Of course, the Colton heiress's realm of reporting was pretty much on social media, but he saw the familiar network logo on the camera and microphone she held. Their interchange would be very public, on a global scale.

For a brief second he wished it was more like Cannes or Sundance, where the focus was totally on the films and any interviews were very controlled in a press junket lounge. What if Skye asked him about Ariella and their disastrous breakup? She'd given no indication that she'd cut him a break when they'd spoken in the ballroom. Anxiety tried to tear down his practiced red carpet persona as he realized that Skye's job was to ask him how his life was going—so how could she *not* ask about his ex?

He had no time left to stew on it as the actress in

front of him walked away from Skye, leaving a cloud of expensive perfume behind.

Skye's gaze met his and yup, there it was. The instant attraction that made him hard with zero effort. Since an erection on television would not behoove him, he willed his reaction into submission. At least that was something he could control. Kind of.

Who knew—maybe he'd make good on it later, if Skye was feeling the same way as he did.

"Good evening. Everyone, this incredible actor needs no introduction, and is the lead in the festival's top-rated film. Welcome back to Roaring Springs, Prescott Reynolds."

"Thank you, Skye. I have to say that of all the times I've been at The Chateau, so far, this has been the most interesting." Why not have some fun in front of the camera? Skye was a pro—she'd give as good as she got, he was certain.

"Uh, interesting? What about it intrigues you, Prescott?" She tilted the mic under his chin, too close, and he wrapped his hand around hers to gently guide it a few inches back. Her eyes widened, and her mouth dropped open, her soft lips dewy pink with a glaze of gloss he desperately wanted to taste.

Your tux pants are too tight to get a boner, dude.

"You intrigue me, Skye Colton. May I?" Before she could respond, he took the mic from her and looked at the camera. "Folks, I know you watch these shows, as I do when I'm not at them, and ooh and ahh at all the beautiful dresses, the actors who've all worked so hard to put together your favorite films. But we wouldn't have the vehicle to get our stories out to you without people like Skye Colton." He looked back at her. "I want to personally thank you on behalf of our film and the entire Hollywood industry for putting on such a wonderful gala each year at the beginning of this film fest. It's the best of all kick-offs." He handed the mic back to her, expecting the woman he'd barely met last year would chime in and riff off his impromptu show of gratitude.

"I, uh, I don't quite know what to, um, say." She clutched her ear, and he hoped the producer was feeding her something decent, because Skye looked like she was about to pass out. Crap. He'd overdone it. It never worked well when he let his testosterone do the talking.

"You don't have to say anything, Skye. We're all enjoying tonight, and I'm looking forward to the gala. It's always such a great start to the week." He was totally lying. Prescott hated formal dances and was far more comfortable on his family's Iowa cornfields than in a fancy ballroom.

"Your film has great expectations around it. How do you manage the pressure?"

Definitely a producer's question. "I hike, preferably with a friend, and spend as much time as I can outdoors."

"Hiking with friends is the best type of exercise, in my book." Score! Finally, she'd figured out that he was trying to enjoy their time together, even if it was in front of potentially millions of viewers.

"It's even better with a bottle of wine, smoked Havarti and a flourless chocolate cake." He hoped she liked the same fancy snacks that he did.

Skye giggled, and it was all Prescott could do to not ask her if he could kiss her on the spot. To hell with the cameras.

"That's not very nutritionally balanced, Prescott. You need some green veggies in there."

"Champagne is made from green grapes, right?" His belly tightened at her smile, the sheer delight on her face. The potent thrill of flirting with her made him wish he could will away the hours until he was alone with her.

"You're teaching me a new way to manage my nutrition, Prescott." She motioned with her hands as she spoke and took a step closer to him.

"Oh!" Her cry wasn't something planned and his hackles rose, always on watch for a possible zinger from Ariella. Skye was already falling into him before he realized she'd tripped on the plush carpet.

Prescott's protective instincts kicked in and he wrapped his arms around her waist, holding her up and saving her from a nasty fall. But before he could look down into her beautiful amber eyes, her arms flailed and he took a hard hit from the top of the microphone. He couldn't stop the grunt that came out of his mouth, or the tooth that followed. He heard Skye utter another gasp of surprise, but it wasn't about her falling this time. It was about the tooth that arced between them and landed on the red carpet.

Dang and double dang. His temporary crown had been knocked off.

Chapter 5

Skye was at once grateful, turned on and horrified as she pitched forward to a certain face-plant, was saved by Prescott's quick, heroic actions and then saw something white fly through the air.

Prescott's tooth.

She'd knocked one of his beautiful, pearly white teeth out. And there was no running from it or editing the tape. The film festival's opening gala red carpet was being live-streamed around the world.

"Go to commercial, now. Skye, get a grip on yourself. What on earth is going on down there? Someone go check the carpet and see what she tripped on." Phoebe heard the familiar jingle of a local attorney who specialized in automobile crash cases but drowned out what the woman was saying as she watched Prescott bend over and pick up the tooth from the carpet. When he stood he grinned at her, the empty space where the tooth had been taunting her.

"Are you okay? Oh. My. Gosh. I am so sorry, Prescott." She couldn't tear her gaze off him and had to ignore the producer's rants or she'd completely lose it. It was all she could do to not rip her earpiece out.

"I'm fine." He looked at the camera and with a start, she realized he was making sure it was turned away and off. "Are we on commercial break, or did we switch back to the camera at the driveway?"

"Both." From the producer's litany of curses, the camera wouldn't be back on her at all tonight. "I've really messed this up. I am so sorry, Prescott. I will cover the cost of your dental work."

He grinned and held the tooth up for her to see. "That's just it, Skye, there's nothing to be concerned about. It's a temporary crown. I lost my real tooth years ago as a kid, playing ice hockey on a farm pond. My dentist suggested that between films was a good time to get a new crown, as the original one was close to breaking off. This goes back in like this—" He placed the white tooth into the space and then smiled, revealing his usual megawatt grin. "I have some dental adhesive in my pocket for just this instance."

Phoebe knew she should feel relieved, but all she felt like was a colossal failure. She'd had one task to get through—to act like Skye for tonight's opening. And she'd failed miserably. Sucking in a breath didn't stop the tear she knew hovered precariously on her false lashes. The warm plop of it on her cheek wasn't muted by the layer of cosmetics, and she quickly swiped at it, hoping Prescott thought she was simply rattled. Not about to become a blubbering mess.

"You're very gracious. I have no idea what I tripped over." She looked down at the carpet where a taped X marked her spot. Only then did she see a long wooden dowel behind the spot. "I must have tripped over this." She bent and picked it up. "This is so odd, how did this even get here?"

Prescott took the dowel from her and tucked it under his arm. "Let's take this to hotel security. Together."

She panicked. "I can't leave my station. I'm the hostess for the red carpet gala."

Prescott wasn't giving in so easily. His mesmerizing blue eyes were on her, and she saw steely determination had replaced the flirtatious light. "I'm a VIP, and I want you with me." He nodded toward the bottom of the steps, where another reporter from a local Roaring Springs television network interviewed each guest and attendee as they stepped out of their vehicles. "It's not as if no one is covering the event, and I was one of the last to arrive. There can't be more than a half dozen or so VIPs left, and none of them are the actors in starring roles." Prescott was the epitome of professionalism, and her attraction to him intensified.

"It does seem that she's taken it in hand." Phoebe wasn't used to relying on a man to help her with anything, but Prescott's warmth and unexpected interest in her made it tempting to walk away from the X and never look back. At least not for tonight.

"Skye, you seem to be struggling tonight. We're

going to let local Channel Seven have the rest of the meet and greet. Stay with Prescott." The producer's voice sounded annoyed but also relieved. Phoebe understood, as it was how she, too, felt at the moment. Frustrated and angry at herself that she couldn't pull off the task of being the consummate media expert that Skye was, and relief that she didn't have to any longer.

But she still had to play the role of Skye.

"I can handle the remaining guests." She didn't break eye contact with Prescott as she replied to the producer.

"Skye, it's Remy. You've already shot the most important VIPs. And Prescott is our number one VIP this week. Forget about the telecast. Keep Prescott happy and mingling in the gala."

"Will do." She quickly removed her earpiece, turned the microphone off and smiled at Prescott. "I have to drop this equipment off at the production booth, but then I'm at your command for the rest of the evening."

"Exactly the response I was hoping for." His voice was even, but the burn of desire in his eyes at once turned her on and reassured her that she was safe. She'd only known him for a few hours, literally, and yet it felt as if he'd always been here. He seemed to know what she needed as he placed his hand on her lower back and escorted her from the red carpet. His touch wasn't too much, as it normally would be if a man she barely knew touched the spot where her evening gown dipped seductively low. The pink sparkles made her feel very feminine, while the halter design allowed for both cleavage and a deeply cut back. The high slits were the real reason she'd bought the dress, though, because her legs reflected all the miles she spent running. Prescott's hands were large, and his palm against her skin threatened her emotional equilibrium but in a way she welcomed.

After she dropped her equipment off with one of the production assistants, she turned to Prescott. "We're free to head inside now."

His hand went from her lower back to her palm, and she allowed their fingers to intertwine. Even their hands fit together perfectly, which made her wonder where else they'd come together so well.

Stop it. You're Skye, and he'll be gone in a week.

"I have to say, this is a pleasant surprise. I wasn't expecting to meet someone I want to spend time with during the film fest." He smiled, and Phoebe ached to tell him the truth—that she was Phoebe, the quieter, less confident twin. Since that was impossible, she summoned her inner Skye.

"I won't let you down, Prescott, I promise." She crossed her hand over her heart and watched his gaze follow her fingers to where her décolletage sparkled with the fine glitter powder she'd applied, just as Skye always did. Prescott's nostrils flared, and she watched his chest hitch up. He leaned in close, his breath on her ear.

"The only thing you could let down is that dress, babe." His voice purred low next to her ear. "I won't be happy until I see all of you." He straightened as quickly as he'd moved in, and to the other guests they'd no doubt appear to be having a fun but inconsequen-

tial conversation. Phoebe knew about Hollywood celebrities—they had women begging to be in their beds,
at their sides. And Prescott was no different, she reminded herself.

But it didn't hurt to pretend he was the one exception, did it? To allow herself the luxury of having him
at her side throughout the gala, and meeting him for a
hike in the morning, as if they were a normal couple
getting to know one another?

It wasn't as if she'd ever forget it was all pretend.
Not while he still believed she was her twin.

Prescott's desire simmered over the next several
hours as Skye led him from group to group across the
grand ballroom, as if they were playing leapfrog and
she was determined for him to meet every single person present.

It was his job to do so, of course, but it wasn't what
he wanted.

For the first time since he'd been brutally used by
Ariella, he wanted to spend time alone with a beautiful woman. And while Skye was tremendously attractive—stunning, in fact—he'd had his share of
physically attractive women over the years. It was
inevitable that he'd date the same women he worked
with, but it also increased the chances of a bad ending,
which he knew about firsthand. Actors had to be self-
involved by definition, and without a partner to keep
one grounded, it was easy to lose yourself in someone
who shared the same profession. Two-actor relation-

ships that lasted the test of constant public attention were rare.

Skye was a public part of the Roaring Springs Film Festival, but she wasn't a true Hollywood type. He saw the depth of her dismay at what happened on the red carpet, had caught the shadow of vulnerability in her gaze when they'd stood in this room earlier, just the two of them and a few dozen support staff.

Prescott wanted to know Skye on more than a business level.

"There are only two more people that I think we should have you talk to. We've done really well tonight!" She appeared genuinely pleased about the social circuit she'd just led him through.

"Thank you for helping me do my grip-and-grin gig, but there's something I can't put off any longer."

Her gaze filled with curiosity before her eyes widened. The false eyelashes were natural looking enough, but he'd prefer to see her bare skin, sans cosmetics. It was as if she wore a mask for the public and he needed to know he had the private Skye all to himself.

"I'm so sorry. Of course. The men's room is to the left of the second, smaller chandelier, over there." She pointed to an area kitty-corner from where they stood, on the other side of the full dance floor.

He laughed. "No, I don't need the men's room, but thank you." He took her hand for the second time since he'd tried to comfort her right after her trip on the red carpet. He'd been so concerned that she was going to knock out one of her real teeth, and had been relieved she hadn't been hurt. Since when did he become emotionally invested in women he'd only met the same day?

Tiny lines appeared on her forehead, and he found the unguarded expression adorable. "Come with me, Skye." He led her through the maze of tables, past many faces that turned to look at them as they strode out of the room and onto The Chateau's main terrace. The huge cement edifice boasted two open bars at either end along with a large hot buffet of gourmet finger foods.

"You're hungry. Why didn't you tell me?" She tugged at her hand but he didn't let go, only kept walking until they were at the top of the steps that overlooked a French garden replete with carved boxwoods, fragrant roses and twisting, inviting pebbled paths. He pulled her up against him and kept ahold of her hand.

"I'm not hungry." And he wasn't—not for the buffet, anyway. He'd asked his security guards to stay in the ballroom unless he texted that he needed them. It was heaven to be out here with her, alone, as if they were any other couple.

She smiled, her full lower lip begging for his kiss. "I'm not used to, I mean, I don't know you well enough to know what your requirements are for an event like this."

"The same as anyone else's. I'm just a man, Skye." He shouldn't have to tell her this—she worked with Hollywood VIPs at each festival. He'd done an internet search on her, as he didn't remember meeting her last year. Skye Colton's social media presence was formidable. This wasn't her first rodeo.

"It's my job to make sure you get all you need. And it's more than just tonight's gala, Prescott. My family prides itself on making The Chateau your home away from home."

"I appreciate that, but I have to ask you something, Skye." He couldn't take his gaze from her large brown eyes, luminous under the full moon.

"Sure, of course." She still had her professional demeanor in place and he wanted to strip her of it—but only if she wanted to.

"I want to walk with you through the garden, but not as Skye Colton, premier hostess. Not as Prescott Reynolds, actor in a film that's being premiered at this festival. Just as Skye and Prescott, you and me."

She blinked several times, and he heard a soft gasp. Either she was as hot for him as he was for her, or she'd not expected his request. He was hoping for the former. After all, she'd have to have picked up on his interest ever since he asked her to meet him tomorrow morning.

"Skye?" Her silence poked through his hope. Maybe he'd overstepped her boundaries. This was supposed to be a professional event, after all.

"I-I'd like to do that, Prescott, but let's face it, we hardly know one another, and aren't we going to go for a walk in the morning?"

He exhaled his impatience. "Here's what I know, Skye. It's not a lot, but it's the real deal. I've learned that rare is the time that I meet someone in this life I lead who I feel might be different from all the others. Who might be someone I could forge a bond with, something more than fancy events, expensive, flashy clothing and cars." He paused, looking deep into her eyes. "So when I do have the rare occasion to get to know someone like you, Skye, I have to jump on it. My lifestyle is transient, and I'm gone for months at a time on film sets all over the globe. I don't have the usual time to allow a relationship to grow—I have to go for it, and if it doesn't work out, we find out sooner."

"A, a relationship?" She repeated a lot of his words, he noticed. As if she was nervous and stalling for time. But Skye wasn't the nervous type, although he had to admit she seemed much more subdued than how she appeared in the media. How she'd flown under his radar last year was a mystery to him. Of course, he'd just broken up with Ariella at the time, and his entire film fest week had been a pressure cooker to meet the requirements of his PR firm while staying sane amid the paparazzi photos and tabloid reports of the breakup. He'd not been paying attention to any women.

He couldn't believe he'd overlooked this amazing woman, though.

"A walk in the garden is all I'm asking for right now, Skye. Walk with me." He held his hand up, giving her time.

She looked at him as if trying to decipher his motives. Prescott didn't blame her—it was always a risk trusting a new person in your life.

After several heartbeats disappointment made an unwelcome appearance in his gut, and he feared that he'd pushed too hard, too soon. It wouldn't be the first time. He lowered his arm.

"No, wait!" Skye reached out and grabbed his hand,

held it with both of hers. When she looked at him again, the lines on her forehead were gone and her lips were turned up without the tremulous quakes he'd noticed earlier, right after she'd knocked his tooth out. "I want to go with you. For a walk."

His gratitude was more akin to elation, but he didn't want to get ahead of himself.

Skye was clearly a woman who needed things done at her pace. If he pushed too hard, too soon, his gut told him she'd sprint off like a deer. Prescott stopped analyzing and enjoyed the feel of her soft, warm hand in his as he led her down to the garden.

Phoebe never knew that portraying her sister would make her life perk up in the romance department as quickly as it had today. In a few short hours, she'd met and been asked on a date by Hollywood hunk Prescott Reynolds. And now he wanted to spend alone time with her in The Chateau's Luxembourg Garden, her mother's pride and joy.

Scents of roses assaulted her as they made their way around the carefully tended landscaping, and she'd never felt safer. At least not since the Avalanche Killer had destroyed her sense of well-being.

Skye's still missing.

No, Skye wasn't missing, Phoebe reassured herself yet again. Her twin was just purposely staying away from Roaring Springs while she nursed her broken heart. Phoebe would only have to pretend to be Skye for a day longer, she hoped. Playing the expert at casual dating didn't come naturally to Phoebe, as she needed to get to know someone well before she made any kind of commitment. And her work at The Chateau had kept her life full, save for the romance part.

It was incredibly tempting to allow herself to embrace her attraction to Prescott. Phoebe couldn't blame anyone but herself for her quiet dating life, but why not take advantage of having some fun? What did they say—no harm, no foul?

Prescott was a man of the world who dated many women, if the tabloid reports were even fractionally true. Posing as Skye, Phoebe would just be another woman he'd have a week of mindless fun with. And when her twin came back, she'd fill her in on what had happened, if anything.

It seemed a sound plan, except for the sick feeling of betrayal in her gut over lying to Prescott. She liked what she knew of him so far and didn't want to keep pretending to be someone she wasn't.

"Did you grow up in Roaring Springs, Skye?" They'd walked to a secluded spot under a huge oak tree. He leaned against the tree and she stopped, leaving a gap between them, even though they still held hands.

"I did. I've also had the opportunity to travel and I went away to college, so I know there's more out there in the big world. But I love it here and have never seen anything as beautiful as our mountain."

"The recent news has to be terrible for you." His voice was full of compassion. Was this the real Prescott, or had he acted the part of the empathetic listener so often that he played the role perfectly?

"Wait—what recent news?" Mara had been clear

that she was to keep the Avalanche Killer case quiet as much as possible.

"The Avalanche Killer. My security detail briefed me on it, and I read a report online this morning."

It was no use, the news was out. Their reservations had tanked, initially, but had picked back up with no further murders. People hoped the tragedies being discovered had stopped the killer.

"It was an awful time. It still is, and will be, until they catch him. He murdered my cousin Sabrina. We don't even have the body yet to do a proper burial, as it has to be examined."

"I'm so sorry." And she decided to accept his condolence as genuine. Because everything about him so far seemed real, full of purpose.

"Thank you. We're managing. I have complete trust in RSPD and the sheriff's office, and as you could see tonight, they're not taking any chances."

"I do have to say that while I'm used to high security at events, the proportion of uniformed security seemed a lot higher than I'd expect."

"Well, there were plenty of plainclothes security officials, too. Our resort runs a top-notch security team."

"I know they do."

"You do?" What had Prescott had to do with The Chateau's security?

He nodded, a shaft of moonlight hitting his dark hair as he moved. "I have my own security detail, who you might have noticed, for every public event. A bodyguard and a backup. It's unfortunate, but it's the reality of life in the public eye today. They have nothing but good things to say about your security."

"They have been like part of our family, really. As long as we've been here at The Chateau, they've looked after my sister and me."

"Your sister?"

"Yes, Sk—Phoebe." Crap, she'd almost blown it! "She's my quieter self, truth be told. Phoebe is a behind-the-scenes type of person. She works the books and manages all of the events, their production, etc."

"Are you identical twins?" Again, genuine interest in his gaze.

"We are, although our personal styles are quite different." Phoebe licked her lips and tugged her hand free of his. He'd start to suspect she was lying if her palm began to sweat…and that would ruin everything.

"It's okay, Skye." Low and gravelly, she felt his voice all the way down to between her legs, where desire pooled into a liquid heat.

"What's okay?" Her voice sounded so breathy, so unlike her usual in-charge self. Being Skye might lure a man in, but who was she to think she could sexually spar with a powerhouse like Prescott?

He reached across the foot or so between them and grasped her waist, pulling her in closer, but not touching. They were a breath apart. Or maybe it was a cry apart, as she felt as though she'd have an orgasm on the spot if he touched her any more intimately. The man had her tingling all over, and not from the anxiety she occasionally suffered. This was pure chemical reaction.

"I know you're nervous. You're wondering if you

can trust me, if I'm going to use you for tonight or this week, then leave without a trace."

"That has crossed my mind, yes." She was pure Phoebe now, as Prescott's gaze reflected the moon with startling brightness. Her knees shook, and she knew he felt it in her trembling arms.

"It's scary for me, too. I'm coming off a bad breakup, and I've had my share of women who've used me for my position."

"Oh, I'm sorry. That's awful."

"It can be. Part of the job. But it puts us on a more even playing ground, doesn't it?"

There was nothing about the ground that felt even to Phoebe. Not with this gorgeous man wooing her, making her feel things she hadn't in…ever. She'd never felt this kind of deep, awe-inspiring attraction to a man before.

"What do you mean by that?" Her lips ached for the pressure of his against them, but she had to keep talking, keep *him* talking. Because once they stopped, there was only one place to go. Would it be as incredible as she anticipated?

"We both are at risk of being hurt." He drew her infinitesimally closer, breaking through any remaining resolve she deluded herself she had against becoming romantically entangled with him, at least as Skye. "Which, as I see it, means we both have the utmost to gain. This could be perfection between us."

She leaned in, needing to be closer to him. Wanting him. Prescott finished the journey by gently tugging her hips toward him, his hands moving to cup her buttocks. A moan let loose, and she leaned her head back, gave in to the sheer sexual heat of the moment. She was accepting herself as Skye, so why not toss all caution away and simply enjoy?

His lips were on her throat at the same instant he pulled her up against his erection, leaving no doubt that they shared the same intense desire for one another. Phoebe wrapped her arms around his neck, lifted her face to meet his and kissed him.

Prescott growled against her mouth, his tongue practiced and expertly arousing her to a level of desire she hadn't dreamed possible. Phoebe's sexual experience wasn't nonexistent but had consisted mostly of dating with sex on an as-needed basis. Nothing this overwhelming or passionate.

She reached down and stroked him through his tuxedo trousers, delighting at how aroused she made him. Whether her newfound assertiveness was from playing Skye or because she was with Prescott, she'd have to figure out later. Phoebe didn't want to miss a single second of this.

"You're so lovely, Skye." He kissed her, and she wondered if they needed to go to her room instead of return to the ballroom, but she was still on duty. And could she really go to bed with a man who thought she was someone else, even if her motives were reasonable?

Footsteps sounded behind them, and Prescott broke their kiss, his profile alert as he slowly released her, putting a finger to his lips.

Phoebe knew to not make a sound, but her heart was still pounding from the rush of emotion at their embrace. Fear racked her body with a shudder, and remorse erased the intimacy of the last moments. She could have put them both in harm's way out here by being distracted.

It was never going to be safe anywhere in the dark, not while the Avalanche Killer threatened Roaring Springs.

Ariella watched them from the shadows beyond the copse of trees where they were bumping and grinding, and she wanted to spit. Prescott had some nerve, throwing away all they'd shared for some hired hotel help.

Okay, so Skye Colton was part of the family-owned business that made up not only The Chateau, but the entire business structure of Roaring Springs. Skye lived the life of a princess with a father like Russ Colton. She wasn't the hired help. Still, Skye didn't measure up to Ariella or any other actor. Prescott didn't want a woman from backwoods Colorado. He'd left his hick Iowa town and provincial family for the opportunity that only Los Angeles offered.

Silly Prescott. He'd gotten so spun up over her affair with another actor. She'd tried to explain to him that the other man was simply a stepping-stone, a means to an end. It was how things were done in Hollywood, at least for women. Prescott had refused to see how she was helping both of their careers by taking up with the son of a legendary director. Didn't he realize that she'd have gotten them both roles in that director's next film? Not that Prescott had to worry about income like she did. Right now she wasn't able to find a job, thanks to the nasty tabloid reports about her and Prescott's messy breakup.

But her time, *their* time, was coming. The furor over how she'd reportedly left Prescott for the other actor had begun to die down, and she expected to land a starring role within a month or so. That gave her a little time to spare—time to make Prescott see how lost he was without her.

A stick snapped somewhere near her, and she jumped. Ariella considered herself pretty damn fearless, but there was a murderer on the loose in Roaring Springs. She'd read that one of Skye Colton's cousins had been among the murdered. Too bad, so sad. It was to her advantage to have the Colton bitch feeling sad and vulnerable, however. It made her easier to spook, and to capture if need be.

She'd thought the message she'd left in her apartment would have been enough to keep her greedy hands off Prescott. Clearly it hadn't, as Skye Colton clung to Prescott like the desperate sycophant she was.

Ariella mentally reviewed why she shouldn't step out of the shadows and stop them, right now. She was the only one who should be in Prescott's arms, the only one he needed to be kissing like that. Come to think of it, they hadn't done a whole lot of kissing. It hadn't been necessary—the sex had been good between them, so who needed all that mushy stuff?

Apparently Skye Colton did, the scheming idiot. What Skye didn't know was that was that Prescott was simply using her, just as Ariella had used various industry types along the way. Sex was a currency to everyone in Hollywood, and Prescott Reynolds was no exception. He'd get whatever he thought he needed from Skye and be gone at the end of the week.

Ariella didn't want to wait seven more days to have Prescott back with her, though. Since Skye hadn't taken her first warning seriously, nor the second one, she was going to have to up the ante to make an unmistakable claim on her man.

Prescott was hers and hers alone.

A rustle of leaves followed by the distinct sound of footsteps startled her, and she quickly looked around for her best escape route. If the Avalanche Killer was out here, she didn't want to be his next victim. She took one last look at Prescott and the Colton bitch, only to find they were gone.

Good thing, because she would have had to warn them off in case the noises she heard were the murderer. As she ran through the night, to the side road where she'd parked her beat-up car, she silently laughed. Her, save the Colton woman from being killed? Now that was just plain silly. Prescott was the only one she wanted alive, with her.

Whatever it took, she was going to get him back in her bed.

Chapter 6

"That was freaky." Skye's gaze stayed on him as she sipped the champagne that Prescott had waiting for her when she returned from the restroom. He watched her lips as she drank and wished he had her alone again, but he'd almost pushed it too far out in the garden. They'd heard a few strange noises while in the midst of their embrace and opted to come back inside the ballroom.

"Did you tell Security?"

She nodded, her hair catching the ballroom chandelier lighting. "They said to not worry, the chances are far greater that it was paparazzi rather than the Avalanche Killer. Not that we can be certain of anything right now." A cloud passed over her lovely face, and he grasped her elbow.

"Let's go sit down." He maneuvered them to an empty table in the back center of the ballroom. Much of the earlier crowd had dispersed, and the band was in the middle of another slow song. There weren't more than half a dozen couples on the floor, and none of them were VIPs. The main purpose of the festival's opening night had been served with the red carpet arrival interviews and ballroom gala. He knew the actors were all striving for max shut-eye, as he needed to be. But being with Skye wasn't something he was willing to replace with sleep. If they hadn't been interrupted outside, he couldn't be sure that he wouldn't have suggested they make love on the spot.

Adventurous even for him.

"We can't go back out on the dance floor, can we?" Skye smiled at him.

"Why not?" He'd jump at any chance to be next to her.

"It'll get us back to where we left off."

"I don't want you to think I usually push things this quickly, like I have been doing with us. But we seem to have something going on here that's bigger than both of us." He couldn't believe he'd said it, but in reality he was giving voice to his thoughts. He'd never been so intensely aware of another woman, not this early in the relationship, if at all.

"Um, yes." She bit on her lower lip, a tell he'd decided meant she was unsure of herself.

"Skye, is there something you're not telling me?"

"Wha—why would you say that?" But she didn't

meet his eyes, focused instead on the votive candles that floated in a crystal bowl in the center of the table.

"Is there someone else?" Realization struck him. "You're with someone already, aren't you? Damn, I'm batting a thousand these days." First Ariella, and now Skye, although if Skye were cheating on anyone, it would be her boyfriend. He didn't like the words *Skye* and *cheating* in the same thought.

"No, no, it's not that. I'm completely single and free." She frowned. "But I don't like that you think I'd be the cheating kind, frankly."

"Anyone can do anything, given the right circumstances." He knew he sounded harsh and hated himself for it. But Ariella's betrayal had battered him, and he still felt a little emotionally raw.

Skye's different.

He agreed with his gut this time. Skye was different from the women he'd casually dated, and definitely from his ex. In such a refreshing way.

"The truth is, there was a bit of a security issue earlier tonight." Her eyes were steady on him as she let out a long, shaky breath. "My sister and I live here, in living quarters apart from the guest rooms. Someone broke into my apartment—and left me a warning message. I think what they wrote was about you."

"About me?" His gut tightened in anticipation of the rest of the story. Dread weighed heavy on his chest.

Skye nodded. "Yes. A note was written, with my lipstick, on a piece of cardboard and it said to stay away from 'him.'"

"'Him'?" If Ariella was up to her scheming ways,

he wasn't sure she would have left her threats so vague. The last woman he'd gone to dinner with had become subject to a social media smear campaign that his security team had traced back to Ariella's account, but nothing could be proven after Ariella claimed her account had been hacked. He hadn't wanted a public legal battle with her, but if she was anywhere near here, and involved in threatening Skye, he'd call in the FBI if he had to.

"I think it meant you, Prescott. I'm not dating anyone else, as I said, and haven't in a long while. It could be a rabid fan, I suppose. Several of the guests aren't associated with the festival, except as fans. We've never had a serious problem with any of them before, save for the occasional overzealous attempt to get a selfie or autograph."

He wanted to tell her about Ariella, at least his side of it, since he was fairly certain that she already knew about the breakup. Except Skye had a refreshing air of detachment from the celebrity buzz. He hated to drag her into the ugly side of fame. Although Ariella might have already done just that.

"I'll tell my security team tonight. They're working directly with them all week long."

"Yes." She smiled, and underneath her ridiculously long eyelashes he saw the woman he thought he'd seen on the running path. A quieter, more contemplative person. But that had been her twin sister, Phoebe. Maybe Skye was the odd extrovert who needed serious recharging after being on for several hours.

"It looks like the festivities are wrapping up. Can I

walk you to your apartment?" He placed his glass on a tray table.

A corner of her mouth lifted, and he noted a deep dimple in her left cheek. He reached out and caressed it, loving the soft femininity of her skin. She turned in to his hand, kissed his palm. Before he'd have seen it as a precursor to sex, but her gesture was so intimate, sincere.

This is something unknown to you.

"I'd love to have you spend your night with me, but I have to stay here until the bitter end. It's my job and will be all week. And I'm pretty sure you need your rest." She stood, and he followed suit. "I'll see you in the morning, Prescott." Using his shoulders as a brace, she reached up on tiptoe and kissed his cheek.

"Good night, Skye." He watched her make her way toward the production area, where a few techies lingered, packing their equipment away and no doubt hoping to catch a few hours of sleep before tomorrow's itinerary had them all running full tilt again.

Prescott stood and signaled for his bodyguards to leave him be. He'd be safe walking to his room alone.

As he made his way into the guest room area of the resort, he went over the past few hours. He'd known Skye Colton for such a short amount of time, yet it felt as if he'd known her, as if they'd been friends, forever.

And had he just thought of their time making out under the stars as making love?

He knew he was vulnerable, as his brother back home would tell him, that the chances of Skye being a rebound were high. But she didn't feel like a relationship statistic to him.

Skye felt like home.

Phoebe went by the security office before she quit for the night and found the team still working, with two assistants laboring over video feed from several cameras. In one frame she recognized the tall, imposing figure of Prescott as he walked down the corridor to his room. Longing hit her low in her belly and rushed down to her most feminine parts, still painfully aroused by Prescott's kisses under the moonlight.

"Evening, Phoebe." The team didn't even pretend to think she was Skye. Phoebe closed the door behind her, keeping unwanted ears from hearing the conversation.

"How do you know it's me and not Skye?" She thought she'd put on a good attempt at playing her twin.

They snorted. "I've watched the both of you grow into the lovely women you are, and it started when you were tiny tots running all over this property. I'll grant you that you are very difficult to tell apart when you want to be, but I still see you as two different women. Why did Skye put you up to posing as her?"

"Long story, but she's taking a bit of a break right now."

"That bastard record producer broke her heart, didn't he?"

Phoebe shrugged. It was Skye's story to tell. "I'm here to talk about tonight. Did you see anything strange, besides what happened in Skye's apartment? And the way I tripped over that stupid stick?"

"That wasn't stupid. It was well placed." He held up the dowel that she'd given him earlier. "This is an exact match for the miniature poles that hold up the resort flags we have in every flowerpot on the property. One of the pots on the back terrace was missing its flag, and we found the banner part in a nearby flower bed."

"It doesn't make sense. Whoever placed it there, if it was done on purpose, took a big risk at getting caught. They had to have put it there while I was talking to one of the VIPs on the red carpet."

The security expert nodded. "We're working to get the video from the network, and I'll go over it when we do. Because we knew that the network was airing the production and their cameras would be on you, we repositioned some of the cameras to catch other parts of the property that otherwise aren't monitored as closely. We can't be too careful with the level of Hollywood superstars here."

"Prescott Reynolds mentioned that his security detail was going to work more closely with you than usual."

"They are, and I understand that you heard what could have been a person outside, in the garden?"

"Yes, we did," Phoebe answered. "I'm hoping it was paparazzi, but with the Avalanche Killer, I can't help but see a murderer lurking behind every corner."

"I had your room swept for anything else out of the ordinary, and the dead bolt is in place on your French doors. I also went ahead and had your lock changed on your room door, too." He handed her a key. The apartments utilized regular keys, unlike the magnetic card keys assigned to each resort room.

"Thanks. I appreciate the extra effort, especially when you're already swamped with this week's doings."

"No thanks needed, but I appreciate that, Phoebe. You look tired. Do you have to play Skye again tomorrow?"

She sighed. "Don't remind me. For now all I want to do is get some shut-eye." As soon as she said it, she shook her head. "Sorry, I have no business whining. Will you and your team be able to call it a night anytime soon?"

"In a bit."

There was nothing left for her to do here, but she wished she could stay and help them look at footage. If she didn't have to get up in a few short hours to meet Prescott, she would do so.

"Good night. Thanks, everyone." She made eye contact with each assistant and let herself out of the tech room.

It was the first time she had to fight to keep herself aimed at her apartment and not veer off to the same corridor she'd watched Prescott walk down.

Skye would go to his room.

She laughed softly aloud. Skye would have taken Prescott back to her room after the hot make-out session in the garden. She'd always envied her twin's ability to live in the moment and enjoy each opportunity that came her way. Of course, Skye was currently nursing a broken heart because she'd impetuously jumped into a relationship with a man known to be a womanizer.

Phoebe ran a bath once she'd let herself into her room. As she soaked, the evening's events swirled with the steaming water. And she realized that if she'd had her choice, she would be in Prescott's room right now. It wasn't like her to move so fast with a man, but she was getting tired of always doing the right thing, taking the time to get to know someone, only to discover they weren't who she wanted to be with long-term. She'd finally met a man she was incredibly interested in, only to find him while playing the role of Skye in order to keep peace with Mara and of course Russ.

She squeezed her loofah in the sudsy water, and as bubbles ran down her arms, she decided she was tired of being such a predictable people pleaser. Phoebe wanted to have fun, and she wanted it with Prescott Reynolds.

But she couldn't do it, not while he didn't know who she really was.

The sun's peach glow framed the mountains as Phoebe left the hotel early the next morning. Prescott's tall figure immediately caught her eye, and the nervous anticipation that had woken her smoothed into delight. She'd decided to let go of her worries about Prescott believing she was Skye, otherwise the week would be too excruciating for them both.

And it was going to be a full week—Skye had texted her in the middle of the night and told her that she needed more time. Phoebe hadn't bothered with a response. One of the things about being a sibling, especially a twin, was that she'd do anything for Skye. No matter what.

As she approached Prescott, she was aware of his heated gaze on her, yet when they stood face-to-face he looked past her, to the tops of the tree line where the dawn's hues smudged the sky.

"Good morning."

"Morning. Is it always this still at sunrise?" He looked around as if he'd landed on Mars.

"Yes. I always feel like I'm the only person out here, in total sync with nature. I can never get enough of the woods and the birds."

His eyes were supernaturally blue this morning against the backdrop of the sky. Phoebe had to remind herself they were talking about the weather, because his eyes communicated something much more significant. Her body answered his silent request, but unlike last night when her desire had swamped her, this was more of a slow, steady pulse. Something that might be able to last if she thought for a minute their relationship was anything more than casual. If she were able to tell him who she really was, and have Prescott call her Phoebe.

"I understand the connection with nature. In Iowa the farm fields can seem endless, and most people passing through might think they're monotonous. To me, the land is teeming with life and energy. In the summer, under a full moon, the corn fields positively dazzle."

She nodded. "You're able to see a lot farther than

we can in this valley. That's one advantage of living on flatter ground."

"Right. Ready?" He didn't offer to take her hand, so they really were going to get some exercise.

"Lead the way. Unless you want me to, as I live here?" She fell into stride beside him.

"I'm happy to do either. But if I'm in front, once we're on the narrower trails, I'll need you let me know where to go."

"Deal."

They were able to walk side by side for the first half mile as the paved portion of the trail led them into the woods. Companionable silence drifted around them, and Phoebe loved that she was sharing one of her favorite things in the world with him.

"What are you thinking about, Skye?" He moved a low-hanging branch out of their way. She ducked under it and kept going.

That I wish you could call me Phoebe.

"It's a nice treat to be able to share this morning with you. I try to tell my sister and mother why it's worth waking up so early, but my words can never do this justice."

He chuckled. "So your twin isn't a morning person? I thought identicals had the same exact DNA."

"We do share just about one hundred percent of the same DNA, but our personalities are different. I like to tell people that it's like living in the same exact house as someone else. The walls and rooms are the same, but we each like to choose our own carpets, wall colors, photographs and artwork."

"That's a great way of looking at it. Have you always been so good at analogies, or just this one?"

"Actually, I love drawing valid comparisons. It's almost a hobby of mine."

"How do I compare to the other men who you've let in your life?" His amiable tone belied the seriousness of his query.

"Whoa, that's pretty intense for before six in the morning."

He laughed. "I'm sorry. I know I've come across as a bit forward, but I can't seem to help myself."

"No, you haven't. You've never done anything I didn't agree to. Whether it's conversation or anything we've done…physically."

"I wouldn't do that anyway." Prescott said it like a vow, and judging from his behavior since they'd met, it was true. He respected women, and she felt safe and cherished around him.

She cast him a sidelong glance and wanted to stop and lie down on the forest floor with him, to heck with the bugs and tiny rodents.

The Avalanche Killer is a lot bigger than any woodchuck.

She couldn't stop the sigh that escaped her lips. Prescott noticed, and true to form, his hand was on her forearm.

"Are you doing okay?" His concern stymied her. She'd never been with a man so attune to her moods. "The festival week is a long one for the film and production crews, and I imagine you're already exhausted."

She paused and put her hand on the nearest aspen tree trunk, the smooth white bark cool to her fingertips. "I'm good, actually. I'm sure by the end of the week I might feel differently. I hike or run out here several days a week, but mostly I come out here for my peace of mind." The hotel administrative office could be a pressure cooker, and she often felt like wilted cabbage by midafternoon.

"Sorry. I don't mean to belabor the point, but it's like this cloud of sadness follows you around. I noticed it last night, too." Prescott's sweet words only served to raise her discomfort. Why couldn't she just be Skye as she'd planned and go with the flow?

Because she was still Phoebe, no matter how well she portrayed Skye.

"I have to admit I'm distracted this week. It's all part of the film fest and making sure our events go off without a hitch." That was exhausting enough. With the strain of the Avalanche Killer and Skye's disappearance, it'd passed into her unavailable-to-take-on-one-more-thing category.

He grasped her hand and gave it a quick squeeze. "I appreciate that you're spending some of your precious time with me. I understand how mentally taxing a long workday can be." He let go, and she missed the warmth as they easily fell back into the hike. Phoebe smiled to herself. She had to take almost two steps for every one of Prescott's due to his height advantage. Yet he never gave her the impression that she was slowing him down.

In fact, he made her feel nothing less than a welcome presence in his life.

"Will your sister be out here this morning, like yesterday?" His question, innocent enough, reminded her that this time with him was based on a lie.

"I have no idea. She's busy with the books and guest accounts. We live in adjacent apartments and I hardly see her during film fest week!" Phoebe hoped her reply sounded more genuine to his ears than hers.

They hiked for a solid half hour into the woods, as they'd agreed they each wanted an hour workout.

"We're getting close to the midpoint. Did you already go up this side of the trail?" She aimed for the crest of the hill they climbed, anxious to share the stunning view of Roaring Springs and the entire valley with Prescott.

"No, I went in the opposite direction yesterday. Last year I didn't make it out of my room much."

"Because some of the paparazzi had broken into the hotel those first few days, right?"

"Yes. We both know there's no stopping someone who's that determined, unfortunately."

"I'm surprised your bodyguards let you come up here by yourself."

"I have my phone, and they have my GPS location at all times while I'm working any public event. I take the right precautions by hiking earlier and keeping a low profile."

She didn't think he'd ever be anything but very visible with his striking good looks and magnetic energy, but kept her thoughts to herself. The last thing she wanted was for Prescott to think she was no more than a blithering fangirl.

Skye would do some fangirl flirting.

Phoebe shoved the thought aside. She might have had to put on makeup before she came up here, and made sure her hair was styled in a fun ponytail under one of her sister's glittery ball caps, but Skye wasn't here now. *She* was, and she was the woman Prescott was getting to know better.

Chapter 7

Prescott usually used his morning hikes as a meditation and a way to center his mind before the day's demands took over. He'd not spent a lot of mornings with other people in his life, but even while seriously dating the one or two women he had over the last several years, this time remained his own.

His desire to have Skye join him on today's walk had been visceral. He wanted this woman to know him as much as possible over the short week they had together, and if it meant giving up his solo time, so be it. Yet instead of feeling as if he'd lost something, it was more like Christmas morning, as Skye fit perfectly into his routine and seemed to enjoy the hike as much as he did.

Who would have guessed it?

The climb up the one side of the mountain was challenging and the habitat spectacular. He couldn't help keeping an ear open for the sound of someone following them, though. Not after last night when he'd been certain someone had been nearby in the garden as they'd kissed. And then when Skye told him about the lipstick message, he'd had to fight to not growl. He'd informed his security team, and they were on top of it. If Ariella was up to her sick actions again, they'd catch her.

He wished he hadn't mentioned the Avalanche Killer, though. Skye had enough on her shoulders this week and already knew about the danger—everyone in Roaring Springs was dealing with the serial killer's devastation, from what his security detail told him.

"Almost there." Skye shot the announcement over her shoulder, as they were on a particularly narrow strip of trail up against the mountain. If they slipped, it would be a long slide through saplings and underbrush to the level they'd snaked up from. Maybe not lethal, but definitely painful. Still, he couldn't keep his gaze from taking in her long legs, shapely from regular workouts. His hands itched to cup her ass again and continue where they'd left off last night.

Chill out or you're going to scare her off.

Nope, he definitely didn't want to scare this beautiful woman off.

"Ta-da!" She stopped so abruptly that he almost toppled over her, so lost in his sensuous memories of last night. He stopped and stepped around to her side on the surprisingly large rock outcropping they'd reached.

Below them spread the entire valley, and with the sun above the horizon, the windows on buildings in Roaring Springs looked like glowing golden orbs. Car headlights inched about on the roads that snaked through and around the town.

"This is even better than the view from the other side." Yesterday he'd hiked to the view overlooking a pastoral, smaller valley.

"Isn't it?" The sun backlit her profile, and he took it all in, from her smooth forehead and high cheekbones to her full lips. As if she sensed his stare, she turned and smiled. "I love coming up here and spending some time by myself."

"I'm sorry we didn't meet last year, but I'm afraid I probably wasn't in a great place then to meet anyone."

"Neither was I, actually. I, uh, I was still getting used to my new position as the events hostess, including the red carpet interviews. The film fest has always been significant, but it's really blown up in the last couple of years. Plus, weren't you dating a certain actress?"

He groaned. Ariella seemed determined to crash his joy, even when she wasn't physically present. "Don't remind me."

"I know you had a bad breakup, or at least that's what was reported." Her voice softened every edge that the bad memories painfully carved.

"That's an understatement. I was betrayed, my heart crushed, and it was public before I even knew it was true myself. It's going to sound hypocritical, but I'm only willing to take my public persona so far. I accept the public facets of my job, one hundred percent. But my personal relationships are just that, and to have something so intensely private become social media fodder was rough."

Her fingers brushed his cheek, and she rested her hand on his shoulder. "I'm sorry that happened to you, Prescott. And it's not being a hypocrite. Who am I to call anyone that, when I'm supposed to be a professional and yet I'm getting involved with one of The Chateau's most important VIP guests?" The gravity of her query triggered his protective instinct. Skye seemed to have the direct line to it. He reached for her, and when she stepped closer, he wrapped his arms around her waist.

"You are doing nothing unprofessional. Neither of us work for one another, and we're together during our free time. I admit that last night, when we were on the red carpet, I almost let my want ruin both of our reputations."

"And you didn't in the ballroom or the garden?" Her smile was genuine, the light in her eyes playful and warm. The heat of her palms seared into his chest where she rested her hands. He grasped one of them and brought it to his mouth, kissing her fingertips and then opening her palm for a kiss.

"I got you out to the garden, at least, before I totally lost it."

"You didn't lose it." Her tongue peeked out as she licked her lower lip, and his erection became painful.

"Can I kiss you again, Skye?" He was losing himself in her luminous brown eyes, and if he weren't so turned on he'd have interpreted the cloud that raced across them as a warning flag. But he wanted her too much, needed to show her how he felt.

"I've been waiting the entire climb for this." She didn't make him wait a second more as she pulled his head down to hers.

How cozy, a nice hike and now they were stuck up on top of the rock that Ariella had explored yesterday afternoon while she knew the hotel staff would be busy with the gala preparations. From her vantage in the hidden ledge of a rock wall just above the trail, she'd only been able to track Prescott and his whore as they climbed, but she knew that they had to come back down the same way, which was fine with her, except now she couldn't see what they were doing at the scenic overlook.

She bit back a laugh at the memory of the expression on the security officer's face when she'd told him she'd been walking in the garden and heard someone following her last night. It was the perfect way to throw them off her scent. She'd registered under an assumed name and changed her wigs and appearance out regularly, but maintained the same disguise for checking in and out, and for talking to any hotel staff. This kept her alibis straight, too.

All good things, since her initial attempts at spooking Skye Colton hadn't worked. It was time to up the ante.

Her plan was going to require more time, and waiting for Prescott and the little bitch to come back down the trail no longer appealed to her. Ariella carefully descended from the sheer rock cliff, expertly using her spiked shoes and rappelling gear. Once on the ground, she quickly changed into the hiking boots she'd left next to her backpack, where she stowed the rock-climbing gear. Turning to leave, she froze as a low growl reached across to her.

A grizzly bear blocked her path. A scream escaped her before she slapped her hands over her mouth. She was going to blow her cover and entire plan if she didn't buck up, pronto.

The bear didn't even turn toward her as it feasted on low-lying berry bushes. Carefully inspecting the surrounding area, she didn't see any other bears but didn't feel relieved that the formidable animal was solo. Keeping her eye on the furry mound, she backed away and made a wide circle back to the trail from the other direction. Once on the trail, she waited until the bear was out of sight and then took off at a full run toward the chalet. As her adrenaline eased and her pace slowed to a comfortable jog, she let her mind refocus on the task at hand.

Ariella had hoped she wouldn't have to risk being charged with assault or worse, but breaking the law was nothing if she had Prescott back in her arms.

Whatever she had to do to make that happen was worth it.

"I want to be with you, Skye, but only on your terms." Prescott's mouth moved over her throat as he spoke, his kisses leaving her dizzy in the morning air. When he called her by her twin's name, she expected it to douse her arousal, but nothing could smother the heat between them. Still, she couldn't deny the guilt that was growing more insistent with each additional moment she and Prescott shared.

Phoebe counted her blessings that no other resort guests had risen early enough to share the trail with, but she knew that she needed to get back to The Chateau.

"I want to be with you, too." Why not admit her truth? She'd never felt this intense an attraction to another man. She owed it to herself to explore it, make the most of it.

"Do you?" He cupped her face in his hands. She sat in his lap and he leaned against a boulder, where they'd sunk to as their kisses had turned tortuously erotic. His aquamarine eyes were half lidded from lust, and the pulsing sensation between her legs made logical thought difficult. "Because there it is again, babe."

"What?"

"Whenever we're together I get the feeling that there's something you're not telling me, Skye."

Yeah, like you're not Skye.

"I'm sorry, I've got a lot on my plate this week." She leaned back in his arms so that he'd see her expression. "It's ironic that it's the worst possible week of the year to meet you and try to spend time together, and yet if it wasn't this week, we wouldn't have met."

"I confess I did an Internet search on you and I'm impressed with your media presence. I can't believe we didn't cross paths before, Skye."

Phoebe's cheeks heated, and she quickly stood up to

avoid Prescott's too-knowing gaze. If this were a game of hot and cold, the partygoers would be screaming. "Hot! Hot! Hot!"

"We were both in different places in our life last year." The cliché was lame, but she had no choice. It was too soon to tell Prescott that she was Phoebe, no matter how much her conscience begged her to. She had to maintain her ruse as Skye for her parents' sake, for The Chateau. Heck, for the entire Colton conglomerate. Russ and Mara were counting on her.

Prescott's gaze was warm, and she allowed herself to soak it in. When he shifted it to the panoramic view for a last look, she felt the chill of its absence.

"I could stay up here all day." His preshave stubble shadowed the cleft in his chin.

"I wish I could." She waited for him to finish absorbing the serenity. A few minutes later, she led them back the way they came. Before they emerged from the woods, onto the part of the path that was totally visible to The Chateau, he called out for her to stop. Phoebe turned and faced him, knowing that she should be worried about how easily they got along. It'd be second nature to allow herself to think that Prescott enjoyed being with her and not her famous twin. If she'd known about this complication, would she have refused Mara's demands to play Skye?

"When can I see you again? I'd love to take you to a restaurant, wine and dine you, but this week makes it impossible to do anything like that without the constant surveillance of the media. Whatever's happening between us isn't something I'm willing to subject to that—not yet."

Not yet. As if they had a future beyond this week. Beyond her stint as her twin.

"I'm booked with meetings and VIP upkeep for the entire day, and I have to attend the premieres. I know that you attend the other premieres, too, right?"

He nodded. "I do like to support my colleagues, yes. But I'm free at any point after the films end. How about you?"

She knew she was risking more than Prescott finding out she wasn't Skye by spending so much time alone with him. But he was the only man she'd ever felt this comfortable around, this soon. "We could take advantage of the later hours after the spa closes and enjoy The Chateau's private access to the hot springs."

"You mean the ones that the hiking trails lead to?"

"No, the ones I'm referring to are exclusively ours, for guests only. They close at ten each evening, and the spa attendants go home. We'd have the entire place to ourselves. It's a wonderful way to wind down from a tense day."

His eyes met hers, and she felt the sexual awareness jolt all the way to her feet, curling her toes in her hiking boots.

"There's nothing I'd love more. See you at ten, Skye."

Before she had a chance to respond, Prescott pulled her up against him in a snug hold and kissed her firmly on her lips. When he released her, he smiled and turned toward the back of the The Chateau. Phoebe watched him for a bit until she finally forced her feet to move.

* * *

Prescott wanted to will away the hours until he could be with Skye again, but business called. He spent the entire day in press junket hotel sitting rooms at the Lodge, another Colton property. He answered the same questions from myriad reporters, always striving to keep the narrative on his premiere. It was a film he'd been honored to be a part of, and while he had no idea how the audience would react, he was hopeful the movie would at least earn back its cost. At best, the story he and the cast had portrayed would touch hearts, inspire people to live their best lives. Or at least take them away from the reality of day-to-day living for a brief two hours.

Once the press gigs were completed, he met his director to attend another film's showing.

"You want to join us for dinner after the movie?" Brian motioned between himself and several other directors who stood around a high cocktail table and waited for the theater doors to open.

"Thanks, but I can't."

His director's eyes narrowed. Prescott knew that his younger self would have jumped at the opportunity to have maximum face time in front of such an esteemed group. But his shooting schedule was full for the next two years. He wasn't looking for a new contract yet. All he needed tonight was the company of a good woman, and he'd found her.

Skye Colton.

"You look like maybe you're having more luck with your personal life, Reynolds." A director who'd turned

Prescott away from several auditions spoke with nosy authority. And reminded Prescott that too much of his life was public knowledge. All the more reason to treasure the private times he could carve out with Miss Colton.

"I'm not the youngster I once was, gentlemen. I need my beauty sleep." This earned him a hearty laugh, followed by a conversation among them about how having kids had totally destroyed their lives while making them better than they ever could have imagined. As Prescott listened to them each basically brag about their families, he realized he was the only bachelor present. The tug of longing in his gut wasn't completely strange to him—one of the reasons he'd stayed in the doomed relationship with Ariella for too long was that he'd figured they'd work things out and settle down together.

But Ariella had turned out to be the wrong woman. Sure, he'd wanted to be with her at the time, but he'd never felt like he did around Skye Colton with any other woman.

Tonight at the spa couldn't come soon enough.

Phoebe sought out her father and found him in his corporate office with the view of the majestic mountain.

"You've done well for yourself, from what your mother tells me." Russ Colton gave Phoebe one of his rare smiles. "If I didn't know better, I'd have mistaken you for Skye."

Of course he wouldn't have—while he didn't spend a lot of time with either of them, he knew his daughters. She recognized the backhanded compliment as the closest her dad ever came to a sense of intimacy with his children. Phoebe didn't have time to play blame-my-father-for-it-all, though. "Thanks. I came in here to ask if you've thought about asking your private investigator to look into Skye's whereabouts. I'm worried about her."

Russ frowned. "Your mother already asked, and my answer is the same. No. Skye wants privacy, let her have it. She's more like me and has an independent streak." Meaning Russ still believed Phoebe was too introverted for his tastes.

"You know, Dad, not all businesses are run by extroverts."

His head reared back, and Phoebe had to bite her lip to keep from grinning. She never called him out, and whether it was her role as Skye or her concern over her twin, she suddenly had the urge to push her boundaries with him.

"That sounds like a slam, daughter." Russ's eyes, the same brown as hers, narrowed.

"It's the truth, *Father*." She shifted in the too-high heels she'd taken from Skye's closet. At least there weren't any new lipstick warnings this morning. "You're aware of the person who thinks they're stalking Skye, but it's really me, right?"

"Security filled me in, yes." She heard him mutter an expletive. "Sweetheart, if I ever catch anyone attempting to hurt you, you know I'll make sure they never do that again. The Roaring Springs jail is a short drive away."

"I do, Dad, and thank you for saying that." She walked around and gave him a quick hug. When she straightened she noticed the creeping blush on his cheeks. Her father was a poker-faced businessman but he loved his family beyond measure.

"I'm glad you're okay."

"They may have placed a dowel on the red carpet last night, intended to trip me. I mean, to trip Skye. Someone might have it out for her, or it could be related to Prescott Reynolds. It seems he has an angry ex. With the Avalanche Killer still at large, everything seems like a lethal threat."

"It's ugly all around, and we're all still grieving Sabrina's death. They haven't even been able to give her a proper burial yet." Her father's usual stone face was crumpled with grief, and she immediately regretted being so hard on him. Sabrina's body was at the county morgue indefinitely until the investigation wrapped up.

"I'm sorry, Daddy. I know, this is a very hard time."

"I've hired a PI to look into Skye's whereabouts— As worried as I am I'm still hopeful she's taken a page from my book and gone on the lam to lick her wounds. She's said as much. Did you know I did the same when I was a younger man?"

"No, no, I didn't." Why did it take a family crisis for her father to share the deeper, more emotional side of himself?

Russ nodded. "It wasn't over your mother, but another woman…never mind. Your mother and I have made a great business partnership over the years." Phoebe ignored that he didn't say "great parents," because her siblings all acknowledged that Mara had raised them. Russ ran the Colton empire, as he referred to it. Now that the kids were grown, Mara proved as formidable a partner in the boardroom as Russ.

"Thanks." She meant it—at least Russ had agreed to do something about Skye's falling off the face of the earth.

"But don't get too excited—she's not looking to come back anytime soon, from the text she sent you. You're going downtown for the two premieres tonight, right?"

She nodded. "Yes. I have to work the cocktail parties and be seen with as many of the VIPs as I can." It was all part of the continuing coverage by the online magazine, plus several other national media outlets were in town. "I'm as much a part of the Colton team as I've ever been, Dad."

"I never said you weren't, Phoebe. Do us proud tonight."

She left his office without a reply. Russ Colton would never change. It was always business first for her father.

Phoebe thought she might run into Prescott at least at one of the social functions that evening, but so far she'd not caught a glimpse of his tall form. Three films had premieres tonight, all along the Main Street where, along with the original Roaring Springs Theater, two additional movie houses had been constructed for the festival. Her feet were killing her in the five-inch strappy silver stilettos as she made her way to one of

Roaring Springs's public parking garages. The summer evening was chilly despite the high temperatures earlier, and she wished she'd brought a wrap as the pink spaghetti-strap cocktail dress she wore offered zero warmth.

Main Street was hopping, with heavy traffic that wove around the pedestrians who spilled over onto the sidewalks. A couple of fans stopped her and wanted to talk about all of their favorite movie stars. Phoebe had no choice but to continue her role as Skye, acting as if she lived to talk about Hollywood. Other than her passion for horses and riding, Skye's only other obsession had been with Hollywood and celebrity culture. As fans asked Phoebe pointed questions, she gained a newfound respect for her sister's knowledge.

Her jaw ached from keeping her chin up and smiling so wide all day. After encouraging a group of tourists from back east to enjoy their stay, she waved goodbye and stepped into the street across from the Gold Rush parking garage. She looked both ways, waiting for the bright headlights on either side to crawl past or flash, letting her know she could cross safely.

The image of soaking her feet in the spa spring pools made her want to weep. As her rendezvous with Prescott approached, nothing sounded better to her than spending more time with him—if only she could be herself.

You would have never caught his attention as yourself.

Phoebe knew it was true but didn't want to accept it. What was happening between the two of them was organic and had nothing to with Skye. Except she couldn't get past the fact that she was lying to him each time she let him call her Skye.

The traffic showed no sign of letting up, so she turned to walk the block to the main pedestrian crosswalk. She stepped back onto the curb, but she found herself blindsided as a rush of warm, stinky liquid assaulted her. She tried to get out from under the stream and inadvertently stepped off the curb. Phoebe heard the oncoming traffic and felt paralyzed on the spot.

"Look out!"

"Skye!"

Several witnesses cried out over the sounds of squealing breaks and car horns. Phoebe's voice joined them as her ankle cruelly twisted in the high heels, forcing her first to her knees and then hands as she landed on the asphalt. Directly perpendicular to the traffic, she didn't see but felt a car bumper hit her shoulder. Knocked on her side, she curled into a fetal position to save herself from the inevitable.

She was about to be run over.

But instead of the hot scrape of metal against her bare skin or the weight of a car smashing her onto the pavement, she heard the voice of life.

"Skye!" Strong hands were on her, removing her hands from her face. She opened her eyes and looked into Prescott's concerned face. "Can you hear me?"

She nodded, unable to speak.

You're in shock.

"Does anything hurt? Can you move your legs?" Warm hands were on her body, feeling for breaks.

"I—I-I'm good." She pushed herself into a sitting position, leaning on her hip. Prescott's arms were around her, holding her. "I think I might have messed up my ankle. And my dress, my hair…" Goodness, her makeup was probably ruined, too. If anyone local who knew both her and Skye saw her, her cover might be blown.

The sound of sirens reached them, and she tensed. "Oh no. I don't want any extra attention." She'd already noticed that traffic was stopped and a crowd had gathered.

"You're going to have to be checked out. I'll go with you to the hospital."

"Is that our only way out of this?" She motioned with her hand to the scads of people surrounding them. Suddenly there wasn't enough air, and she had a strong urge to run, anywhere, away from this scene.

"They're almost here, hang on. I've got you." He half held, half cradled her in the middle of the street, and she kept her face buried in his chest. He'd probably ruined his tuxedo helping her, but she'd get the resort dry cleaning to fix it.

Phoebe pulled her head back and looked up at Prescott, who was staring at her. The concern on his gaze made her forget about her twisted ankle and the fact she'd almost become roadkill. He should know who she was before this went any further.

"Prescott—"

"Nothing to see here, folks, we're good." The loud announcement by the arriving EMTs stopped her from breaking her role as Skye.

Chapter 8

"This feels like heaven." Skye's voice was stronger than it had been in the ER, and relief allowed Prescott to let go of the taut rope that he'd clung to since he'd witnessed her accident.

Skye sat next to Prescott in the large hot pool, the water bubbling around them in the empty spa. Prescott was still shaken from seeing Skye hit by the cab but hoped his concern didn't upset her. He wanted her to know she could lean on him.

"It'll do wonders for your muscles. Hopefully you won't be in as much discomfort tomorrow."

She smiled. Her eyes were closed, her hair soaked straight, and her makeup had long ago faded. "You sound like the EMTs and ER docs. Why don't you just say it like it is?" She opened her eyes and turned her face toward him. "I'm going to be in a world of hurt tomorrow morning."

He leaned over and kissed her lips. She accepted his gentle caress, and while he'd planned to do a whole lot more than smooch tonight, there was no way he'd make love to her right after a car accident. At least, not the way he'd planned. The champagne in his room was going to get warm. And the rose petals—he'd have to clean those up, too.

Prescott wanted Skye to be fully present when the time came for them to be together in every sense of the word.

"That's nice." She curved her lips against his, and he fought to keep from grasping her waist and hauling her closer.

"It sure is." He looked into her eyes and acknowledged again that he'd easily lose himself in her.

Skye blinked. "Let's go out to the springs. It's prettier out there, and the water's even hotter." She stood, and he took in her beautiful form, perfectly feminine in a two-piece suit. He'd have expected Skye to wear a frilly bikini, based on her usual fashion choices, but the well-cut red polka dots with navy trim suited her better. At least, the part of her he was getting to know.

They donned the spa's custom fluffy terry robes, and he put his arm around her waist, wanting to be a support to her with more than just his strength.

"How are you feeling now? How's the ankle?"

"It's sore, which is why I'm wearing these ugly plastic clogs instead of flip flops. But I've had my share of sprained ankles before, with the run—um, hiking I like to do. It's nothing I haven't dealt with."

"You told the deputy sheriff that you never saw who dumped the water on you. Is that true?"

"Of course it is. Trust me, Prescott, if I'd seen who'd done that, they'd have had to deal with me. I totally trust Daria—she's a consummate professional. But she's overworked, along with the rest of the sheriff's department and RSPD. I feel awful that she had to worry about me in the middle of tracking a serial killer. We don't know that someone dumped that water on purpose, anyway. It could have been kids horsing around in one of the apartments above Main Street, or someone dumping their dirty dishwater out, for whatever reason." Her voice trailed off, and that familiar shadow appeared over her expression again.

"You think it was personal, though, don't you?" They stopped at the smooth rocks that surrounded the steaming hot spring. The sky was open above them, and as The Chateau was several miles out of town, the lack of light pollution revealed a fantastically glittering sky.

She nodded. "Yes, I'm afraid so." Skye undid her robe's tie, and he got out of his.

"Here, let me help you." He braced his feet on the rock steps, clearly man-made to accommodate the mountain's treasure. Skye accepted his assistance and slowly lowered herself into the pool.

"Ahhh, this is even better than the hot spa."

"Is that sulfur that I smell?" He settled in next to her.

She giggled. "Rotten eggs, yes. But a sulfur soak is very good for the soul, and it helps with skin ailments. Whenever we scraped our knees as kids, my mother had us take a dip. It'll wash out my injuries, that's for sure."

He never wanted to be as afraid as he was tonight

when he'd left the one premiere early and within seconds witnessed Skye tumbling into the very busy street. It was as if he'd felt her alarm, the way his gut had cramped.

"Skye, I don't want to put any additional pressure on you."

"But…?"

"But I'd like to take you to the awards ceremony as my date, at the end of the week. I know you have to work some of it, but when you're through, I'd love to have you sitting next to me."

She didn't respond, and he let the soft bubbling of the spring ease his fear that he was moving too fast, that she'd think he was desperate. And he knew he should have more concern for himself. He'd been used in the ugliest way by Ariella; Skye could prove just as deadly to his heart.

But he didn't believe it for a single second. Skye was different, even different from who he'd thought she was, who she portrayed herself as on-camera.

"I'd love that."

Three words, softly spoken in the Rocky Mountain night air. Prescott wanted to punctuate them with a shout of elation or a fist pump. He settled for allowing a rush of warmth to settle in his belly.

"Prescott?"

"Hmm?"

"Do you find this as romantic as I do?" She placed her hands on his chest and floated over him. He reached up and held her waist so that the gurgling spa didn't carry her away from him. Her breasts were brushing against his chest, the fabric of her bikini top a barrier to what he wanted.

"You're sore, Skye."

"Not that much, really." She watched him, and Prescott groaned with need as his fingers moved up and unhitched her top. He held one of her breasts in his hand and brought her mouth to his, giving in to the need he couldn't deny.

Prescott's tongue wasted no time rediscovering every nook and sensuous spot of her mouth, and when he gently squeezed her breast and ran his thumb over the nipple, Phoebe cried out. The freedom of being alone in the spa's hot springs, under such a dazzling sky, left her a throbbing mass of want.

And she wanted Prescott.

"Do you have condoms, Prescott?" As the words left her mouth, her doubts returned.

Is this how you want to be with him, posing as Skye?

He opened his eyes, and she saw the struggle he waged with his desire. "Not tonight, babe. You're going to feel your bruises tomorrow, and I don't want your memories of our first time together to be associated with any kind of pain."

She leaned in and kissed him. The water was over Phoebe's head, and she held onto his shoulders to stay afloat. They stayed together in an embrace for a few more moments. It was long enough for Phoebe to know she had to come clean with Prescott.

"I have to tell you something, Prescott, and it can't wait."

"Why don't we can talk later?" Desire blazed in his gaze.

She put her hand on his arm, stopping him from moving his hand to her breast. "No, please. I've waited too long as it is."

A frown marred the handsome lines of his face. "This sounds serious. Tell me something—is this going to put an end to the wonderful time we've been having together so far?" He tensed under her hand, and she recognized defensive posturing. Prescott thought she was going to end it with him. When they hadn't even really begun anything yet, hadn't approached the topic of being a couple. It was too soon for that, but she couldn't go any further without telling him the truth.

"I—I hope this won't end what we're beginning to share. But I won't blame you if you change your mind about me."

"That's just it, Skye. What we have is—"

"No, *stop*! I have to tell you now. Please, let me get this out." Her entire body shook as if she were on a mile-high precipice with no vision of what lay below.

"Tell me what?" Prescott's wariness contained the beginnings of exasperation. "Spit it out, Skye."

Now or never.

"I'm not Skye. I'm Phoebe, Skye's twin."

Prescott heard her say it, saw Skye's—no, *Phoebe's*—mouth form the words, but it took a full heartbeat for the realization to travel from his brain to his heart. And back again.

He'd been falling for the wrong twin. Or rather, the

right twin but under the wrong assumption. Either way, he'd been betrayed. Again.

"You *are* the woman I saw on the trail that very first morning. With longer hair, no makeup. Were you stalking me then?" Sick revulsion twisted his gut. How could he be so damned stupid the second time around? And with the first woman he'd dated seriously since the Ariella fiasco?

Phoebe—he actually liked that name, it suited her—stared at him, and as she registered his accusation, her eyes widened as if she were afraid of him. Which only made him angrier.

"No, of course I wasn't stalking you!" She shook her head, and he knew it had to pain her to do so just days after being pushed down the stairs at The Chateau. "I was on my regular morning run. When I got back that day, it was clear Skye wasn't coming back in time to host the red carpet. My mother—Mara—flipped out. You've met her, you saw her in action at the hospital. My mother's very persuasive."

"You could have told me who you were, once it was clear I was interested in you."

"I wanted to, but please understand I wanted to support my family, too. It's so important to them to save the Colton empire, and The Chateau's been suffering a loss since the Avalanche Killer struck. We had fewer reservations this year for the film fest, which is unheard-of. Normally we're sold out a full year in advance."

"I don't give a damn about any of that, *Phoebe*." He tried to sound disgusted over her parents' scheming, but he had to admit, at least to himself, that he wasn't as surprised as he should be. Her parents were in the midst of a heck of a struggle, business-wise, and they were worried about their missing daughter. It was hard to shake his sense of betrayal, though. He'd seen in Hollywood how people could manipulate the truth to suit their own purposes. Ariella certainly had done so.

Now Phoebe was part of that kind of manipulation, too.

You know she's not like Ariella at all.

No. He was not going to do his own interpretation of the truth. Phoebe had deceived him. There wasn't any valid excuse for that, except, she was doing it for her family.

"I'm so sorry, Prescott," she choked out. "I can't say that enough. I know you're upset, and you should be. I don't know what I'd do if I were you—"

She's different. Special.

Phoebe's tone was calm, but he heard the quaver, knew with all of his being that she was suffering over this. And hated himself for caring so damned much.

"Whatever."

She'd lied to him. Just like Ariella.

"I'm not going to stay if you don't want me here, but maybe a night to process this would help both of us."

"Both of us? From what I can tell, I'm the one who was betrayed. I never lied to you about anything, Phoebe. The man who asked you to coffee in the grand ballroom? That was all me. No pretending. Hell, you almost let me make love to you thinking that you were another woman!"

"I did." He didn't risk looking at her, because damn if he wasn't impressed with how she was owning up to it, now that she'd told him. And hadn't he suspected something was amiss, all along? He'd even thought about the possibility of a twin switch.

"I felt it in my gut that something was off with you, that you weren't telling me everything. I hate when I find out I was right, in this way."

"I haven't given you reason to trust me, Prescott, but even though I had to pretend to be Skye, everything I told you about me, how I behave when I'm with you, how you make me feel—it's all me. Phoebe. With you, I'm one hundred percent Phoebe. Well, except for the stupid false eyelashes. And the makeup. I've actually found out more about myself these past few days, thanks to your patience and the time we've spent together. I'm realizing that I'm the best version of myself with you."

"Words are cheap, Phoebe." His words were harsh, but he didn't miss how his anger was slowly abating. As if in the big scheme of life and this newfound relationship, maybe Phoebe acting as Skye, for good reason, wasn't the worst thing.

Still, he couldn't condone his own behavior. Why didn't he call her bluff as soon as he'd thought she might not be Skye?

You were afraid she'd disappear. That you'd lose her.

He hadn't wanted to step out of the comfort zone he'd found so readily with her. So while she'd misled him, this betrayal was nothing like what he'd suffered at the hands of Ariella.

His pride was dinged, but he knew that once he calmed down, the truth was inevitable.

The woman he'd known as Skye, who was in reality Phoebe, had gotten under his skin. He wasn't ready to let her go, not until he figured out where this was headed.

The rest of the week, all Phoebe wanted was to be alone with Prescott so that she could reinforce what she'd told him in the spa. That while she'd pretended to be Skye, her feelings toward him were real. After she'd told him the truth, he told her he needed some space to process it. He'd insisted she get to bed, alone, and rest. Prescott had assured her they'd go to the awards ceremony, that they weren't done, and emphasized his concern for her healing. To Phoebe this only underscored the integrity that attracted her to him in the first place. Prescott was the real deal.

Having to play Skye for several more days took on a different perspective for Phoebe since Prescott was in on her secret. It was actually a relief to not have to put up a false persona in front of him any longer. She looked forward to attending the awards ceremony on Sunday with Prescott, because her role as Skye would be nearly over by then.

Attending as Skye actually made it easier, because she could enjoy her very intense, very private feelings for him without turning any more heads than expected. Skye and Prescott were the perfect it couple, as they

were both in the entertainment industry and understood one another's careers. No one would give their
being together a second thought. Whereas if it were
Phoebe that Prescott was with, it might cause more
of a stir. She was certain most people didn't think she
was Prescott's type.

What Phoebe hadn't planned on, though, was all the
questions about her accident Tuesday night. At each
and every venue she went to, playing Skye—albeit
with her own lower-heeled shoes instead of the ones
in her twin's closet—Phoebe was asked three main
questions. Did she see the person who dumped water
on her, forcing her into traffic? Did she really believe
it wasn't on purpose? Was there a chance someone
didn't want "Skye" seen with Prescott and they were
sending her a message?

Phoebe had to dig deep to use her own calm demeanor while still portraying her twin well enough to
be convincing on camera. She assured each and every
reporter, and every civilian who stopped her on the
streets of Roaring Springs, that she was certain it was
no more than an accident caused by her high heels.
Then went on to say that Colton Enterprises had the
best security money could afford, and they were doing
their utmost to prevent any further upsets during the
film festival.

All the while one part of her, a bigger part each day,
remained focused on Prescott, whose presence was becoming something more than companionable.

Who was she kidding? Their relationship had been
so much more right from the first time he'd walked up

to her in the ballroom the afternoon before the first red carpet event. The subsequent hikes, meet-ups and shared glasses of wine and coffee had condensed what would have otherwise taken two months of dating into less than a week.

As she walked through the afternoon crowds on Main Street, dressed more like herself with no makeup and her hair hidden under a ball cap, Phoebe knew she was going to have to face the fact that after tonight's awards show, Prescott was getting on a plane and leaving Roaring Springs for good. She hoped that before he left they'd have time alone together— all night long. As Phoebe and Prescott: no more masks.

She slipped into the local coffee shop and went directly upstairs to the more private booth area where she'd agreed to meet Prescott. Climbing the steps still smarted, from her bruised knees to her still-swollen ankle, but she relished being out and about without being accosted by well-meaning fans and intrepid paparazzi. It was almost as if she were Phoebe again, no pretending needed.

At first she couldn't find Prescott, until she realized the person slumping on a booth bench with his ball cap pulled low wasn't some skateboarding teen but was in fact the man who'd so completely filled the empty part of her life.

It's only for another day.

Her conscience kept reminding her to not take any of it too seriously, that it was only going to lead to heartbreak.

"Hey." She slid onto the worn red leather seat and

tried not to think about next week, when the festival was over and Prescott gone.

He looked up from his phone and smiled. It was hard to see his eyes under the brim of the ball cap he wore, and she laughed at the logo on the dark blue fabric.

"What's so funny?"

"I never pegged you as a Yankees fan. It takes courage to wear that in Rockies territory!"

He shrugged. "I've followed the Yankees since I was a kid running through my dad's cornfields."

"Your father's a farmer?"

"I thought you already knew this."

"You said you were from Iowa, but there are some large cities out there, right?"

"Yeah." A waitress appeared and took their orders. She seemed to pause when she recognized Prescott but didn't react. A swell of pride warmed Phoebe's insides. Roaring Springs knew how to throw down with the most cosmopolitan cities.

"Not a lot of coffee shops have someone taking your order at a table these days." Prescott had noticed the extra service.

"We don't, either, but for film fest week, Roaring Springs pulls out all the stops. There are workers taking orders in most of the restaurants, including fast food places. It's a way to keep the momentum going, as this week represents at least fifty percent of all profit for the downtown establishments. That's saying a lot for a ski resort." The mountain town brought in a hefty profit during the prime snow months.

"So Roaring Springs is mostly a tourist-driven place?"

"Yes. Thank goodness, or we'd still be a backwater, two-lane town without the modern amenities we enjoy now." She thought of how her parents had done without cell phone service not much more than ten years ago.

The waitress returned with an iced green tea for Phoebe and iced latte for Prescott.

"This is what I want to do more of with you, Phoebe." Prescott looked at her, and Phoebe felt as though he was really seeing the real her, but she was setting herself up for a huge fall.

"Drink tea and coffee?" She stirred stevia into her drink. "We haven't had time to talk much since the other night at the spa. Are you okay with who I really am?"

It took all her courage to meet his gaze, to see the answer in his eyes.

"I'm more than okay with it, Phoebe. Do I wish you'd told me right away? Of course, yes. But I understand the need for discretion. And let's face it, no matter how natural it feels to be together, we didn't know one another less than a week ago."

Relief surged so strongly that she dropped the spoon on the table. It clattered and Prescott reached across and took her hand.

"It's okay, babe. I'm not going anywhere, and I hope you're not, either." His aquamarine eyes took on a bright blue intensity as he smiled at her. "Are you?"

She swallowed. "No, not at all. Thank you, Prescott."

"Nothing to thank me for. I wish we had some time

together, living a normal life. No cameras, no crowds." His wistful expression tugged at her.

"Are you tired of your profession, Prescott?"

"Of acting? Never. Of Hollywood and all the entertainment industry's trappings? Sometimes." He released a breath. "But I don't think it's fair to whine about the few negative aspects of my dream job. No career is without its pain-in-the-butt parts."

"True."

"I am getting a little burned out on the film schedule I've been on. I'd like to get back to the stage."

Her eyes widened. "I didn't know you were once a stage performer."

"That's how it all started—junior and senior high school productions. I've actually been on Broadway in between shoots, but always for a limited engagement."

"It seems to me it would get old in a Broadway show, with months and months of the same performance, eight or nine times a week."

"First of all, when you're in front of a live audience, nothing is the same," he explained. "Each appearance is new to most of the theatergoers, and if I'm doing my job right, I'll give them the performance of a lifetime."

"You put a lot of pressure on yourself." She liked that he took himself seriously, though. It was refreshing from the many celebrities she'd met over the years, and especially the dozens she'd interacted with this week as Skye.

"No more than any other professional. A surgeon gives it their best every procedure, why wouldn't I with each role?" He squeezed her hand. She turned her palm over and they intertwined fingers, their elbows on the table. Prescott leaned in close across their drinks. "I've been planning to take a two-week vacation, starting next week. Actually, tomorrow morning, as soon as the festival ends. I want to bring you with me, Phoebe." He kept his voice low whenever he spoke her name, and while she appreciated his intention to not have anyone overhear it, the low vibration of his tone made her achingly aware of her attraction to him.

Phoebe blinked, her mind racing. Trepidation racked her, because she knew that on paper it was too soon to go with him to Los Angeles. At the same time, a sense of pure joy burst in her chest, knowing that Prescott felt the same bond growing that she did. But how could she be certain this wasn't just a relationship that blossomed because of the way she'd had to pretend to be someone else?

"Before you get all worked up over it, please don't. Let's keep it simple. I'm not ready for this to end between us, are you?"

"No." She shook her head. "Not at all."

"Why do I get the feeling you're not really into going with me?"

"I'm sorry... I'm still feeling guilty for deceiving you about my identity. I absolutely would love to spend more time with you, away from here. I just can't help but wonder that once we're out of Roaring Springs maybe we'll discover that our attraction has been more about the glamorous trappings of this week and not about who we both really are."

Prescott's eyes narrowed, and she fought to maintain eye contact as he scrutinized her. Darn it, she'd overstepped. He needed time, their budding relationship needed time, to reach a new equilibrium now that she'd admitted that she wasn't Skye.

"As I'm looking at you now, without a lick of makeup on, in your beat-up workout clothes, I find you more desirable than ever. I love seeing you in your fancy clothes—no one looks sexier in a pair of heels than you do—but I'm interested in the woman beneath the professional facade, Phoebe. It's *you* that I care about." He pointed at her heart, and it was as if he'd shot a lightning bolt through her.

Prescott was the real deal.

And you've lied to him all week long.

"You know how to cut to the heart of things. I want you to be sure that you want to be with me, Prescott, not the person I was pretending to be all this week." Phoebe let go of his hand and gripped her glass, not wanting him to feel her trembling. Why did the one time she met the man of her dreams have to be the one week in her life that she had to play Skye for all the world to see?

Prescott watched Phoebe retreat into her emotional cave and wished he could reel back some of his comments about taking her with him after the festival ended tonight. All because he'd asked her to join him on vacation. Did she expect to go to his beach house in Malibu? He'd deliberately not mentioned Iowa, as he didn't want to scare her off with his confidence in how he felt toward her. He was certain that she felt what he did—the ferocity of the attraction between them was too strong to be one-sided. Unlike his previous relationships, being with Phoebe was easy, as if they'd already known one another for months, years, instead of a handful of days. Even when he'd thought her name was Skye.

Except when he got too close, like now. Something about the promise of total freedom and intimacy together, away from the rest of the world, freaked her out. He wanted to chalk it up to her fear that he'd find out that she wasn't Skye, but now that he knew, she was still being reticent.

"I'm the one who's sorry, Phoebe. You've had a rough week, and not just with the festival. It can't be easy to know there's a possible serial killer on the loose." Plus she was still mourning her cousin Sabrina. If Prescott could hit himself upside the head without drawing attention to their table, he would.

"When I've been with you, none of that is so burdensome." She smiled, and the strong woman he'd been getting to know better all week shone through her doubts. She reached across the table and clasped his forearms. "I never expected what's happening between us. It's been wonderful."

"*Wonderful* is the perfect descriptor." He wanted to be alone with her more than he'd wanted anything in a long while. "I don't suppose we have any chance of being together before the awards ceremony?"

"I'm due back at The Chateau in twenty minutes to start the prep for the red carpet." Regret lingered like maple syrup on her words. "But we'll have all night after the ceremony."

His own regret sucker-punched him. "I'm on the hook to attend the post-ceremony parties. We'll still be together, but not alone."

Her mouth twisted, and he suddenly knew that she wanted to come with him, but she was afraid of something. Maybe Phoebe was afraid of being hurt.

"Do you still plan to leave early tomorrow morning?"

"Yes." Before daybreak he'd be wheels-up in a private jet his director had provided for him to get back to Iowa with minimal discomfort. "You don't have to answer me now, Phoebe. If you're not there with me in the morning, I understand. You can change your mind at any point over the next two weeks and I'll have you flown out to be with me. All you have to do is call me."

She nodded, offered up a small smile. "As long as the number you gave me isn't for a burner phone."

He laughed. "No, not at all. That's my real number. You'll never have to go through an assistant to reach me."

Phoebe looked at her phone to check the time and then up at him. "I've got to go. I'll meet you at the ceremony, right after I finish with the red carpet festivities."

"I'll be waiting for you."

She looked around the packed café. No one appeared to be looking at them, or paying attention. "Is it okay to give you a quick kiss or too risky?"

"I'm willing to take the chance." He stood and met

her as she rose, pulling her close for a too-brief embrace. Her lips were warm and supple under his, and he fought with his desire, which only wanted to turn the embrace into an all-out passionate kiss that would lead to him and Phoebe in between his resort guest room sheets.

When he pulled back, he watched her slowly open her eyes and meet his gaze. "Oh."

"Yeah, this is the tough part. You go, and we'll make up for lost time later." He managed to keep his hands at his side as she left, ignoring the instinct to pull her back.

However long it took, he hoped that Phoebe would eventually want to be in his bed as much as he wanted her there.

"Hey, honey." Mara walked into Phoebe's room with several shopping bags. "I know I shouldn't have taken the time during the festival, but two baby stores are having huge blowout sales. I couldn't resist."

"Did you ask Wyatt and Bailey if they're okay with you buying all of that stuff?" Her older brother and his partner were expecting a baby soon.

"Bailey's getting too far along to care about this. She's realizing how much work it's going to be. And Wyatt is going to have to swallow his pride and accept my gifts. I'm the grandma!"

Phoebe met her mother's gaze and smiled. With all the recent sadness, some good news was welcome. As she watched Mara, her gaze sobered.

"Your father told me you asked him to find Skye."

Mara sat on Phoebe's bed as Phoebe applied her makeup and did her hair. After a week of posing as Skye, she'd memorized how the salon stylist had transformed her into her twin. Another evening gown from Skye's closet lay across her bed next to her mother.

"I did." She met her mother's gaze in the vanity mirror as she twisted her hair around a piping-hot curling iron. "I'm worried about her, Mom."

Mara's dark eyes glittered with the same apprehension Phoebe had felt all week long. "I know, honey. I am, too. As much as I keep telling myself this is just another one of her trauma-drama displays, my heart doesn't believe it. It's not like her to miss professional commitments, and this week has always been such a highlight for her."

Finally her mother was on the ball about Skye's whereabouts.

"She'll be okay, Mom, but it won't hurt for Daddy's team to put some feelers out and find her."

"You're right." Mara's half smile broke Phoebe's heart. "It's hard for me whenever one of you has even just the appearance of being in trouble. It's my mother's third eye."

"Why on earth do you think Skye's in trouble? No one knows her like I do, Mom. She's gone off on her own after every major breakup from a guy. Remember when she went camping for two nights when we were nineteen?"

Mara frowned. "You mean the time she came back at three in the morning because of the bears?"

Phoebe smiled, the memory jarring a happy thought.

"But instead of bears, it was a herd of pronghorn?" They both chuckled, but the strain of their worry pitched their laughter a bit too high. "Daddy will find her, Mom, don't worry."

"I suppose you're right." Mara stood. "I'm going to head out and make sure the caterers and our staff are all getting along well, and that the food is ready to go. You're on in less than twenty minutes!"

"Okay, well, I'll see you later, Mom." Phoebe thought of telling her mother that she'd been asked to join Prescott on vacation but it wasn't as if she was going to go. No need to upset Mara as the reality that Skye had been out of touch with them for a week now sank in.

After her mother departed, Phoebe looked over her extensive note cards one last time. She'd written out notes about each actor and festival VIP after she spoke to them all week, from the first red carpet, to the various premieres, to the cocktail receptions. While she was relieved that her facade was coming to an end, Phoebe understood why Skye liked her job so much. Getting to know and follow each actor was similar to following a sports team. Add Skye's natural effervescent nature, and it was the perfect career for her twin.

Phoebe grinned to herself. She knew that she relished keeping track of the numbers and being the behind-the-scenes person who put things together. Production was her calling when it came to the film festival and resort events. She only had one more event in which to portray Skye. One more night with Prescott, unless she made a decision to put herself first for once and go with him in the morning. LA wasn't a place she'd been to very often but she'd be happy in the Arctic with Prescott. Her conscience tugged at her, reminding her that she had a duty to her family. This was a rough time to make her own disappearance, when Skye was gone and with Sabrina's death still so recent.

Prescott could be a once-in-a-lifetime man.

Skye would encourage her to go for it, and would help her pack her bags. Wasn't Skye always telling her to live a little, to add more romance into her life?. This was the difference between Phoebe and Skye, though. Her sister enjoyed each man who came into her life with gusto, whereas Phoebe was slower to trust, and never felt comfortable entering a relationship until she knew the man fairly well. And while on paper she'd not known Prescott long, less than a week, it felt as though she'd been with him for much longer.

The sensation of butterfly wings fluttering in her stomach confirmed what she already knew. This thing between her and Prescott was never going to be a fling for Phoebe. Getting on the plane with Prescott meant she had to be willing to risk heartbreak.

Phoebe tapped her phone and saw that there wasn't any more time to fret over her decision. The last ceremony of the festival was about to start.

She slipped into the shimmery white evening gown that hugged every curve. She and Skye had each worn it to different functions over the last couple of years—it was one of the rare dresses that they both could wear. It hung a little loose on Skye's frame, giving off more of an Art Deco–era flair. On Phoebe it turned into an

'80s disco dress, emphasizing her fuller breasts with a deep cleavage and flaring from her hips while following the dip of her buttocks to perfection.

Excitement curled in her belly as she anticipated the light in Prescott's eyes when he saw her tonight.

Chapter 9

The festival's final red carpet event went so smoothly compared to the first evening that even the producer offered reluctant praise to Phoebe, whom he still believed was Skye.

"I have to hand it to you, Skye, whatever was bothering you last Sunday night is gone. Good job."

"Thanks." She handed the microphone and headset over and headed into The Chateau. A local network was broadcasting the event with a famous emcee flown in from New York, so Phoebe, or rather "Skye," was by contract not working the actual event.

The ballroom was a cacophony of excitement when she entered, the ceremony still a few minutes from its start. She looked for Prescott at his assigned table, but their seats were empty. She'd interviewed him on the red carpet again and thankfully this time hadn't knocked out his tooth. The local dentist had worked a miracle and glued it back in place.

"Skye Colton." A petite woman with familiar features, dressed in a killer green dress, addressed her. Phoebe didn't remember seeing her at all this week, and certainly not in the last hour during the arrival interviews. But somehow, she knew this woman.

"Yes?" Phoebe tried to keep her features relaxed. She was still Skye until the festival was over, which meant until this awards ceremony finished.

"You've got some damn nerve, going after Prescott the way you have. Who do you think you are?"

"I beg your pardon?" Her nape tingled with warning.

"Prescott is a man who has very particular tastes. To throw yourself at him when he's so vulnerable, and to think he's going to be around after this week, is wishful thinking on your part."

Ariella Forsythe. Phoebe hadn't recognized her with a different hair color and style. But Ariella's usual beauty was marred by the pure hatred on her face.

"I'm sorry if you got the wrong impression, but Prescott is a grown man. He can make his own choices."

The other woman's face became pinched, her eyes narrowed to mean slits, and Phoebe wondered if the woman was about to slap her. She tensed, trusting her body's instincts that she was under attack, even if it remained solely verbal.

"There's a name for women like you, Skye." Ariella spat the words at her. "*Slut* comes to mind. Stay away from Prescott or I'm going to ruin your professional reputation. You'll never land anything more than the Roaring Springs Film Festival whore."

"*Escort* sounds more professional, doesn't it? Although *date* and *companion* work for me. Prescott, too." Phoebe wasn't going to give in to this woman. She was acting as Skye, after all, and her twin wouldn't take any guff off a jealous ex-lover of Prescott's, either. "If you have a problem with Prescott, you need to take it up with him." She looked past the much shorter woman's head and nodded. "In fact, I think I can see him walking in now. Why don't we—" She looked to meet the frightful gaze again, but only an empty space existed where Ariella had uttered her ugly words.

"What. The. Heck." She searched for the actress and strained to see if she was heading for Prescott. No such luck.

Prescott caught her attention with a wide smile while he was still several yards away, on the other side of the dance floor that had been turned into the awards podium. She involuntarily smiled back, the attraction that simmered between them palpable despite everything that had just happened.

He wove around several groups of guests, and she wondered if her favorite childhood princess, a mermaid, had been the right choice. Because right now she was acutely aware that her life was about to be diminished to pumpkin status in a few short hours.

Relief soothed any angst from Ariella's threats. Thank goodness she'd 'fessed up to Prescott. It was as though by revealing her true identity she'd made the first step toward being more committed to whatever it was that they shared. For tonight it'd be Phoebe and Prescott, no more secrets. At least she'd have a memory to cherish for the rest of her life.

Prescott's gut clenched when he saw the shorter woman talking to Phoebe. From a distance it looked like Ariella, and he panicked. She wasn't involved in any of this week's events, and if she'd approached Phoebe, it probably wasn't a good conversation. A fierce sense of need hit him. All he wanted was to be next to Phoebe, protecting her from the angry woman.

He kept his game face on, smile included, as he made his way to Phoebe as quickly as he could without causing a stir. The other woman had disappeared.

When he reached her, he knew from her steely posture that she'd been shaken.

"Babe, what's going on?"

"You tell me, Prescott. I just got a tongue-lashing from Ariella."

"I thought it looked like her, but I'd hoped it wasn't." He was already texting his security team and motioned to one of his bodyguards.

Phoebe stood next to him while he filled in his bodyguard. When the guard walked off in the direction Ariella had taken, Phoebe turned to Prescott. "I didn't recognize her at first, as she's dyed her hair and is wearing a completely different look than what I've seen her wear in photos. She wasn't on my radar because she wasn't on any of the guest lists for this week, and she's not on the list as a VIP or otherwise for the awards ceremony."

He swore, and Phoebe's eyes widened at the string of very nasty words. "She's been stalking me, on and off, since our breakup."

"But I thought she broke up with you? I mean, she left the relationship."

"Yeah, she stepped out on me big-time." He leaned in close, and it looked like they were having an intimate, private conversation. Prescott didn't need any of the tabloids or more reputable news sources picking up on his frustration, especially if they'd identified Ariella. "But I'm the one who broke it off. She thought I should be able to understand that sleeping with other men was part of her job, as she put it. The price to pay for getting ahead with her career."

"She didn't really have sex for a role, did she?"

"Honestly, I have no idea what she did before she met me," he muttered. "My friends warned me that she was using me when we were on the same film set, that she only wanted in with the director, who happened to be a good friend of mine."

"He must have thought highly enough of her to cast her in a role to begin with."

"You'd think so, but it turned out that she'd gotten the extra role by her agent pulling strings with the production company. I wouldn't put it past her to bribe an exec or two."

Prescott watched Phoebe's expression as she digested the sometimes sordid reality of the entertainment industry. Her dismay was evident in the lines between her brows and the way she pressed her lips together in a straight line. "None of this is a surprise to you, Phoebe, is it? You've been working in our industry for several years yourself."

"Yes, but, um, I'm still centered here in Roaring Springs, and Denver. Skye's the one who travels to LA and New York frequently. I've been around the industry for years, yes, but, I'm not an actor, trying to get ahead with each role. It has to be a tough place to be in."

"It is, and frankly, more so for a woman. It's always been harder for women in the entertainment biz."

"You said she was stalking you—what do you mean by that?"

"She's showed up at some of my public events, and if she thinks I'm dating someone, she's sent messages to me through my PR team that she needs to talk to me. I won't speak to her directly at the recommendation of my friends, and my lawyer. That's why I was so concerned about the note in your room that warned you away from me. I'm concerned she's escalated her behavior toward me."

"You think she dumped the water on me, too, don't you?"

Pain seared into his gut at the memory. "I don't know. I'd like to think she's not so far gone that she'd actually do something so blatant. Although the lipstick message was damned obvious."

"I hope it wasn't her, too."

"What did it feel like to you, Phoebe? When the water hit you?"

She shook her head almost imperceptibly. "It happened so fast, I have no idea. Did I feel like it was personal? Yes. But as I remember it, it was a heck of a lot of water that dumped on me. The woman I just met is too short to have been able to lift a container with that much weight. Plus I was wearing my super-high heels, which made me stumble. If I'd had sneakers on, all that would have happened was that I'd gotten wet. It wasn't a well-planned prank, if that's what it was meant to be."

Prescott pulled out his phone. "My protection detail and The Chateau's security will figure it out."

"If they don't, Daria and the sheriff's department will. Plus with all of the RSPD covering the event, we'll get to the bottom of this."

"Agreed." Prescott grabbed two flutes of champagne from a server's tray. "Let's put this behind us for the next few hours and enjoy the ceremony. Here's to the most beautiful woman I've had the pleasure of getting to know this past week."

They clinked glasses and Prescott had the sense he'd never been so happy, even with the specter of Ariella's bad behavior hanging over him like a twister cloud in Iowa.

Phoebe had never attended the awards ceremony as a guest, and while it still felt odd to not be behind the scenes and working the production end of things, being seated next to Prescott as his date was more than a dream come true. She'd never been enticed by celebrity and pop culture like Skye, and it wasn't lost on Phoebe that if she hadn't had to fill in for Skye this week, she'd never have viewed Prescott as more than another handsome actor. The thought that she'd have never met him pierced her with unexpected melancholy.

He wouldn't have sought her out, either, if she weren't dressed to the nines like Skye every day. As the days had gone by, she'd let her guard down a little bit, like earlier in the café when she went without makeup and wore clothing more typical of her style. Prescott hadn't seemed to notice. That was what was so admirable about him. He made her feel special for just being herself.

"You've been quiet, babe." His mouth nuzzled at her ear, and she relaxed into the arm he'd kept around her shoulders for most of the last hour.

"We're not supposed to talk unless it's a commercial." She smiled up at him. "Aren't you worried about more photos getting out of the two of us? It'll give Ariella more ammunition to come after you. I think the pics of us when you carried me out of the street enraged her."

"I am past caring about photos of us together." His eyes blazed with red-hot need, and her breath caught. What was he going to ask her?

"Phoebe, have you given any more thought to spending time with me for the next week or so? I've been up close and personal with you, and I've seen how hard you've been working. It's unhealthy to keep pushing yourself at this pace. You need a break as much, if not more than, I do."

He had no freaking idea. Not only had she had to manage her usual tasks with production and accounting, but she'd had to do her sister's strenuous job as well. Her nerves were at their breaking point, and she was exhausted. But knowing she'd see Prescott each day and night had kept her going.

"I appreciate your concern. You're right, I need a respite. But you've only known me for a week, Prescott. You just found out my real name."

His eyes darkened, and she felt him tense. No doubt he wasn't used to women turning him down.

You know that's not true. You playing Skye has messed this all up. Caused both of you to doubt the feelings between you.

"I've already put your pretense behind me. That's why I'd hoped you'd join me on vacation. The offer stands, Phoebe. But I'm on a plane in the morning no matter what."

"I understand." She looked around the ballroom. This was the long intermission break, so she had at least another five minutes. "I need to use the restroom. I'll be right back."

"I'm going with you." But as he responded, his director and executive producer walked up to their table.

"I'm perfectly safe going to the ladies' room, Prescott. These gentlemen want to talk to you." She stood, took her clutch purse and made her way back toward the women's lounge. The crowds and lines had cleared, so she took care of business quickly, and when she emerged, she saw that Prescott was still engrossed in conversation with the film staff. Her thoughts were racing, and she needed a minute to take a few deep breaths and figure out her next moves.

The terrace was full of ceremony attendees, so she

walked around to the side where she knew few would venture, as the VIPs were here to be seen and no one but hotel staff knew how extensive the terrace was. In the shadow of The Chateau and several large potted plants, she walked to the edge of the back staircase and took in the full moon.

More than anything she wanted to hop on that jet with Prescott. But her responsibility was to her family, and she hadn't heard from sister since earlier in the week.

The announcer signaled that it was time to go back inside for the second half of the ceremony, and she allowed herself a few more seconds of peace, trying to separate her feelings and wishes from what was expected of her.

Her sister's well-being was obviously a top concern right now, but what could Phoebe do that her father's PI and law enforcement weren't already doing? Besides, odds were that Skye would call Phoebe when she was good and ready.

It was difficult to consider leaving her parents, especially Mara, alone while they tried to find Skye, but neither of them was as concerned as Phoebe, and it was as if Phoebe's life were an afterthought to them.

Skye's love life had always been the center of attention, and Phoebe's life had been a blur of pleasing her parents and being there for Skye whenever her heart got broken. For once, Phoebe wanted to take a cue from her sister and do what was right for her. It was Phoebe's chance to have something more than her life at The Chateau. And the regret she'd have if she didn't pursue her attraction to Prescott might last a lifetime—and drive a wedge between her and Skye.

She walked across the top of the stairs on her way back to the ballroom, her heart full of hope and her nerves tingling with the anticipation of Prescott's reaction when she agreed to go to away with him.

Her concerns about their relationship being based upon pretense tried to derail her optimism but all she had to do was remember the way Prescott looked at her. Going away with him after the festival was the right thing for her to do, even with her family in emotional chaos.

The ballroom lights were beginning to dim as the spotlights came up, and she turned to take a more direct route to the nearest French doors.

The hit came out of nowhere, directly to her back and over her right kidney. She screamed out in pain and abject fright as she sailed through the night air, her arms instinctively coming up to protect her face. But it wasn't enough as the back of her head met a stone step, and with a sickly mix of instant nausea and excruciating pain, her awareness turned into total nothingness.

Prescott gave Brian a last grin before he sat back down. He'd skimmed the room the entire conversation, his senses on alert for Phoebe's return. He didn't want to believe that Ariella's antics had escalated into criminal behavior, but she'd been amping up her threats on the texts and voice mails she'd left on his phone. She'd used burner phones so he'd never picked up the calls, and in fact blocked them immediately, but he was going to have to get a new phone. Right after the police traced one of the calls, if that proved possible.

The awards began again, and he looked at his watch. Phoebe had been gone for ten minutes. He texted her a quick *you okay?* And waited. In three more minutes, he was going to leave the table and find her.

When both his phone screen remained blank and his smart watch didn't ping with a text, he excused himself and walked out of the room, keeping his blank expression in place while his mind reeled with the possibilities of why Phoebe was delayed, none of them positive.

The lipstick message, the wooden dowel that she had tripped over on the red carpet and then tonight's personal message from Ariella. Most of the incidents were intrinsically shady and broke the law, but none had irreparably harmed Phoebe. The problem was that Prescott had no idea if Ariella had become totally unhinged, and if she had, how far was she willing to go to keep him under her perceived control?

Phoebe wasn't in the lounge area or at the back bar. He circled back to the ladies' room and stopped an actress he knew from a film they'd worked on together years ago.

"Bonnie, I need a favor."

"Hi, Prescott —sure, what is it? Are you okay?"

"I am, but I've misplaced my date. Can you do me a favor and check the ladies' room for me? She's tall, red hair—"

"She's Skye Colton. Everyone knows you're an item. I'll be right back. Don't worry, Prescott, she's probably right under your nose." Bonnie hurried into the restroom, and he paced, unable to stand still. In less than thirty seconds, Bonnie burst through the door.

"No one's left in there. Let me help you look. Have you tried the terrace? I was just out there getting a breath of fresh air. Even designer perfume can become way too much for my sinuses." She was trying to buoy his spirits, but Prescott's anxiety was at an all-time high. He had a sinking sensation in his gut, and his heart was slamming against his rib cage more than any cross trainer had ever made it do.

Something was wrong.

"You go left, I'll go right. This patio goes around the entire building. We'll meet back here." Bonnie acted as if she did this every day, and belatedly he remembered that she now worked on one of television's top detective series. But he was already moving away from her, circling The Chateau's huge form. Several couples remained here and there, and a full-service bar was serving up custom cocktails and champagne. Phoebe was nowhere around, but he kept moving, past where the decorative lighting illuminated the terrace and toward the dark shadows that covered the far side of the extended balcony.

He made it almost to the front of the building before he stopped, turned and retraced his steps. He and Phoebe had gone down the main stairs that led to the garden earlier in the week. On one of their many morning hikes together they'd swung around back here, closer to the gym entrance, and taken a set of steps that were narrower, not so well traveled.

Maybe Phoebe *was* under his nose, sitting on the

steps where they'd shared confidences. He understood needing a break from a crowd.

Please let her be there.

He was running now, his legs moving with effort, as if the Colorado mountain air had turned to sludge that he couldn't push past. His entire focus, the very beat of his heart, was on finding Phoebe.

Once he reached the stairs he found nothing—no one sat on any of the steps. Disappointment crashed over him. He'd been so certain—

A flash of light as the moonlight hit something white below caught his eye, and his gut clenched. Phoebe's dress was white. He ran down the steps, his hand skimming the concrete balustrade for balance.

"Phoebe!" The strangled shout tore out of his chest as he drew nearer and recognized her crumpled form at the base of the steps. Her head and upper torso lay on the soft mound of lawn while her hips and legs were askew on the concrete tiling.

Phoebe didn't respond, didn't move a muscle. He grasped her face, turned it toward him, spoke to her in urgent queries. No response.

"Prescott!" Dimly he heard Bonnie's voice, and he called to her.

"Call 9-1-1!"

Bonnie ran down and stood next to him while she called for help. "Prescott, let me look at her. I have EMT training—I got certified when I was auditioning for a role."

He allowed enough room for Bonnie to evaluate Phoebe, but he wouldn't let go of her hand. It was cool to the touch, but he felt her pulse under his fingers and willed her to be okay. She had to be. Somehow, in only one week, Phoebe Colton had become the center of his life.

Chapter 10

She knew she should beat feet out of town, but it was too delicious to watch Prescott's shocked expression when he found his precious little plaything on the ground, knocked out cold. Ariella couldn't really see his expression or hear what he'd shouted when he'd found her, but she knew by his body language just how distressed he was.

He'd been that way with her, once. When she'd admitted that she'd had an affair. His freak-out that day had been louder, more dramatic. Tonight he looked like a little boy who'd found out his puppy was sick and dying.

She bit the inside of her cheek until she tasted the copper tang. It reminded her to stay quiet and not laugh. If she got caught now, she'd never get to see her plan to fruition.

The trees immediately surrounding The Chateau weren't as tall and offered less in the way of camouflage than the aspens on the hiking trail. But it was night, and since she was dressed fully in black, in the climbing gear she'd changed into right after she'd warned Skye to stay away from Prescott, Ariella knew no one would see her. They'd have to be looking for her in the first place. All the security footage would show would be a figure dressed in black knocking Skye down the steps.

Ariella had wanted to completely cover the camera, but it would have been too risky. Plus she had no idea where or when she'd be able to take care of Skye. She'd been on her way to that bitch's apartment again when she'd decided to monitor the terrace in case Skye and Prescott came out for a drink during intermission. Prescott had always liked to enjoy a night like this when they'd been together, and they'd shared many cocktails under the stars.

Rage threatened to overcome her. Tonight should have been *her* night with Prescott. She gripped the tree branches with her leather-gloved hands, willing herself to hang on, literally. It was a fifty-foot drop to the ground and then at least a half mile run to safety. She couldn't lose it now.

Prescott would figure it out, once Skye was out of the picture. Ariella had hoped Skye would maybe die from her head injury—the sound of the crack to her skull had been a delightful treat—but even if she lived, she'd be stuck here in Roaring Springs. Prescott couldn't stay in this two-bit town, not with his schedule. She knew he spent an entire month back in Iowa with his hick family each year, and he hadn't been yet. His assistant had let it slip that he was heading there after the film festival when Ariella had posed as a PR rep for a fictitious movie company. Her shoulders relaxed as her rage dissipated. Prescott was hers, and she'd soon have him all to herself. Even if it had to be in the middle of a cornfield, she'd convince him that he couldn't live without her.

"Thanks for giving me your statement…Skye." Deputy Sheriff Daria Bloom smiled past what had to be exhaustion. She sat on a flimsy stool next to Phoebe's hospital bed in the trauma center as she took notes. Phoebe didn't remember the life flight to the hospital, but when she'd regained consciousness, both Prescott and Daria had been at her side. Prescott had been shooed from the room so that Daria could take her statement, and to see if Russ and Mara were here yet. They were en route, at last report.

Daria had driven in from Roaring Springs to interview Phoebe in the hospital. Phoebe had no idea how the deputy sheriff was managing it all with the Avalanche Killer to catch, bodies to identify and the whole town up in arms over what tragedy might befall them next.

"I do have a favor to ask you, Daria. I can't let anyone else know that I'm not Skye, not until the festival is completely over."

"Hey, I think it's brilliant that you were able to fill in on such short notice without being discovered. I mean, no one has even breathed a hint that they think you're not your sister." Daria's golden eyes were full of compassion as she spoke to Phoebe. "I do have to ask, for my own edification, does Prescott Reynolds know who you really are?"

Shame pained her more than her head trauma and body bruises. "Yes. I had to let him know the truth."

Daria assessed her with an open expression. "You two seem to have gotten real cozy this week, in the best of ways. I'm glad you came clean with him."

"Me, too." Phoebe tried not to grimace at the thought of how her plans to go away with Prescott might be jeopardized due to her fall. Her parents would be even more reluctant to agree to her leaving The Chateau. "And thanks for keeping it quiet."

"Denver's not in my jurisdiction, so if you've told the hospital that you're Skye, it's none of my business. Just get it straightened out with the hospital's billing office, so that you don't commit insurance fraud."

Their conversation was interrupted as Mara pushed past the curtain, followed by Russ. Both of her parents appeared harried.

"Honey, how are you feeling?" Daria stepped back and allowed Maria to get close to Phoebe.

"I'm fine, Mom. They're checking me out, but I doubt it's anything serious." She knew she'd ache like hell tomorrow, but besides the hit to her skull she thought she was doing okay.

"Glad to hear it." Russ adopted his usual calm demeanor, but she saw the worry in his eyes.

"I'll let you folks get to it." Daria nodded at them.

"You haven't told anyone she's not Skye, have you? We've made it this far and—" Russ put a restraining hand on Mara's forearm.

"It's not Daria's problem, Mara."

Daria gave them both a small smile. "I've got bigger fish to fry back in Roaring Springs. You all work out who's who on your own." She looked back at Phoebe, and if her head didn't pound so hard, Phoebe would have giggled at the deputy sheriff's expression. Daria knew Russ and Mara all too well and took their manner in stride. "See ya."

"'Bye."

Mara waited for Daria to be out of sight before she looked back at Phoebe. "You look upset. What's bothering you?"

"That was ridiculous, Mom." Phoebe struggled to stay calm and in the relaxed reclining position on the hospital bed that suited her best, but Mara's insistence that she maintain her ruse as Skye was a bit much.

"It's only for another twelve hours, Phoebe." Mara hissed her name, and while her mother's behavior was vile and unusual for her, Phoebe knew that her fall had shaken both of her parents.

"If I'd known you two were going to do this, I wouldn't have agreed." Russ Colton stood at the foot of her bed, his imperious bearing in direct contrast to the worry in his eyes.

"That's totally false, Dad, and you know it. You've never done anything but whatever it took to keep your empire on top."

"Phoe—" He stopped speaking at the sound of the

footsteps approaching her bed, curtained off from the huge trauma bay. She'd been flown to Denver because of her head trauma and had undergone a battery of tests over the last several hours.

Phoebe didn't have to see Prescott walk through the curtains to know it was him. She'd learned his gait this week, along with a lot else. The man had saved her life tonight.

"I asked for cream and sugar for yours, Ms. Colton, and here's your black, Mr. Colton." He handed her parents coffee from the square cardboard carrier and brought a covered cup to Phoebe. "Chamomile for you, Phoebe."

"Thank you." She made a weak motion with her hand to the bedside tray table. Right now the nausea had abated, but she was afraid to introduce anything new to her stomach. She'd only agreed to give Prescott a drink order because he'd seemed so damned lost when her parents arrived and basically told him he wasn't on her medical consent forms and ordered him out of the room.

"'Phoebe?'" Mara's face was ashen.

"It's okay, Mom. I told Prescott the truth. He's not going to say anything."

"I hope not." Russ's expression matched Mara's.

Familiar anger welled up, mixed with the usual dose of resentment and something else as Phoebe stared at her parents. Regret or sadness, she wasn't sure. All she knew was that she was tired of being their obedient daughter and Skye's agreeable twin. She'd filled in for Skye all week long; where was Skye when Phoebe needed her most?

The missing piece of her heart that was Skye ached as much as her sore head. Somewhere, wherever Skye was nursing her broken heart, maybe she had a flash of Phoebe's discomfort. Good. Maybe she'd call or text. Or even better, come home.

Prescott's hand was on her shoulder and she reached for it, needing the warmth.

The attending doctor entered the room, taking in Prescott and Phoebe's parents with an air of impatience. "Hello, folks. Glad you're all here, but I need to speak with Skye alone. Unless you give them permission to be here?"

"It's fine, they can hear whatever you have to say. And on a very confidential note, I'm not Skye. I'm Phoebe. Long story, we're identical twins." She was Skye until Mara and Russ deemed the pretense was no longer needed, but not here, and not with Prescott. Her jaw tightened, but a shooting pain in her temple stopped her from fully gritting her teeth. Forcing her muscles to relax, one by one, she closed her eyes and sank into the hospital pillow, a sore substitute for her own bedding at The Chateau.

"Okay, Phoebe." The young resident who served as the attending physician approached the spot next to her as Prescott moved to stand behind the bed. She wore her white coat over blue scrubs and appeared hopeful as she smiled at Phoebe. "How are you doing?"

"I'm hanging in there. Do you have any results yet?"

"I do." She looked down at her smart tablet. "Good

news—your concussion is mild, and while you've sustained some hefty bruising, you have no indication of any fractures."

"Thank God!" Mara let out a strangled cry, and Phoebe was aware of her stoic father actually putting his arm around Mara's shoulders and pulling her close. It was as rare as a yeti sighting in Roaring Springs.

Prescott's hand had returned to her shoulder when the doctor appeared, and he gently squeezed. He'd been worried, too.

"So I can go now?"

The doctor shook her head. "No, we want to keep an eye on you overnight. Which really means just until noon tomorrow."

"Can she fly, Doctor?" Prescott's query jolted through Phoebe's semi-hazy state, and she groaned as her stiffening made her head throb.

"Ah, I wouldn't recommend it, not for at least a week or so. Is there somewhere you have to be in the next few days?"

"No." She'd be happy enough to return to The Chateau and nurse her wounds for the next several days. Her heart was about to be added to the list with Prescott leaving.

"Actually, there is. I'm taking you with me." Prescott spoke quietly but there was no mistaking the steel in his tone.

"What? We already—"

"You're not safe at The Chateau or in Roaring Springs any longer. Since you can't work, why not come home with me as I've offered?" Prescott was back behind the doctor now, watching her. He didn't seem to care if her parents, the doctor or anyone else heard their discussion.

"Because your time is valuable, Prescott. I'm not intruding in on your vacation. Besides, you heard the doctor, I can't fly." He was due to leave within a few hours if the clock on the wall was correct.

"We're going to take the best care of her at home, Prescott. You've been generous with your time and all you've done tonight, thank you." Russ spoke for himself and Mara. But Prescott either wasn't listening to her father or didn't want to speak to him. Prescott's entire focus was on Phoebe.

"I'd like to speak to Phoebe alone, please." Prescott's voice suddenly went from concerned to commanding authority.

"Yes, please. Thank you, Doctor, for all you've done."

"It's my job." She paused. "As for flying, no, you can't. But driving…" The doctor looked from Phoebe to Prescott. "I think if you're willing to take it very slowly, and make frequent stops to include a full night's rest as needed, a drive shouldn't be a problem. You might want to book yourselves a hotel with a whirlpool, as your muscles are going to start complaining and won't let up for several days."

"Thank you." Phoebe didn't look anywhere but at the doctor. She didn't want Prescott to see the anticipation in her eyes. Time alone with him, without the stress of the festival or of being stalked by anyone, sounded pretty dang good right now.

The doctor nodded. "I'll be back to check in on you before I'm off my rounds at seven, and then barring any unforeseen complications, you'll be released by lunchtime." The physician left, but Phoebe's parents lingered.

"We have this, Prescott." Mara reinforced what Russ had stated.

"I understand that you're both on edge, but Phoebe could have been injured far more seriously this evening." Prescott's voice bore a steely undertone she hadn't noticed before. "I can provide top-notch security, and actually the best security is getting her out of Roaring Springs. Whoever did this means business."

"And whoever did it is most likely your ex." Russ looked at Mara before continuing with Prescott. "It's true, my detail told me that Ariella Forsythe threatened him from the moment he dumped her several months back. Then she confronted our daughter tonight right in our grand ballroom!" Russ's ire seemed authentic, and Phoebe felt sorry for her father. It wasn't easy, trying to keep the business afloat with family worries.

"Then if Prescott goes, Phoebe is safe." Mara nodded.

"Hold on a minute. No offense, Russ and Mara, but your security wasn't enough to protect Phoebe tonight. And if the same person was behind the warning note in her apartment, dumping water on her and forcing her into moving traffic, not to mention the first red carpet tripping incident, we can't risk them upping the ante. She'll be safer with me."

Russ and Mara opened their mouths to reply, but

Phoebe had had enough. Her head pounded, and the only thing that soothed her discomfort was Prescott.

"Mom and Dad, Prescott's right, I'm afraid. I'm not going to be safe back home anytime soon. You won't need me for at least another couple of weeks, as the festival is over." She always took the week after film fest off, at her parents' insistence, in fact. She saw their befuddled expressions and forged ahead, using what they'd both taught her. Strike when your opponent was most vulnerable.

"I love you both so much. Thank you for dropping everything and driving in. I know it was a shock and inconvenience with the awards ceremony going on and film fest week wrapping up."

"Honey, all we care about is your well-being." Russ walked to her side and planted a kiss on her cheek, his version of acquiescence to her wishes. Genuine affection shone in his eyes, and if pain wasn't spiking through her head and down her limbs she'd have reached up and hugged her father. Deep down he cared, it just wasn't apparent much of the time.

"What your father said." Mara kissed her and, while still leaning over Phoebe, looked at Prescott. "Thanks for taking such good care of our little girl."

"Mom." Phoebe thought her mother needed more rest than she did. Maybe the worry over Skye was weighing heavy on her, too.

Don't go there. Take care of yourself for once.

Phoebe watched as Russ shook Prescott's hand and Mara kissed his cheek, then left. As much as she hated admitting that she needed time out for just herself,

Phoebe knew that she'd be no good to anyone, including Skye, if she didn't keep herself safe and far away from Ariella. The fact that the Avalanche Killer was preying on women throughout Roaring Springs didn't make her decision hard.

"Are you sure you don't mind having to drive all that way?" She wanted to be sure Prescott wasn't making a rash decision. He'd moved back to "his" spot next to her bed and held her hand as he sat on a folding chair.

"I love driving cross country. It'll be part of my vacation. And we can enjoy it all together." His eyes gleamed with determination, and Phoebe wanted to give in so badly. To just go with what she wanted for once.

Phoebe smiled and looked at Prescott. "I'm in."

"Really? Great." His smile did more for Phoebe's spirits than anything else could in the moment. Prescott reminded her that she was her own person with her own life to live.

Time away from the stress of Roaring Springs sounded like a good idea, but being alone with Prescott was her idea of pure bliss.

After Phoebe was moved to a private room for the rest of her stay, Prescott chose to catch a catnap in the easy chair next to her bed rather than leave her alone again. As soon as she was released from the hospital, he had his driver take them back to Roaring Springs in order to gather his luggage and for her to quickly pack.

They were on the road by 2:00 p.m.

"How did you find this to rent on such short notice?"

Her voice reflected her incredulity at his efficiency and he grinned. He'd settled Phoebe into the very roomy leather passenger seat of the Cadillac Escalade SUV and made certain she was completely comfortable before driving out of the rental lot and away from Roaring Springs.

"You must have taken a conk on your noggin, because it's kind of obvious." He looked at her but saw that she only looked straight ahead, and immediately recrimination washed over him. Phoebe was just coming off an awful attack and had to be struggling to stay focused, much less think about something as mundane as car rentals.

"I'm sorry, Phoebe. You're hurting over there, and I'm trying to yank your chain. They had a slew of rentals available, as many of the festival attendees have left town."

"That's right. A lot cleared out last night, right?"

He nodded. "Yeah. I'd considered it, earlier in the week."

"But?"

"But then I met you."

He knew he was risking it to put his feelings out there for her to examine, but he wasn't about to pretend he didn't have them.

"I hope you don't decide this was all a big mistake." Her voice was filled with such longing that he pulled the car over onto the shoulder. "Hey." Gently he cupped her faced and turned it toward him. Her eyes were full of tears, and anxiety clawed deep in his chest. "Babe. Are you in pain?"

"Not physically." She blinked, her long lashes damp and emphasizing the circles under her eyes. "I just don't know what we both are hoping for in this. You don't know me very well at all, Prescott."

"I could say the same about me. Listen, if you've changed your mind—"

"I haven't." She sniffed. "I want to get out of here, and I do want to know you better." Prescott wondered if she meant it. He hoped so. Each time they'd been together this past week, he'd sensed she was holding a part of herself back from him. Except when they kissed, and more. Then he knew he had her all to himself.

"I'm glad." He lowered his lips to hers, trying to keep the kiss as chaste as possible, because he figured the last thing she needed was to be jostled. When she wrapped her arms around his neck and pulled him in closer across the seat divide, he silently cursed whoever had hurt her. He could have lost this, lost Phoebe, all in one horrible instant. The kiss deepened and his erection strained against his cargo shorts. Prescott fought not to growl in distress when he pulled back.

"Babe. I want nothing more than to make love to you, but not here, not when you're not one hundred percent."

"That's the second time you've had to say that to me in a few days. As corny as it sounds, finally being alone with you will cure me, I'm certain." She gave him a cheeky grin, and he couldn't help laughing.

"You must be feeling better already."

He gave her a quick kiss on her forehead before

shifting the car back into Drive. As the miles fell behind them, he told himself it'd be a great time with Phoebe in Iowa. He couldn't wait for his family to meet her, and her them.

But the image of Phoebe at the bottom of the stone steps remained on constant replay in his mind, and he knew he wouldn't rest until Ariella or whoever else might have done that to her was caught.

Chapter 11

Phoebe couldn't believe she'd done it. After twenty-five years of being the good twin, only leaving home for college, she'd taken off with a man. A Hollywood heartthrob, no less. She smiled with her eyes closed as Prescott drove them out of Colorado.

"What's the grin for?" His voice wooed her back from her doze, and she peeked through her sunglasses at the ribbon of highway ahead of them.

"This is the first time I've ever gone away with a guy. And I'm looking forward to going back to Los Angeles."

"About that, Phoebe." His tone was so serious she opened her eyes and looked at his grim profile.

"What is it?"

"We're not going to California. I'm taking you home with me to Iowa."

"*Iowa?*" Belatedly she checked out the highway signs and realized they were heading east, not southwest.

"Yes. My safe place. It'll be safe for you, too."

"Okay." She took the news like another hit to her kidneys. He was taking her home to meet his family. She was grateful she'd told him who she was—this could have proved disastrous otherwise.

"You said you've never gone on a vacation with another man?" He sounded so surprised that she turned to face him again, ignoring the protesting discomfort from her head.

"Nope, never. As in I've not gone off with a guy—Skye's the one who does that, usually."

"Sometimes I wonder if you and your twin sister switch places every other day." He smiled, but she saw a flash of steel in his gaze.

Phoebe sat up straighter, her attention held by the wisdom of Prescott's words. Was he finally becoming angry over her deception? Allowing himself to feel the full depth of her betrayal? He'd told her he was over it, but she couldn't help the fear from creeping in, the fear that Prescott would change his mind about moving forward with her.

"What do you mean?"

"I mean that ever since you've told me you're really Phoebe, I'm wondering why I didn't know something was off sooner."

"How could you? You'd never spent any time with either of us before. And isn't that the purpose of this next week? To get to know one another better?"

"It is." He nodded, and as she drank in his handsome profile, she appreciated how relaxed he was with her. Prescott had never put on any airs with her, or played his VIP celebrity status. He was the real deal.

Guilt marched along her spine, up to her nape, and she rested her head on the back of the seat again. Even if Prescott forgave her for betraying him this week, she still hadn't exonerated herself. Her stomach started to feel off. Queasiness was a common symptom of concussion, and she didn't want to get sick on the road.

"You feeling bad again?"

"Not really. I just don't want the nausea to come back."

"There's a bottle of ginger ale in your door handle."

"Is there anything you don't think of?" She reached for the bottle and held the cold plastic to her forehead for a minute before opening the beverage.

"Your mother had it sent out, along with the picnic lunch in the back."

"She feels bad that she and Dad were such butt heads at the hospital."

"They weren't that bad. I imagine they were pretty shook up." He adjusted his posture as he drove, and she wondered how often he was in the driver's seat.

"They were, but I'm okay and it's behind us now."

"Why didn't any of your siblings show up at the hospital?" She paused mid-gulp of delicious, soothing ginger ale. Prescott had unwittingly dug deeper with his question than she wanted to share.

"Skye's out of town, obviously. And I'm guessing my parents didn't tell my other siblings, to avoid my cover being blown." She and Skye were often insepara-ble, and her older brothers and she had a genuine bond when they shared the same space. Phoebe had no doubt that Mara made sure no one was notified about her fall because of the risk of her being outed as herself and not Skye. None of her family would ever mistake her for Skye, even with all the appropriate cosmetic changes.

"You said that besides Skye, you have three older brothers?"

She nodded, noticing that it didn't hurt her head too much. "Yes, and then we have two cousins that my par-ents took in and raised after my aunt and uncle were killed, so they feel more like siblings."

"Your parents don't look old enough to have raised all those kids."

"They're not, in many ways. But it's my mother and the nannies who did the raising, to be fair. My father has always been focused on the Colton empire, as we call it at home. Building the largest resort conglomer-ate in Colorado, and eventually North America, has always been his goal." She tried to keep resentment from her tone.

"I can see where you get your single-mindedness when it comes to your work from. And I mean that as a compliment."

"Thank you?" She teased him, needing to lighten up the conversation. "What about your family?"

"We're Iowa corn farmers, to be truthful. My fa-ther has dabbled in various other jobs on the side, to keep the cash flow looser when times are tough for the crops. He's a man who can do just about anything he sets his mind to, and I learned everything I know from him."

"Did it bother him that you didn't want to stay in Iowa and work the farm with him? I'm assuming it's a large farm?"

"It's good sized, yes. No, he wasn't upset about it at all. I guess in Dad's mind he feels if I ever decide I'm done with acting, I can come back and take over. But if I don't, he's okay with that, too."

"You're lucky to have that. Parents who let you be you."

"What part of you can't you be around your folks?" Prescott was using their time together on the drive exactly as he'd promised—to get to know her better. And it'd sounded like a good thing, back in the middle of the mess in Roaring Springs. But as they blew past the Welcome to Nebraska signs, she felt the intimacy loom large between them in the large SUV.

Phoebe knew in her gut he was going to eventually feel his anger toward her for deceiving him. Which meant sending her packing back to Roaring Springs was a very real possibility.

"There's a lot, but I don't want to get into all of that right now. Tell me more about your family, Prescott"

Prescott drove the last mile of the first day's route in quiet, soaking up the rolling hills that were this part of Nebraska. He would have easily made the drive home to Iowa in one longer day if solo, or if Phoebe didn't have a bruised body to heal.

The sun began to set behind them as he drove directly east, and its parting rays set the road and brush aflame with gold. The timing of their arrival at the bed-and-breakfast would be perfect; they'd be there before dark. His only concern was Phoebe's safety, and worry that Ariella had somehow followed them here. But he'd taken all the precautions his security detail told him to, and they'd helped him with the vehicle rental so that he'd lose anyone who'd tried to tail them.

Of course, if all of the vicious actions were by Ariella, nothing would stop her from showing up at his parents' farmhouse, where he'd stupidly taken her last summer. She'd only flown in for two days and had left such a poor memory in his family's collective minds that he didn't think he'd ever live it down. After that last debacle, he figured they were going to be reserved with Phoebe. He heard it in his parents' voices when he'd called to tell them he was bringing Phoebe Colton home. His parents weren't big on television and especially not celebrity culture, but they did try to catch his interviews. They knew Phoebe as 'Skye' from the red carpet.

He glanced at Phoebe as she lay sleeping. Away from the harsh lights and glittering nights of the film festival, sans cosmetics, she was more beautiful than ever, even with the various cuts and bruises on her face and forearms. Turning his attention back to the road, he had a hard time ignoring the question that had bothered him since he'd first seen Phoebe on The Chateau's fitness trail. How had he missed meeting her last year?

While Phoebe had explained that she was more of the behind-the-scenes sister, he clearly remembered seeing both twins at last year's film festival. He'd been involved with Ariella at the time, so of course he'd been distracted. The more he thought about it, the more he remembered about Phoebe from last year's festival, as she'd actually helped him with a technical issue when his and Ariella's room keys stopped working. She'd quickly fixed the problem and offered him an enchanting smile. A smile he'd never forgotten, in retrospect.

He looked at Phoebe again. It would be easy to believe she was always part of his life and always would be as she dozed peacefully. Prescott shook his head and turned back to the road, determined to stop allowing his overactive mind to get too far ahead of reality. His brain was firing on all cylinders, was all, because of the sudden appearance of Ariella after thinking he'd finally convinced her to stop stalking him.

He blamed himself for not seeking to get a restraining order issued against Ariella. But he knew that it wouldn't have been enough to keep her away from Phoebe, not when Ariella was so clearly worked up. Would it take her being arrested, if she'd left any evidence behind, to leave him and those he cared about alone?

"You look so serious, Prescott." Phoebe slowly stretched and sat up more fully. "Wow, that was the quintessential power nap. It almost feels as though I didn't hit my head last night. Oh, wait, nope, there's the pounding." She laid her head back on the rest and turned her face toward him. "You must be exhausted. Did you get any sleep in that awful chair at the hospital last night?"

"I'm good. It's surprising how waiting in trailers during a shoot has conditioned me to grab sleep wherever I can. Besides, we're not more than fifteen minutes out." He motioned at an exit sign. "We're getting off here."

"I didn't notice any hotel signs, or restaurants."

"Because there aren't any."

"Please tell me we're not camping. Not that I'm adverse to being outdoors, but right now with my concussion I don't think I'd be the best tent companion."

He laughed. "No worries. I found a nice B&B that had a vacancy. It's a little remote, but that's a good thing right now, don't you agree?"

"Totally."

"And I can't wait for you to feel better, Phoebe."

"Why's that?"

"Because I want to find out just how companionable you can be in a tent." He thought he was keeping it light and playful, trying to rouse her out of the aches and pains he knew had to be settling in from her fall. Speaking the words and her sexy glance did nothing but make him hard.

No way was he going to make love to her when she was hurting so badly.

"It doesn't have to wait for a tent, you know." Her husky voice elicited a groan that started in the middle of his chest.

"I have no idea how much privacy we'll have here, and you need at least another day or two before you're going to feel more yourself, much less want to do the horizontal two-step with me."

"Horizontal two-step?" Her laughter, while a bit softer than usual, was a balm to his anxieties over her well-being. "We must be getting closer to the country."

"We could call it the double-backed dragon." Prescott continued to come up with the corniest expressions he knew for sex. He could listen to her laughter all day.

"Stop!" Phoebe clutched her belly, and he thought he saw a tear or two seeping from her eyes. She pumped up his ego by finding his jokes funny.

"I will, but only because I'm starting to think my original dreams of being a stand-up comic could still come true."

She immediately sobered. "No way. You? Comedy? Now this is just my opinion, of course, but you're a classic actor through and through. I know that you've gained popularity with a couple of romantic comedies. But Prescott, your best work is in your dramatic films."

"You think so?"

"Yes, totally!" She sighed. "When you played the role of the US cavalry soldier who stood up to his commanding officer in order to protect the native tribe he was guarding, I about died. Your ability to project that character's angst was beyond acting. I really thought you were robbed of an Oscar nomination that year."

If he hadn't needed to focus on the tiny dirt road he'd pulled onto, he would have given her a huge hug. He swallowed around the lump in his throat. "Wow, thank you, Phoebe. That means more to me than anything any film critic said about it." He'd received accolades for that role, but he'd been too new into movies, fresh out of a five-season television series that had nearly typecast him as an average Joe. Not that he minded playing any character, average or exceptional, but he wanted more, believed that he had more to offer a part.

"You earned it." Phoebe leaned forward and pointed. "Look, is that the B&B?"

The rough road opened unto a large clearing that boasted a Victorian house overlooking miles of hill country.

"I believe it is." He peered through the twilight and saw the swinging sign on the front post. "Sand Hill B&B. Yup, this is it."

They both got out as soon as he parked.

"Wait for me to help you." But Phoebe wasn't listening or didn't hear him—she was apparently as eager to stretch her legs as he. He drew her to him next to the SUV, wanting to feel her warmth and know she was okay. "How are you holding up, babe?"

"I'm good." She nodded but didn't meet his eyes for longer than a second. He figured her bones were aching, and he knew that he wasn't very good company when he wasn't himself.

Giving her one last hug, careful to not squeeze too hard, he lightly kissed her lips. "Welcome to your vacation, Phoebe."

Phoebe allowed herself some space from Prescott and took in the interior of the inn as he registered. She'd been expecting fully antiqued-to-the-gills decor but was stunned by the completely contemporary interior. The downstairs had been redone to allow for a very cozy reception area, complete with a fireplace for the colder months, wine bar and hot beverage service. A large, flat-screen television was on mute in the tavern, where a few couples lingered over cocktails. The license plates in the parking lot indicated travelers, like she and Prescott, were from out of state.

"I have our keys." He handed her a key card.

"I have to admit I was expecting an old skeleton key."

He nodded. "I would have, too. My security team found it. As much as I want to take you to a real-deal historical B&B, this isn't the time for it." His jaw tightened, and she knew he didn't want to bring up Ariella or whoever her stalker was.

She put her hand on his arm, the strength of his bicep giving her reassurance. Prescott was her anchor—she wasn't sure exactly when, but sometime over the last week she'd learned she could completely rely on him.

If only he had reason to trust you.

"D-don't worry, it's okay. I'm the one who's making all of these extra security measures necessary. Stop blaming yourself."

"You don't know that it isn't Ariella. She wouldn't just show up at the awards ceremony for nothing."

"She told me off, which is pretty much what she wanted to do. But we have to remember that there is a serial killer on the loose in Roaring Springs." She shuddered, hoping that the Avalanche Killer would be caught before more lives were lost.

Stop. This is your time away from everything.

"I wanted this time to be a true respite, for both of us." Prescott's warm smile erased much of her worry. "I'm sorry that it started off on such a lethal note."

"It wasn't lethal. We're both still standing here, right?" She tried to tease him back into the relaxed Prescott she'd witnessed on the drive. "Let's put it behind us and head up to our room."

He wrapped his arm around her, their single shared bag in his other hand. They'd consolidated luggage back at The Chateau to make this stop easier. "I'm impressed with how well you've planned this on such short notice."

They made their way up the stairwell, the historical parts of which were intact. It was a bit incongruous with the rest of the modern decor but also made the hand-carved balustrade stand out, emphasizing its beauty.

At the landing, which was surrounded by five different rooms, he winked at her. "It wasn't as spur-of-the-moment as you might believe. I started dreaming of bringing you home with me about two minutes after we met in the grand ballroom that first day."

"You did?" Warmth suffused her, making her cheeks hot and shooting down to her center. Prescott's direct gaze conveyed what she'd felt all week. Their attraction was primal, the chemistry elemental, but they'd developed something much deeper. And it had happened as if by default. Even with a serial killer and Prescott's stalking ex-girlfriend.

"I did." He bent his head toward hers and very lightly touched his forehead to hers. "Does this hurt?"

"Not at all." Her breath made her voice wispy. Alone on the landing with Prescott, she allowed her body to melt against his.

"Let's get inside." Prescott quickly moved to door number five and unlocked it. "Wait a minute." He disappeared in the room, and she thought it was a little bit of overkill that he was doing a security sweep. As he'd said, they were off the beaten path, he'd booked it under an alias and his security team had approved it. But it still made her feel special. Protected. Thank goodness she'd finally fessed up about being Phoebe. Because intimacy, true connectedness, had to be based on the truth.

She'd not been truthful with Prescott from the start and it still tore at her heart.

Chapter 12

Prescott came back to the door and looked at Phoebe, who had those two little worry lines between her brows again.

"Are you in pain?"

Her eyes widened. "Pain? No, no, I'm doing okay. It's better to be moving around, even if I'm sore."

"Then is it okay if I lift you up?" He waited for her to comprehend what he meant. Her eyes went from him to the room and back to him.

"You mean, to carry me?" Her voice squeaked, and he let the thrill of knowing he'd surprised her shoot through him. Pleasing Phoebe had become his delight.

"Yes. I want to carry you over the threshold, Phoebe." He kept his gaze locked on hers, let his eyes do the talking. He wanted this woman in his bed as soon as possible. If they had to wait for the full-course menu because of her injuries, so be it. But they were far from the pressure of the festival, away from Ariella and the Avalanche Killer. "It's just us now."

He saw her lick her lips, and her pupils dilated despite the brightly lit chandelier in the center of the landing. "I, I don't want you to take this wrong, but—"

"I'm not asking you to marry me, Phoebe. I'm telling you that I want to make love to you."

She answered by throwing her arms around his neck and pulling him down for a long, sexy kiss. Before the heat built to an inferno, he squatted down and lifted her in his arms, never taking his lips from hers. As he carried her across the threshold, he knew there was no other place he wanted to be. It was a feeling he hadn't experienced in way too long.

Phoebe knew she shouldn't give in to her desire for Prescott before they'd had a chance to work through her deception in the early part of their relationship. That way he'd know she was committed to their bond and wanted to make a go of it, for as long as they both wanted to.

As their kiss deepened, she squirmed in his arms, needing to be on her feet, up against him, pressing against his hard length. He'd closed the door behind them and she had a vague impression of a large four-post king bed and a wide picture window that showed the shadowed hills in the distance. The only view she wanted was Prescott, naked.

"Put me down, please." She gasped against his

mouth, and he lowered her to the floor. Phoebe tried to close the gap again but he was there before her, grasping her hipbones and pulling her up against him. Her knees shook, and she clung to his shoulders in lieu of collapsing in a puddle of need.

"Babe." He ran his mouth over her throat, his end-of-day whiskers scraping just rough enough against her skin to heighten the pleasure to a fever pitch. His tongue made whorls along his journey to her collarbone, unbuttoning her blouse as he moved to her breasts. Impatience overcame her and she reached for the hem of his T-shirt as she shrugged out of hers.

She couldn't stop the groan of pain when her shoulders sent sharp needles through her arms.

Prescott immediately froze. "Oh no, Phoebe, I'm sorry. Where does it hurt?"

"Babe, let me." Prescott moved her hands away and helped Phoebe onto the four-poster bed, then removed her yoga pants. She'd dressed comfortably for the drive, and he'd been unable to take his eyes off her bottom as she'd walked upstairs.

"Hurry, Prescott." Phoebe moved back on the bed and rested on her elbows, watching him with her half-lidded sex goddess expression.

"We'll get there." He shucked his hiking shorts and underwear. Her gasp when she saw his erection only made him harder, and he couldn't remember ever being this turned on before. Except for the mineral springs, where he'd had to employ every gentlemanly skill he had to not completely ravish her.

"It looks like you're already there."

He lay next to her, his hands moving over her curves, his fingertips on fire with the sheer softness of her skin. "I don't want to hurt you, babe. You're still in the rough part of your healing."

"Let me worry about that, will you?" Phoebe's eyes were languid with her need. He lowered his head and kissed her then, their mouths coming together in a perfect connection that allowed tongue-on-tongue action that had Prescott fighting to not move to the next step. But he wanted to pleasure her first. When her hand grasped his length and stroked, he groaned into her mouth.

"Babe." He worshipped her with his mouth, took his time as he gently lifted her arms over her head and then moved over and down her length. "You're exquisite." He gave careful attention to each of her nipples, already puckered from their kisses. Using her soft exclamations of pleasure and the way she undulated her hips as his guide, he kept licking and kissing his way to her mound, where he stopped and looked up at her.

"You ready for this, babe?"

"Yes!" Her fingers were in his hair but moved to the quilt as she clenched her hands. Phoebe's excitement gave him the most intense satisfaction without an orgasm.

He tugged at her lace panties, and she helped him by arching her back and lifting her pelvis. Prescott took advantage of the pose to bury himself in her very center, where her sweet musk almost undid him.

"Prescott!" Her hips rose to meet his tongue, his

mouth as he stroked her languorously—craving more, knowing he'd never have enough of her. They were on fire for each other and when she cried out her release he kept licking, kept loving her until the spasms abated.

"That feel okay, babe?" He was next to her again, caressing her stomach and breasts. Phoebe was the epitome of feminine as she lay back in complete sensual abandon, the blush across her chest and cheeks evidence of her orgasm. She turned her head and opened her eyes, and he knew he could spend forever right here with this woman.

"Your turn, Prescott."

"I don't want to push this tonight, babe. It's our first time together, and I don't want to hurt you." He felt as if he'd crush her, he wanted her so badly.

"There's more than one way to satisfy each other. This is not going to be a repeat of our spa time, because you're going to let me make love to you." She slowly rose to her knees and pushed him all the way until he was on his back, his desire unmistakable in his erection.

Skye kissed him and spoke against his lips as she reached town and again grasped him, moved her hand in delicious synchronicity with his need. "I'm going to make you come, sweetheart."

The groan that erupted from his throat was followed by more as she teased him with her tongue, not unlike what he'd done to her only minutes earlier. As she kissed him on his pecs, nipples and then down the path of dark hair past his abs to where her hand worked him, he again wondered if he was going to last until she put her sweet mouth on him.

As her warmth engulfed him, he hissed, his hands itching to bury themselves in her long red locks, but he couldn't risk touching her head.

"Relax, Prescott. I'm okay." As if she had read his thoughts, he took the permission she offered and did something he so rarely allowed himself to do.

Prescott let go.

Phoebe thrilled to the power that Prescott finally relinquished. She moved her mouth over him and used her hands to reciprocate the pleasure he'd generously given her.

Prescott's shout of release set off a rush of warmth through Phoebe's body. She was connected to him in a way she'd never expected. How could she? He'd taken her to new heights with his masterful mouth, and now she'd received as much if not more pleasure from bringing him to his climax.

Whatever this was between them, it was the real deal.

"Come here." He opened his arms, and she snuggled into him, careful to place one of the very fluffy pillows under her head in the right place for maximum comfort. She felt his lips on her hair, the softest of kisses on her temple. "You okay?"

"Mmmm." She was beyond good, better than ever.

Even her worries that he hadn't fully processed her earlier deception seemed inconsequential as she lay in the safety of his embrace.

"Prescott, I hope you don't end up regretting this."

"Shhh. Not possible. Let's take a quick catnap and then we'll get room service. I'm a little beat from the drive."

With a start of guilt that she'd only been worried about her own pain, she lifted his hand to her mouth and kissed his palm. "I'm sorry—of course you are. Rest."

Soon his even breathing managed to erase all her sense of foreboding and worry. With Prescott, everything seemed promising.

Dinner morphed into an early night asleep, as they were both burned out from the previous week and the drive. Phoebe had wanted to make love fully with Prescott but he'd told her she needed at least another day to heal. When she woke up the next morning, Prescott had already showered and their breakfast was waiting downstairs on the B&B's wraparound porch. She dug into her biscuits and gravy like a lumberjack.

Prescott's rumbling laugh made her pause midbite. "What?"

"I'm glad to see your appetite is back." His eyes sparkled with deeper blue pigment than the camera picked up, and she counted herself lucky to be able to know this intimate detail about him.

She gulped down her tea and refilled it with the small pot their server had brought. "I've never had a problem eating before, except when I'm sick. I guess the hit on my head was worse than I thought."

"Concussions are serious business. I'm relieved the doctor assessed yours as minor."

"Me, too."

Her phone pinged with a text, and she quickly looked at it. It was from her mother.

Hope your travels are safe. Let us know when you get there. Your father's still tracking down all leads on Skye.

"Everything okay?" Prescott must have seen her frown.

"Yes, just a note from my mother. She says for us to travel safe, that Dad is working on finding Skye. I'll let her know when we get to your parents' place, later."

His gaze searched hers, and she froze. Was this when he told her he'd made a mistake, that he could never forgive her for pretending to be someone else?

"I like you better as Phoebe. Without all the makeup, you know. Don't get me wrong—you're a beautiful woman no matter what you're wearing, or not." He gave her the look that let her know he'd seen her naked and very much enjoyed it. "But it's as if you're more accessible without all the glitter and gloss."

"I have to admit I prefer to be more casual. My role in our family necessitates that I play the part of celebrity expert whenever I'm in public, though."

"I understand." He reached across the small table and held her hand, his thumb absently moving in whorls around the inside of her wrist, right above her pulse. "I want you to be completely comfortable with me, Phoebe. Always."

She swallowed, doing her best to not let tears fall at his tenderness. Prescott was always surprising her with his warmth. "You couldn't tell how at ease I am with you last night?"

"Mmm." He kissed her hand, each of her fingertips. The heat of a blush ran up her throat and face, and she quickly skimmed the area with her gaze. None of the other patrons seemed to even know they were there. Apparently the B&B catered to people who wanted to be alone.

"Prescott…" The now-familiar heat that only he brought pooled between her legs, and her nipples strained through her bra. When his liquid eyes glanced at her breasts, she knew that he saw her arousal through the thin white T-shirt.

He let out a long sigh and put her hand down with exaggerated reluctance. Phoebe laughed, and his brows rose.

"This is the first we've been truly alone, Prescott. I'm trusting that you're not acting because of the sincerity of all these beautiful sentiments you're sharing with me."

He grinned but the heat in his eyes didn't lessen. "I wish I was playing it, but the truth is that you turn me on like no other woman I've ever met." He looked at his watch,. She knew that it was reported he'd made millions over his last few films, but he didn't seem to invest his earnings in the trappings of high fashion or expensive jewelry, wearing the same smart watch as anybody else. "We need to get on the road."

"I can drive if you'd like a break." Though she was still sore she'd do anything for him.

"No way. This ride's on me."

He stood and held his hand out for her. Phoebe felt like Cinderella at the ball as she took his hand and walked next to him through the hotel to the reception desk, where they checked out.

It was almost too perfect.

Chapter 13

As they pulled up in front of a large white traditional farmhouse, Prescott's parents stood at the top of the few steps and waved. Two large dogs barked and jumped in circles until Prescott helped her out of the SUV and gave first the chocolate Labrador and then the golden retriever their due scratches and rubs. Phoebe watched his parents approach, his father long and lanky like Prescott and his mother equally fit but shorter, with Prescott's trademark aquamarine eyes.

"Honey, it's so good to have you home." She hugged her son and placed a sound kiss on his cheek. Prescott kissed his mom on her cheek, too, and Phoebe immediately warmed to the entire family. Open affection was something she missed in her own.

"Son." Prescott and his father hugged as Jeannie Reynolds approached Phoebe.

"And you're Skye. We saw you on television last week, and it's so nice to meet you in person." Jeannie held out her hand and shook Phoebe's outstretched hand. She wasn't expecting as warm a reception as Prescott received, of course, but it was clear that his mother wasn't impressed with him bringing home another celebrity. Ariella had really done a number on the entire Reynolds family.

"Nice to meet you." She shook the woman's hand and then turned and did the same with Lance Reynolds, who was a little more welcoming than his wife.

"Glad to have you with us, Skye. Welcome to our home."

"Thank you both so much for having me." Phoebe wanted to correct them immediately, but maybe when they first met wasn't the right time. She looked around the land at the cornfields that seemed to fill every speck of scenery and smiled. "This is beautiful."

"You've caught us in the middle of a slow period, so we'll be able to spend a little more time together than we normally do."

"What Mom means is that they're waiting for the corn to grow. It won't be harvested for another couple of months."

"Funny how your visits home seem to be at this same time each summer, son." Lance grinned and Prescott shook his head.

"Dad, I'd come home for harvest if you asked me."

"Stop. Let's get inside and have some dinner. Are

you hungry?" Jeannie was already back inside the farmhouse, and Phoebe followed, curious to see the place that had shaped Prescott. And she had to admit that it was nice to be away from Roaring Springs and the worries that had plagued her there—Skye's whereabouts, the Avalanche Killer, Sabrina's death and now Ariella's apparent stalking.

Phoebe felt safe in Iowa with Prescott's family.

"Good morning, sleepyhead." Prescott pushed into the guest room, carrying two cups of coffee, one with cream, just how he knew Phoebe liked it. Her hair was a glorious mass of copper in contrast to his mother's pale yellow linens, and the slight blush in her cheeks relieved his worry about her injuries.

Phoebe was healing.

"Hey." Her brown eyes blinked up at him, and she smiled, curled into herself as if she'd go back to sleep. "What time is it?"

He set her mug on the nightstand and sat on the edge of the bed. "Six."

Phoebe's eyes widened. "In the morning?" Groaning, she shoved her head back under her pillow. Her sharp groan put a halt to his assumption she was feeling better. He lifted the pillow from her face.

"You're still in pain."

"No, actually, I'm doing better." She sat up, revealing the thin ribbon straps to a pale pink chemise. He knew the exact term because he'd been part of enough historical productions.

"You look better, but you just acted like you're hurting."

She moved her head to the left, right, up and down. "I had a brief flash of discomfort, is all. It could be so much worse, Prescott. I'm lucky I didn't crack my head open. Now that would have been a bloody mess!" Her grin and giggle were infectious, but he didn't find anything funny about Phoebe being attacked and hurt. She reached for the coffee and sniffed it with an expression of sheer bliss on her face.

"This is wonderful." Her eyes watched him as she took a healthy drink. "Mmm. Perfect."

"I'm glad you like it." He sipped from his own mug, hoping she'd like what he'd planned for the day. "If you're up to it, I thought I'd take you to one of my favorite places."

"I thought the farm was your favorite place. Or hiking in the mountains."

"There's another place." He loved watching the curiosity play out across her stunning face. "But if you need a day to rest, that's cool, too."

"Are you kidding? We've been trapped in a car for the past two days. It'll be good to get out."

"Great. Pack a bathing suit. You can bring sneakers or hiking shoes, too. But don't worry—we're not going to do anything that tires you out."

She put the mug back on the table and wrapped her arms around his neck. "Nothing with you tires me out." Her lips were softly parted, and he kissed her. She tasted of coffee, cream and the promise of a new summer day.

"As much as I'd like to spend the first part of today right here, in bed with you, my folks are down the hall." He should have thought about the barn apartment but wanted her to get to know his parents.

"I need to tell them I'm not Skye."

"We will, but not yet. Let's take off on our own and worry about it later."

And truth be told, it was a bit daunting bringing home the first woman since Ariella. He wasn't up to dealing with his parents' suspicions when he revealed who Phoebe really was. Especially when he knew in his gut, and maybe even his heart, that Phoebe was nothing like his ex.

Phoebe was a keeper.

"I can be ready in ten minutes." Her head rested on his chest, and he leaned to put his mug next to hers so that he could fully embrace her. Her skin was smooth under his fingers as he massaged her back.

"We'll eat breakfast and then we'll go."

He'd been back in his childhood home for less than a day, and it already felt as if he'd come home for good. With Phoebe.

Phoebe tried to get Prescott to tell her where they were going, but he was all smiles and tight-lipped anticipation. Secretly she hoped it would be somewhere private, so that maybe they'd be able to at least share a repeat of their time in the B&B. But as they passed through very public lands, reality set in. There wasn't going to be enough privacy to make love to Prescott like she wanted to, not today.

"It's only five more minutes." He spoke over the wind and highway noise, as he'd rolled back the sunroof and the windows were down. Summer was a whirlwind of scents from fresh-cut grass to manure, pure country. Phoebe associated the invigorating bouquet with all the times she'd accompanied Skye to a horse barn.

Where are you, Skye?

"Here we go." Prescott's words cut her worry short and she read the sign for a park he turned into.

"Geode Lake?"

"Yes, ma'am. Best spot on the planet to swim, hike and find a treasure."

He grinned, and she was glad to be the one with him, right now, as he looked happier than she'd seen him before. It was probably a combination of being away from the spotlight and being at home with his family, but she hoped that at least some of it was because he had her by his side.

"What kind of treasure are you talking about?"

He pulled into a graveled lot that appeared to be the head of a trail. "The fun kind."

"Well, since the sign said Lake Geode, I'm going to guess we're going hunting for rocks."

"You've already done this?" His disappointment made her laugh, his face was so adorable.

"Actually, no. We studied them in school, of course, as Colorado boasts a good number of places to go find them. I love those science units when we got to crack them open and find the glittering crystals inside such an ugly lump of rock."

"No rock is ugly. It's all in your perspective." They got out of the car and walked to the back, where they sprayed themselves with sunscreen and bug repellant. Prescott filled a small backpack with water, a small shovel and snacks.

"I can carry some of that. You don't have to handle the load all the time."

"If you hadn't taken the tumble you did the other night, I'd have no problem giving you a backpack. But we're not going far, no more than a quarter mile, and we don't need that much."

"Okay." She adjusted the hat that was supposed to protect her from the sun and any wayward insects like ticks. As she tied its cord around her chin, Prescott leaned in and kissed her. He kept doing this, giving her warm kisses whenever he could. She loved it, but her body craved so much more.

"Let's go, Phoebe." He closed the back door and hit the car's locks, the beep sounding through the quiet area.

Phoebe caught up to him.

"Ready?" Prescott watched Phoebe's face as he held up the chisel, the fruits of their geode search splayed out in front of them on the ground. They squatted next to the Escalade, which he'd kept for the week. It was more comfortable than his old pickup, but Phoebe told him she wanted to ride in his high school vehicle before the week was out, too.

The day's sun was burning through the morning

clouds and tree line. A swim in the lake was his next destination to take Phoebe. But first, a little fun.

"What if you end up smashing them?" Phoebe held one of the roundish dark brown rocks in her hand as if feeling for the weight of it. He'd shown her how to determine if a rock was just another piece of limestone or might be filled with wondrous crystals—by the weight. A rock weighed more than a geode.

He shook his head. "There might be a little damage, but as long as we take our time, they'll break open and leave most of the crystals intact."

"Hmm."

"You're thinking about more than the rocks. Tell me, Phoebe." He'd been looking forward to this so much. Last week he'd only dreamed that Phoebe Colton would accompany him to his birthplace, to the land that was home to him. Now that he had her here, no matter the circumstances that had convinced her, no matter that he'd thought she was Skye for most of last week, he longed for her to open up and bare her soul to him.

Prescott had a burning need to know all he could about the woman who'd captured him so fully in such a short time.

"It's silly." She pursed her lips, tossing the rock from hand to hand. "It's like our hearts. We have to put up with some damage, some heartbreak, to get to the best relationships." She stared at the rock as she spoke, and he held his breath. Was she finally going to believe him when he told her he didn't care about what she called herself when they'd first met? That it was her, Phoebe, he was falling for?

"Here." He handed her clear safety goggles before he took the rock she held and placed it on the concrete block he'd brought for this purpose. With practiced movements, he used his chisel and hammer to carve out a groove all the way around the rough sphere, until he'd scored a circumference. Phoebe had removed her sunglasses and he wanted to see her reaction to the geode, if indeed it was one.

"Go ahead, open it." He nudged her with his shoulder, watching her face.

"Okay." Phoebe picked the rock back up and grasped it with both hands, her knuckles white from the pressure she exerted with her fingers. "This isn't that easy."

"Keep pulling, give it a little twist."

Her wrists moved, and with a soft scraping noise, the rock came apart.

Phoebe gasped and Prescott smiled at her sweet surprise. The inside of the rock was covered in white crystals, opaque to diamond clear. "It's lovely, Prescott." She held it to the sunlight and the crystals came alive then, reflecting iridescent lines of light. "Wow."

"Just like you, babe." He took the rock from her hand and placed it on the ground in one quick movement. She met him halfway when he reached for her, standing and pulling her up against him in one needy motion.

Heat exploded and his erection swelled, his desire for her demanding release. The kiss went on and on. Prescott wondered if she'd think he was a louse if he asked her to make love in the back of the car.

"Get a room." The snicker reached his ears, and he

pulled back, looking over her head toward the source— a group of teens walking past and heading for the geode site.

Phoebe pushed back, her face flushed with embarrassment. "Oh my gosh. That was, um, way too close."

He met her startled gaze and nodded. "I'm sorry."

"There's nothing to be sorry about. It's ironic that the very kids that you'd expect to find doing what we were are the ones who called us out on it, isn't it?" She was all common sense and practicality. "Let's clean these up and go for that swim you promised. We can eat lunch on the beach."

Prescott joined her in getting everything back into the SUV, and once they were at the lake they took turns going into the pool house to change.

She walked toward him in flip-flops and her red polka-dot bikini. He softly swore under his breath. He definitely needed to get them some privacy from his folks. He'd never last a week in Iowa without having Phoebe completely.

A woman running along a path caught his eye, and his stomach dropped until he realized it wasn't his ex. With a start he knew why he was strung so tight. When they'd been kissing by the car and the teens had called out, his first instinct had been that it was Ariella, out to harass them.

His relief was short-lived as he watched Phoebe enjoy the sunshine and clear lake water. If anything ever happened to her, he'd lose a huge piece of himself.

He vowed it wouldn't happen. He'd do whatever it took to keep her safe.

* * *

"I'd love for you to see the July Nights festival downtown, Phoebe." Prescott spoke over the home-made strawberry shortcake his mother had made, served with her secret family ice cream recipe. They'd come back from Geode Lake, and she'd taken a shower and nap before dinner. The slow pace of Iowa farm life after the rush of film festival week in Colorado was a delightful gift to Phoebe. "They light up the sidewalks with fairy lights, and the vendors are open late."

Jeannie nodded. "It runs through this week, but you'll want to go tonight if you're up to it, before the crowds hit this weekend."

"Sounds like fun. What do you think?" She looked at Prescott. She'd honestly rather be in bed, snuggled up in his arms. But she needed to try to reach Skye. Phoebe hadn't had a minute to herself since they'd left Roaring Springs, and she wanted to try to contact her sister. If Prescott took her downtown, she'd be able to catch a moment to herself and text Skye again. Her sister wasn't answering texts but Phoebe couldn't stop trying.

"Let's freshen up and go, then." Prescott gave her the smile that made her toes curl with want before he turned to his parents. Phoebe wondered what they made of their son bringing her here, of his history with women. "You coming with us, Mom and Dad?"

"No, no, you two go on. Your dad and I have to go on Wednesday night, as we're volunteering at the 4-H's hot-dog stand."

"They do it every year." Prescott's pride in his parents' community involvement was evident. "I love this about my hometown. Everyone pitches in with no expectation of getting something in return."

"Maybe we can help you then, too?" Phoebe couldn't resist offering .

"No, son, we're fine, really. This time is about you two getting to spend time together, away from the bright lights. You'll take your pickup instead of that modern rental, won't you, Prescott?" The way she said *modern* let Phoebe know that his mother was teasing him. Prescott had waxed on and on about how he'd learned much of his acting craft by watching old film classics from the 1930s and 1940s as a kid. He had an appreciation for history and the classics that rivaled only Phoebe's love of all things vintage.

The weight of her conscience was too heavy to bear at the same time as a concussion. She'd let the ruse go on for way too long. But Prescott showed no indication of wanting to correct his parents' assumptions about her identity, so she let it go. For now.

It's okay, you're going to tell them soon.

The cowboy hat itched Ariella's scalp, and the baggy clothing she wore to disguise herself was hot in the summer evening. But it was worth it, because she'd just spotted Prescott with the bitch. Ariella's annoyance at having to wait an extra day for them to show in Iowa made it especially difficult to stay on task. She'd had to be super careful about staking out the farmhouse, as Prescott had security people and the whole damned town knew him. They'd arrest her in a heartbeat.

All she really wanted was to confront them both and point out all the reasons why Prescott had made such a big mistake by dumping her.

But he wouldn't listen, not with Skye Colton next to him. Which led her back to her objective. As she watched them move from store to store, she bided her time. It took almost a half hour, but finally Prescott and the whore walked right past her as she sat on one of the town's long benches. They didn't even notice her. Or if they did, they didn't recognize her in her ridiculous disguise.

Skye was smiling up at Prescott, and for a moment Ariella's animosity faded. Who could blame the woman from crushing on him? He was a catch. But Skye didn't deserve him. She didn't know the demands of his career like Ariella did. No one knew Prescott better than she did. Didn't he know that? She'd remind him soon enough.

All that was between her and Prescott was Skye Colton. Skye wasn't as easy to ditch as she'd anticipated, but Ariella had gotten a great idea when she'd followed the two of them into Roaring Springs, the night someone had dumped a barrel of dirty water on Skye and she'd tumbled into oncoming traffic.

Ariella was jealous that she hadn't thought of it—until she saw that the figure who'd poured the water from the second-story office building hadn't timed it right. It would have been nice if Skye had been taken care of then and there. It would have saved Ariella a heck of a lot of trouble, and she'd never have had to confront the stupid woman at the awards ceremony.

That had been tricky, timing her meeting with Skye so that Prescott didn't get to her. He was under whatever spell Skye had put on him.

A spell that Ariella was about to shatter.

Prescott loved being back in his hometown, and even better, with a woman he cared about beside him. He and Phoebe walked easily together, holding hands. It was still light out at eight o'clock, and the young kids were out in abundance. He'd often wished that Ariella would want to have a family, which she never did. Now, as he was with Phoebe, he realized he'd dodged a bullet with his ex.

"Your parents are nice. I hate lying to them." Phoebe stopped and admired the window of one of the town's nicer boutiques.

"They like you. I agree that we need to tell them the truth, but trust me, it'll result in a long discussion and I don't want to take the time for that now. I want to be with you, period. Do you want to go in here?" He nodded at the store, lit up and ready for night business.

"I don't want you to be bored." She smiled, and he knew he'd never grow tired of spending time with her.

"Tell you what—the bookstore is two blocks down, across the street." He pointed. "See it?"

"Yes."

"I'll be there, and I'll come back to get you in maybe fifteen minutes? But take your time—I'll wait out here on this bench until you'll ready."

"Great." She leaned up and kissed him. "Thank you, Prescott." He had the distinct feeling she was thanking him for more than the brief look inside the boutique. As relaxed and happy as he felt with Phoebe, he still couldn't shake the feeling that something was going to go wrong. He tried to chalk it up to Ariella's antics and the dark cloud that the Avalanche Killer had placed over last week.

"See you in a bit, babe."

He left her and meandered over to the bookshop, stopping to talk to several locals he'd known his entire life. Unlike in LA, where fans would stop him at every corner, his hometown left him alone, unless they knew him personally. He hoped that he could raise his future kids away from the glare of Hollywood.

Holy cow, he was thinking about children. Whatever Skye wasn't telling him he needed to know now, before he actually began to believe in a future with her. His heart couldn't take what he'd gone through last year when Ariella cheated on him.

Thumbing through the historical fiction shelf, his hand paused. Losing Ariella had seemed like the end of his world last year, but he'd been mistaken. He'd never cared for her with the depth that he now knew he was capable of.

If things didn't work out with Phoebe, it would be catastrophic. His heart throbbed with an emotion he wasn't sure he was ready to acknowledge.

"Hey, Prescott, how are things going?" Kirsten LaBrand, a high school classmate he'd been in the drama club with, stood next to him. She juggled an infant on her hip and held the hand of a small girl.

"Good, thanks, how about with you?" His mind was

reeling with his discovery about how deeply he cared for Phoebe, but he tried to stay in the present and focus on Kirsten, who'd always been a good friend, as had her husband, Jeb, who owned the bookstore.

She motioned at her baby and then the toddler with her head. "I'm living the dream!" Her laugh reminded Prescott of what he wanted—someone as happy and content as Kirsten, who wanted to raise a family with him.

Man…he had it worse for Phoebe than he'd ever anticipated.

"Well, you look good. I saw Jeb when I came in and said a quick hello, but he's too swamped to talk to tonight."

"Just wait until the weekend, when it gets insanely busy."

Prescott looked around the bookstore, more crowded than he ever remembered it being years ago. "I can't imagine it being more busy than this. It seems the festival gets bigger crowds each year."

Kirsten nodded. "This was the size the weekend crowds were only a few years ago. With online access to accommodations and local folks renting out their places for the week, we are seeing huge numbers. Did you notice the traffic jam down Main Street?"

"I did. It must be gridlock on the weekends."

"Not anymore, as the town blocks the downtown and makes it pedestrian-only Thursday through Sunday when the festival ends. It is too much of a safety hazard otherwise."

As if on cue, loud squealing followed by an audible

gasp echoed through the shop's constantly opening and closing door. Prescott stiffened in fear. Not again…

"Jeez, it sounds like another close call out there. Maybe they need to reroute the traffic starting today." Kirsten bounced the baby on her hip as the tiny little boy started to whimper.

"Will you excuse me? I'm meeting a friend—" Prescott shoved the book he'd been perusing back on the shelf and made a beeline for the shop's exit. He looked up and down the street, and at first nothing seemed amiss— until he saw the crowd of pedestrians gathered around what looked like an older-model car. They were standing on either side of the street, about two blocks down, in front of the boutique where he'd left Phoebe.

Fueled by a rush of pure adrenaline, he pushed past every onlooker, winding up in the middle of the street where the traffic had been forced to stop.

A huge construction dumpster blocked his view of the road in front of the boutique, and he had to squeeze back onto the walkway, excusing himself through and around the throngs of gawkers.

Sirens sounded and flashed against the whitewashed storefronts, adding to the gravity of whatever had happened.

Phoebe.

Phoebe screamed as her knees and hands slammed onto the street pavement. It wasn't from pain but pure frustration. How many hits did she have to take before she would catch the stalker first? Confident that the

Mack truck she'd been shoved in front of had stopped, along with all the downtown traffic, she scanned the crowd over her shoulder, still on her knees. No one matching the description of Ariella Forsythe was on the sidewalk or in the street, where a crowd was quickly forming.

All she'd wanted was to text Skye, enjoy the inviting boutique, and instead her life had almost been cut short. Was someone after both her and Skye? If Skye had been abducted, did the same person want Phoebe dead, too?

"Hey, you okay?" A man in jeans and a blazer was at her side. He had kind eyes, and she smiled.

"I'm good. Honest."

"Are you with someone? Is there anyone I can call?" He had his phone out, and she had the impression he'd already called in the almost accident. "I'm Detective Tom Briscoe. I don't think we've met."

"My, my boyfriend brought me here. Prescott Reynolds." Describing Prescott as her boyfriend came naturally.

The detective's eyes squinted with his grin. "Prescott's a good buddy of mine. Let's get you back with him."

Prescott finally managed to get to the accident scene, only to have a large hand on his chest halt him.

"Sorry, Prescott, we can't let anyone past here." His former wrestling teammate Tom Briscoe was a detective with the local police. Tom was in civilian clothes, but his lightweight blazer and the way his shirt seemed tight at the buttons let Prescott know he was carrying a weapon and had body armor on. In the small town Prescott had grown up in—it seemed wrong. His anxiety ratcheted.

"Tom, who got hurt? My girlfriend was meeting me here—"

"I know, bud, I was coming to find you."

"Is she okay?"

"Wait, is your girlfriend *the* Skye Colton?" Tom's eyes narrowed. "Of course it is. I didn't even recognize her, and she told me her name. My fiancée watches all the celebrity programs. Go ahead." Tom moved aside. "Clear a path, folks."

Prescott's head buzzed, and it wasn't from the crowd's murmured speculation. It was pure fear at what he'd find in the middle of the street, past the first responders and his friend Tom, who held Phoebe's arm.

Her glance caught his, and she smiled broadly.

"Prescott!"

He closed the small distance in a few strides and had her in his arms, ignoring the slight protests from Tom and the EMTs to take it easy. From what he could see, though, Phoebe wasn't hurt this time.

"Babe." He inhaled her scent, pulled back. "Are you okay?"

She nodded emphatically. "I am. Thanks to the quick reflexes of the truck driver." She looked over her shoulder, searching the crowd. "He's over there. I need to thank him."

"You will, but first, what happened?"

"Ma'am, can you walk? We need to clear the street."

A uniformed officer worked in tandem with another to restore order.

"Skye, when you're ready, I need to get a statement from you." Tom was back, and he had another police officer with him. They all walked to the front of the boutique where Prescott was supposed to meet Phoebe. He looked at his watch. They'd agreed to meet about now—as if whoever was behind this knew that Prescott would be looking for Phoebe right at this moment.

"I was walking back to the boutique, after taking a few minutes in the silver jewelry store over there." She shot Prescott a guilty glance, as if he'd disapprove of her leaving the boutique. He didn't, of course, but wished she'd stayed in one place for safety's sake. "After a few minutes it was almost time for me and Prescott to meet back up, so I walked along the sidewalk. There was a group watching a street performer, so I got around them by stepping onto the street, and there were two cars parked in front of the boutique so I had to walk around them. Someone was in between the cars, and then the next thing I knew I was shoved in front of the truck." Her breathing was still hitched, but she appeared calm for someone who'd almost been run over for the second time in less than a week.

"Did you see the person who pushed you?"

"What were they wearing?"

The cops fired questions at her, and she answered them all thoroughly and with far more patience than Prescott had. He gritted his teeth, blaming himself. It had to have been Ariella—she knew where his parents lived from that one time he'd brought her here when they'd been together. He'd told no one but his immediate staff and closest friends where he'd be this week, but Ariella would have taken the chance he'd show up here. In her sick mind it would be worth it.

"I have to speak to you, privately." He spoke to Tom, who raised his brows and nodded. "We're done here. Ms. Colton, you're free to go. Where are you staying?"

"At Mr. Reynolds's family home."

"We'll be in touch if we find anything out."

"Can one of you stay with Skye while I talk to you?" No way was Prescott going to leave Phoebe alone again.

"Why don't I walk you both back to your vehicle?" Tom knew, as did Prescott, that finding a quiet place to have a conversation while the festival was happening would prove impossible.

"Sounds good. Skye?" Phoebe looked up at him and took his hand. The walked the half mile back to the high school parking lot, and he mentally kicked himself.

"I should have had you wait in town and brought the car around."

"I'm fine, Prescott, really." She squeezed his hand and looked at Tom, on his other side. "Thank you for being there and getting me off the street so quickly."

"I'm just the police officer. The EMTs are who helped you right away. We keep them stationed in the center of town all week for just such an occasion. Not that we like it when it happens."

"It could have been so much worse. I'm grateful to be able to walk back to our car."

They came up on the truck, and Prescott helped her into the passenger seat. "Here." He handed her the keys. "Go ahead and start the engine, get the AC going. I need to talk to Tom for a bit."

"Sure." She looked tormented. "I told him I was Skye because we haven't told your parents yet. I have to let them know, Prescott. This has gone too far."

"We'll take care of it." Prescott was so grateful she was unharmed that he didn't care about what anyone called her.

"I trust that you'll let me, ASAP." She smiled at him.

Another reason he was falling for her. The power of a woman who trusted him was immeasurable. He gave her a quick kiss before he shut the passenger door. Tom stood on the other side of the truck, at the driver's side.

"Tom, I think I know who it was who did this."

"Oh?

"Ariella Forsythe. She's an actress I dated, then lived with, for a while. We met when she was an extra on one of my films. I'll spare you the details, but it turns out that she wanted to sleep with industry professionals, supposedly to get both of us better roles. We broke up last year, but she can't get it through her head that I'm not going back to her. I've had a lot of odd things happen, and more recently, since I've been spending time with Skye, more dangerous things have occurred." He filled Tom in on the happenings in Roaring Springs. Prescott had to admit, at least to himself, that he didn't like calling Phoebe by her sister's name.

"Your security team that you mentioned—are they with you here, in Iowa?"

"No. Stupidly I thought we'd be safe enough here, out of the spotlight."

Tom put his hand on Prescott's shoulder. "You are, man. We'll make extra security patrols past your parent's place, and you keep us informed on anything suspicious you notice. We'll get a good description of Ariella to our force."

"I'll send you photos of her as soon as I'm back at the house. But she's been wearing disguises, changed her hair."

"No problem. Better to have something to go on than nothing. Do you have a weapon out at your place?"

"I don't carry a handgun, no, but Mom and Dad have hunting rifles, mostly to scare the bears away in the winter."

Tom laughed. "Your dad still goes deer hunting, too. He went with my father last season."

"That's right. I'd forgotten."

"I'd suggest you keep the buckshot handy, just in case. File a local restraining order in the morning, and with a little luck we'll prevent anything else from happening."

"Thanks, Tom."

Chapter 14

Phoebe couldn't hear what Prescott and Tom were discussing, but she assumed it had something to do with Ariella. The fact that she'd been pushed into traffic again made her angry—at herself. Not that she'd been expecting it, but after being knocked into the road in Roaring Springs and the fall down the stairs, shouldn't she have been more cautious?

She leaned back against the seat and forced a long breath out. Prescott was so sure that Ariella was behind all of her mishaps this past week. But with Skye missing and the Avalanche Killer still at large, she wondered if they were looking at the wrong person.

She sighed. The concussion had to be making her paranoid. The Avalanche Killer picked off victims in and around Roaring Springs—he wouldn't follow her to Iowa, would he? And truth be told, other than the note in Skye's apartment and Phoebe's fall down the stairs, everything could be explained as a sheer accident. The red carpet incident with the wooden dowel could have been innocent—a child at the resort playing around, tearing apart one of the potted plant flags, leaving the dowel in the wrong spot. Both times she'd ended up in oncoming traffic as a pedestrian could be explained by large crowds and simply being jostled, in the right place at the wrong time.

But none of this *felt* coincidental—in fact, it all felt very personal. Phoebe's nerves were thrumming, and she wanted to blame it all on Ariella or whoever was doing these awful assaults, but there was no use pretending.

Phoebe had no one to blame but herself for feeling so awful over how she'd misled first Prescott and now his parents.

Add the local police to the list.

"See ya." Prescott's low goodbye to Tom vibrated through the closed window, and she watched as he walked around the front of the SUV. As he neared the driver's side, she hit the locks to let him in.

"I like that you locked the doors as a precaution." His white teeth flashed in the dark front seat, and he shut the door, then turned to face her. "It's just us now. Are you sure you're okay, Phoebe?"

"Physically I'm fine. My head didn't appreciate falling down again, but I didn't hit it on anything." She let out a dry laugh. "My body seemed to react on instinct. I guess it's getting used to falling."

His fingers were on her jaw, under her chin. "You're the bravest woman I've ever met. I'm going to make this right for you. If we find out it's Ariella, she's going to face the full extent of the law."

Phoebe thought Ariella was a better evil when compared to the Avalanche Killer but didn't express it. There was only one thing that she needed to tell Prescott right now. She was falling for him, hard.

Unlike her true identity, this wasn't a fact she was going to keep from him.

"There's so much I want to say to you, Prescott."

"Me too, babe, but can we table it until we get back? It's turned into a crazy night." He gave her a kiss that temporarily calmed her urge to blurt out her feelings on the spot. But she'd tell him what he meant to her as soon as possible.

Prescott got lost in his thoughts as he drove them home. Phoebe was quiet, no doubt calming herself down, too. He didn't know how he'd live without Phoebe now that he'd found her.

Not that he was going to tell her right away, not after such a fright—he was only human. He needed the drive to shake out his nerves over her being hurt again, and maybe a long walk around the farm under the stars. The road became twisty, taking them through the rare hills around farm country, and he used the need to concentrate as his excuse to end the conversation. Telling the woman he wanted to be with for the rest of his life that he believed she was the one for him wasn't something he wanted to do under any kind of stress. He wanted it to be perfect for Phoebe.

Phoebe couldn't help her self-doubt from creeping back in as they drove in silence back to the farm. She didn't deserve Prescott, the man who'd awakened the part of herself she'd ignored for too long. The sexual part, of course, but so much more. The facet of her personality that longed to belong to someone else, to forge a bond that would last a lifetime.

She bit her lip. Judging from his silence, he wasn't very happy over the night's events, no matter what he'd just told her, no matter how he'd kissed her. He had every right to want to send her back to Roaring Springs. Her presence here, with his family, was too much of a liability.

"I'll pack tonight and be on the first flight out." She spoke quietly, as if he were an unpredictable wild animal instead of the man she'd totally relied upon this week.

"What?" He shot her a quick glance and she saw the surprise in his eyes. "No, don't go there. You're feeling low because of what just happened. Besides, you can't fly, remember?"

Stunned, she blinked back the tears that she'd fought against. "That's typical of you, being so generous to me."

"Actually, it's selfish. I'm not going to let you go, Phoebe. Not over Ariella's criminal behavior, and not over your false identity with me last week."

"But your family is at risk as long as I'm here."

"I'll worry about my family. Is there any news on Skye?"

"No, we still don't have any idea where she is. It's not unlike her to go off on her own after a breakup, or after she's fought with our parents. She's always needed a lot more space than me to cool down, to be herself." She released a breath. "I know you saw me as Skye this week, but I am totally not an extrovert. I'm the introverted twin, and I thrive on recharge time alone. All of this attention on me is draining and I'm afraid I haven't been at my best with you." She'd felt her best with him, though, a fact she couldn't deny.

"I picked up on that. You were always a bit strained when you had to be on, whether it was the red carpet or at the cocktail meet and greets, before the premieres. When you told me who you were, it all made sense." He'd really watched her, taken the time to know her, and more than anything, she wished she'd told him sooner. Remorse threatened to make more tears fall. She sniffed and tried to cover it up with a cough. A good cry was a comfort, something she didn't have time for right now.

Without warning Prescott's hand covered hers as he navigated the curving highway with one hand on the wheel. "It wasn't an ideal start for us, and yet it was perfect."

"Maybe." Her reply was a strangled whisper, and she couldn't stop the tears if she wanted to. She tried to wipe them away, but she must have missed a few, because Prescott's hand left hers and he lifted the center console's hatch.

"There are tissues in here."

"Thanks." She blew her nose. "I like this truck way better than the rental we drove from Roaring Springs."

He patted the dash of the restored pickup, as if it were a favorite pet. "This old girl has seen me through a lot of life's ups and downs."

Another reminder that she'd put Prescott in a definite low. Sure, Ariella was causing a lot of the trouble, but Phoebe had brought her Roaring Springs life along with her to Iowa.

And yet, Prescott claimed to still want to be with her. Had anyone else ever put so much faith in her?

Ariella got up from the position she'd had to stay in for the last half hour, to be certain the cops had left the scene. The cornfields that surrounded the high school's parking lot had been a perfect hideaway right after she'd taken care of business.

Of course, she'd thought shoving that stupid bitch into the street would be enough. And it wasn't. She hated to admit it to herself, but her pride stung at that one. Tripping Skye on the red carpet hadn't worked; neither had the note scared her.

Once she was certain there were no more festival goers in the parking lot, she walked to the nondescript rental she'd grabbed in Roaring Springs at the last minute. She hadn't expected that it would take this long to convince Prescott what a mistake he'd made by dumping her, but she was resilient. It was one of the affirmations she told herself every morning. Right after she uttered "Mrs. Prescott Reynolds" several times, followed by "Ariella Reynolds" repeatedly while looking in the mirror. The best self-help books talked about being the person you wanted to be, and she wanted to be Prescott's wife.

She was the best, the only woman for him. If he couldn't see that, she'd have to take care of it, once and for all. Because she was never going to let go of Prescott or what they had together.

Never.

Chapter 15

A quiet descended between them as he drove home. Prescott knew it had to be difficult for Phoebe to be preyed upon at the same time her family needed her to pretend to be her twin.

When she'd started crying it had kicked him in the gut. Her pain was his pain. She wasn't the type to fake her emotions, as much as she'd faked being Skye all week.

His anger at Ariella reared again, and he vowed that when they got back to the farmhouse, he'd make sure they moved in to the barn apartment, to keep her more hidden until Ariella was apprehended.

He risked a quick look at her but in the darkness only made out her silhouette as she gazed out the windshield.

"Prescott, watch out!" Her shout shook his attention back to the road, and he braked and swerved as a herd of deer meandered in front of them. They were at least a half mile off, illuminated by the full moon.

"It's okay, they're pretty far off." Maybe her hit to the head had put her on serious edge. She'd seen deer cross the road in Colorado, surely.

"They're beautiful." Phoebe breathed out the observation as they drove slowly past the herd, but he wasn't paying attention to them, as they were off on the shoulder with many already disappearing into the surrounding fields. As soon as they cleared the animals he accelerated to the speed limit, and heard a slight change in the truck's engine. His truck seemed to be handling differently and he made a mental note to spend time under the hood tomorrow. That was exactly what he needed to—

He saw the red taillights a split second before Phoebe's scream filled his ears.

"Prescott!"

He slammed on the brakes, knowing it would lock them up but not wanting to crash into the car that had appeared out of nowhere. To his shock, the truck that he'd worked on and driven since he was sixteen didn't respond, even with his foot holding the pedal to the floorboard. The brakes failed him, and combined with the quick maneuver to the right, it was too much. As the car he'd tried to avoid raced off ahead into the night, the momentum of his jerk to the steering wheel combined with their speed flipped the truck.

He'd been in enough action movies, watched enough stunt drivers who'd performed as his double to know that while he wasn't as good as a professional stunt driver, he was a decent defensive driver. Even so, there was no stopping the half-century-old steel frame as it turned airborne, rotated and landed in a sickening crunch on the driver's side.

Prescott felt Phoebe's warm weight slam into his side and had a brief flash of gratitude that he was able to save her from the worst of the impact. His seat belt kept him from doing any more as pain shot through his left shoulder and he realized it was going to hurt like hell tomorrow morning, just as stars exploded in his vision and he lost consciousness.

"We were driving back from the local summer festival when my brakes went out." Prescott's voice sounded even as he spoke to Daria, whom they had on Phoebe's speakerphone. A wave of relief rolled over Phoebe that he was okay. They both were, thank goodness. "The local police have to confirm it, but someone had to have cut them. And they knew I'd be on a long stretch of highway, with no safer way to find out that they weren't working, at a lower speed. And there was a car that pulled out—did anyone talk to that driver?"

"Detective Tom Briscoe here, Sheriff, nice to meet you. We have indeed confirmed that Prescott's brake lines were cut, but there are no witnesses. The vehicle that he's described was nowhere on scene when the first responders showed up."

Tom stood with them in the hospital ER as they waited to be discharged. He'd shown up at the scene when Prescott's license had been reported. No other

Iowa resident had the vanity tag SHT4STZ. Phoebe was relieved that she hadn't suffered any more head trauma, thanks to Prescott's body stopping hers mid-fall. But she was worried about Prescott, as he had stitches over his left eye and his arm would be in a sling for the next several days. He'd only suffered a dislocated shoulder, another minor miracle considering the impact they'd survived.

"I'm so sorry to hear that. Phoebe, are you okay?"

"I'm okay, and so is Prescott."

"Oh, good." Daria's relief was muted. No wonder, with first a serial killer to find and now someone who was stalking Prescott and, in turn, Phoebe.

"Wait, what?" Tom Briscoe looked at Phoebe, head tilted.

"I had to impersonate my identical twin sister Skye this past week, in Roaring Springs, for our annual film festival. She's taking time off for personal reasons, and my mother thought it'd be best to keep things going more smoothly, without paparazzi being distracted. We wanted the entire focus to remain the film festival."

"Thanks for filling me in." Tom nodded.

"Phoebe, have you told your parents about this latest accident yet?" Daria's cautious tone sent prickles of warning down her spine.

"No, I haven't had time yet. Why?"

"They've asked us to quietly file a missing persons report on Skye. They don't want it public yet, especially since some of the film festival tourists are still in town. Your father's PIs came up with nothing other than the possibility that she's been abducted."

"Oh no." She was glad she was sitting on the edge of an examination table or she'd have collapsed. "What did they tell you?"

"Not a lot. We're working with your father's security to piece together Skye's movements over the last week."

"I'm coming home as soon as they release me from this hospital." She'd rent a car and drive herself back if she had to. Prescott wasn't in any shape to spend hours in a vehicle, and his truck—

"You can't travel yet." He interrupted her racing thoughts.

"Prescott's correct, but more importantly, you're safer where you are, Phoebe. We have to take every precaution in case…" Daria didn't want to say what Phoebe knew too well.

"In case the Avalanche Killer is involved in Skye's disappearance."

"Yes."

"I'm praying that's not the case. If she'd been taken by him, she wouldn't be alive to send me the texts she did earlier in the week, right?" Phoebe couldn't go to the dark, scary place that would be her life if anything awful had happened to Skye.

"That's what we're hoping." Daria's concern reverberated through the phone's tiny speaker. "And we're not going to let anyone know it wasn't Skye this past week, or that Prescott is dating you and not Skye. The more quiet we keep things, the better, for the time being." Phoebe respected that Daria couldn't tell them all the reasons she had for conducting her investigation the way she chose.

"I'll send you a list of all the horse ranches I know in the area that Skye likes to escape to. She's close friends with a lot of horse folks, from her dressage club. I'm hoping she's escaped to one of their bunks to lick her wounds."

"That would be great, Phoebe. Again, I can't reiterate the importance of you staying put for now. It lets me have one less civilian to protect at the moment." Daria's voice was strained with exhaustion.

"There's another reason Phoebe needs to stay here." Tom spoke up, meeting first Prescott's then Phoebe's gaze. "This recent accident with Prescott's truck, and the fact that Phoebe was pushed into oncoming traffic on our Main Street, makes this case highly sensitive. I'm going to need to examine both her and Prescott's phones for recent activity."

"Why our phones?" Phoebe wasn't getting it. She and Prescott had done nothing wrong.

"With your permission, of course. To look at all of your contacts, see if there's any cell call activity that corresponds to anyone you know."

"I think Ariella has expanded her stalking of me to hurt you, Phoebe." Prescott's eyes were full of remorse…and something else.

But how could he show her any compassion after she'd so blatantly betrayed him?

"Can you please share that intel with me once it comes through?" Daria asked.

"Sure thing. We'll keep a close eye on both Prescott and Phoebe, and we're using all the resources we have to catch the culprit." Tom's phone dinged, and he looked at a message. "And I just received verification that FBI has been notified, so we'll have their resources to draw on, as well."

"They agreed because Ariella, if it's her, has crossed state lines?" Phoebe had worked with the Colton empire's security enough, and sadly been privy to far too many horrible crimes against her family members, that she understood what it took for a federal law enforcement agency to get involved.

The weight of her circumstances, of her sister's possible lethal situation, shot adrenaline through her body.

"I can't stay in Iowa. I have to be closer to Skye, in case she needs to reach out to me."

"She'll text, call or email you, right?" Prescott spoke quietly, his aquamarine eyes shadowed with the responsibility they'd both been saddled with. Neither of them could go anywhere until his stalker, most likely Ariella, was caught. And hopefully the Avalanche Killer would be caught in Roaring Springs at the same time.

All Phoebe wanted was Skye to be back at The Chateau, safe and sound.

"Prescott and Detective Briscoe are spot-on, Phoebe. I need you to promise me you'll stay put until the all clear is given for you to leave Iowa. If anything comes up about Skye, I'll call you ASAP. You know that."

"I do. Thank you, Daria."

"Phoebe." Daria's prompt almost made Phoebe smile. Daria clearly understood that where her twin was concerned, it was easy for Phoebe to not follow whatever was deemed the best course of action. But smiling wasn't something Phoebe felt she could do, not with Skye still missing.

"Yes, Daria, I promise. I'll stay put in Iowa. But only until we catch whoever's after me and/or Prescott."

"Good. I think I've gotten all I need from you and Prescott. Just promise me again you'll stay put until we figure out more about who's stalking you in Iowa."

"I will."

"Great. Take care, Phoebe. Detective Briscoe, can you give me your contact information?"

"Sure thing." Phoebe turned off the speaker and gave the phone to Tom. Prescott's attention hadn't wavered from her, and she had no idea if he was still angry with her, as he should be, for lying to him about her identity, or if he blamed her for the accident. The stalker had only ever aimed the bad things at her, not him. Until tonight.

"How's your shoulder?"

He shrugged, then winced. "Still attached. I've dislocated it before, in high school wrestling. It's going to be sore, but I'll survive. How's your head?"

"Still attached." This time she did smile, in response to the shadow of a grin her reply coaxed from Prescott. "We're both lucky, although I can't help feeling guilty about all of this."

"Why?" The crinkles around his eyes deepened in puzzlement. "None of this is your fault."

She let out a derisive sound between a snort and a laugh. "First, whoever's after me, or Skye, is not aiming at you. I think you were collateral damage tonight, so yeah, that's my fault."

"Phoebe." He said her name as an admonition, but it sounded like a caress. Hearing her given name on his lips sent warmth through the coldest parts of her soul.

"You said we'd talk about it later, at the house. You never expected I wouldn't legally be allowed to leave. It's too risky for your folks. I can find a hotel or B&B or—wait, didn't you say there's an apartment over one of the barns on your parents' property?"

"Stop." His took her hand, covered it with his good one and brought it against his chest. "You're staying at the farm, no arguments. I've already decided we should stay in the barn apartment."

"Excuse me for butting in, but I'm in agreement with Prescott here. With our local festival, our police force is stretched, and having to monitor two extra locations would be a strain. I need both of you in the same place." Tom had ended his call with Daria. "Although I do like the idea of the barn apartment. Did you ever show it to Ariella when you brought her out here last year?"

"No. She could barely tolerate staying at my parents'." Prescott's face reverted to the grim expression she'd noticed whenever he discussed his ex.

Tom either ignored Prescott's angst or was trying to get his lifelong friend to ease up, because he laughed. "I remember when she asked the boutique if they carried Jimmy Choo's. As if she couldn't last a week in the sticks without a new pair of fancy shoes. Your face turned beet red that night."

Prescott nodded, but Phoebe thought he might want

to deck his friend. "I was embarrassed at her behavior. I don't know why I didn't see through her sooner."

"Because you're a nice guy, Prescott. You haven't ever changed, no matter how successful you become. It's why you remain such a good friend." Tom's seriousness seemed to make both men uncomfortable, but Phoebe was glad he'd voiced what she suspected. Prescott was beloved not only by his family but by the town he'd grown up in. It said a lot about his character.

He'd seen her in her hometown, too. But she'd been acting as Skye, and other than a few close friends, Skye kept her relationships with school classmates more on the surface. It was how she protected herself from getting hurt when the inevitable jibes came out from those envious of her very public success.

As Phoebe watched the two men loosely embrace in a brotherly hug, she realized that Prescott only knew the part of her she'd shared in private with him. He still didn't know her as well as she wanted him to before she confessed how she felt, not yet.

Maybe these next days were some kind of gift from the universe, a second chance for her to be totally herself with him.

As long as neither of them got killed before they reconnected.

Prescott stretched his long legs on his mother's ottoman and leaned his head back into the leather sofa. He ached from head to toe, but nothing hurt as badly as his heart.

"Do you want to talk about it?" His mother sat opposite him in an easy chair, and his father was perched on the edge of the sofa. Mom had brought a tray of coffee and muffins in from the kitchen, as he'd not been able to stomach much breakfast. Dawn had just broken. The family room was lit up by the peachy gold only a summer sun in Iowa gave. His father had delayed going out into the fields to check for rodents so that he could spend time with Prescott in the house. Phoebe was still sound asleep in the guest room.

"Not really."

She waved a hand in front of her face as if ignoring him. "Do you think Skye's comfortable in her room? And you two can sleep in the same room, you know. I get it."

"She needs her own bed right now, until she's over the aches and pains of all she's been through."

"So do you."

"True." He stretched his good arm. "Tom wants us to move to the barn apartment for the next few days."

"That makes sense. We never showed Ariella the entire farm." His mother sniffed, and he knew her opinion of the actress he'd been involved with for too long.

"You were right, Mom. I never should have lived with her."

"It wasn't a matter of me being right or wrong, honey, it's the fact that I see that you want to settle down, as much as your career will ever allow you to. You rushed it with the wrong person—that's not an uncommon thing to do."

"It was a mistake."

She quirked a brow. "What about Skye? Is she a mistake, too?"

"No. I think I found the one woman who gets me. I'm hoping that maybe we'll make more of this than a film festival fling."

"Honey, if after being in what could have been a life-threatening accident doesn't make you want to be with her forever, nothing will."

"You have a point." He wrestled with telling his mother the truth. It was Phoebe's story to tell, though. If she wanted his parents to think she was Skye, that was her deal.

His mother smiled. "You've never been this happy when you've come home, not in several years. And I can't help but feel it's because you brought a woman with you who is making a difference in your life. A good difference."

"I've only known her less than two weeks, Mom." He was paralyzed at the thought of moving too quickly again. "If I'd waited another few months to move in with Ariella, I never would have." He'd have found out about her cheating ways by then.

"Stop living in the past, Prescott. I raised you better."

His mother was a big proponent of conscious living and staying present. He eyed her as she sat cross-legged on her favorite chair, obviously comfortable with herself, her life.

"You did. You and Dad have made such a great lives for yourselves, and you gave me and Kimmy such a great childhood." He smiled as he mentioned his older sister, a family doctor in Des Moines.

"We tried. There were bumps along the way, just like anyone has. And if you ask me, that's what you're having here, honey. A few bumps in the road with Skye." She grimaced. "Sorry, bad choice of words. I was so scared when we got the call from Tom last night."

"I know, Mom, and I'm sorry." He motioned to his sling and looked at his father. "I'm really bummed that I'm can't walk the fields with you today, Dad. Even to just watch the corn grow. I look forward to that more than anything each year."

"You'll feel better in a few days, son."

"It's not forever, honey. Your shoulder will heal but the pain from a crash that hard will last for more than a few days. And the torture at losing your baby the longest." His mother grinned.

He couldn't help the laugh that his mother's astute observation triggered. "I haven't called that old truck my baby since high school, Mom."

"It was an integral part of your childhood, your adolescence, and it was destroyed in one quick crash. That's not fun."

"No, but I'd do anything to have stopped sooner, to keep us from the actual crash. Ph—Skye's been through too much this week. We're lucky she survived and didn't hit her head again."

"Skye seems a lot stronger than you're giving her credit for."

"I am." At the familiar voice, his body reacted before his brain, making his desire flare and then tighten into a ball of need. Phoebe walked into the room and plopped down on the chair next to his mother's. At the same moment, his father strode into the house, coming into the living area.

"Did you sleep okay, dear?" His mother waved his father in, drawing her family close.

"I did. And I have to tell you both something, since I'll be staying here for the near term." She looked at his parents, giving each a long look, and in that moment he'd never seen a more beautiful woman in the world. "I'm not Skye Colton. I'm her twin sister, Phoebe."

Chapter 16

To their credit, Prescott's parents didn't gasp or even sneeze at her pronouncement. Lance remained detached and Jeannie smiled, actually grinned, as she clapped her hands together.

"I thought you seemed far too quiet for a woman who gets up in front of cameras on a regular basis."

Phoebe wasn't sure what Jeannie meant by that; Skye needed recharge time, too, and could be quite different off camera. But it wasn't the time to explain the intricacies of her personality. First, she had to figure out how or if they'd ever trust her after this.

"You didn't have to tell them." Prescott spoke from the sofa, and she knew he had to be hurting as he hadn't stood when she'd walked in. His manners were impeccable under the worst circumstances. Concern for him immediately superseded everything, and she went to sit on the edge of the sofa next to him.

"How are you feeling?" His skin was pale under his tan, and his eyes had unfamiliar bags under them. "You didn't sleep well, did you?"

He shrugged with his good shoulder. "I drifted."

"It's the pain meds." As his expression remained resolute, suspicion dawned. "You didn't take them, did you?"

"There's an opioid crisis, haven't you heard? No way do I want to take something I don't have to."

"But they're not for the long term, just to get you through this patch." She sighed, knowing she sounded like a mother hen but unable to stop her genuine concern for Prescott.

Something she'd have to look at later, away from the observant gazes of Lance and Jeannie.

"I did take some anti-inflammatory meds, and I've been icing it." Prescott defended his modified pain management routine. "It's just going to take a few days for the aches to ease up. Now, tell me, how are you doing?"

"I'm actually much better, after a good night's sleep." She heard how boastful it might sound and shot him a grin. "Sorry."

"There's all kinds of choices for breakfast, Phoebe." Jeannie didn't miss a beat, never even came close to calling her Skye. Maybe she was making a bigger deal of it than she needed to, at least with Prescott's parents.

"I'll help myself. You've been way too kind as it is."

"I was just talking to my mom." Prescott looked at Lance to include him. "Phoebe and I are going to move into the barn apartment for the time being. It'll make the local police's job easier, with having to monitor us and anyone coming in and out of the farm property."

Lance nodded. He looked so much like Phoebe expected Prescott to appear in another thirty years. Tall and well built, with darker blue eyes and the same full head of thick hair. Only Lance's was silver all over, while Prescott's had only begun to gray at his temples. "We keep saying we're going to make money off it by renting it, but either you or your brother and sister show up and ruin it for us." Lance's words were somber, but the shadow of a grin on his handsome face revealed he was yanking Prescott's chain.

"The linens are all clean and folded on the bed. I just haven't had time to get in there to make the bed and put the towels away. Your sister brought her boyfriend with her when she stopped in last week." Jeannie smiled. "I think they're serious."

"Kimmy has been serious about each guy she's ever dated. Until she dumps him and moves on." Prescott explained the situation to Phoebe, but she wasn't so interested in Prescott's sister. What had her attention was that he looked at her with unabashed affection. As if he'd either forgotten she'd lied to him for over a week, or had forgiven her.

No way. Wasn't it too soon for him to let go of her betrayal?

"Good thing you kept your rental SUV, son." Lance helped himself to a cup of the coffee Jeannie had brought out sometime earlier, and he swallowed at least half of his mug in one gulp. Phoebe once again watched the man who was unmistakably Prescott's father. They even shared the same capable, strong hands.

The memory of how Prescott's hands had burned her skin wherever they touched, back at the B&B, made her hot all over.

Prescott leaned forward to stand, and she quickly stood, giving him the steady hand he needed. Bright eyes met hers.

"You shouldn't be even thinking about taking care of me. You've got yourself to worry about." His expression remained grim, and his lips barely moved as he spoke.

Prescott was hurting.

"Where are you going?"

"Getting our stuff to take to the apartment." He slowly walked toward the hallway that she'd just left. "If you need anything in the way of toiletries, take them from the guest room here. I don't know how stocked the barn is."

"I have all that I need." And she did. She had a month's supply of vitamins, ten days' worth of underwear. The Reynolds' had a washer and dryer. As far as she was concerned, she could stay here in Iowa with them for the next year if she had to.

But does Prescott want you to?

She had no freaking idea. But she supposed she was about to find out.

"Watch your head." Prescott spoke as they slowly climbed the stairwell to the barn apartment, which was more like a completely finished contemporary loft far above the original barn floor. While the scent of hay still lingered downstairs, it was clear that the barn hadn't been used for live animals or hay storage for a long while. The concrete floor gleamed, and the doors and windows were all locked tight.

"Welcome to my home away from home." Prescott gave her a smile before opening the door and ushering her inside. Moving to the barn seemed to lift his mood and ease the discomfort from his shoulder injury.

Once up in the loft, she had a hard time reconciling it with the 1840s-era farmhouse his parents lived in. Sure, parts of the house had been redone and even were additions to the original plan. But this—this was fantastic.

She wandered over to the small kitchen set in the far corner of the loft. The major appliances were sleek stainless steel, but the smaller coffee machine and toaster, and what she thought was a blender, were covered with quaint custom fabric cozies. It was the perfect blend of modern and country charm.

"You haven't spoken a word since we left the farmhouse." Steady eyes on her, Prescott leaned against a butcher-block island counter, next to two high bar stools.

"There's not a lot to talk about. I mean, the police and FBI are taking care of finding your stalker, right?"

"It's not just my stalker, Phoebe. They've come for you. While we can be pretty sure it's Ariella trying to scare you off, some of the attacks seem way past the pale, even for Ariella in one of her worst moods."

She walked over to a large semicircle window and took in the morning view. "You grew up surrounded by all of this. It's beautiful."

"It's flat and nothing like the mountains you're used to." His steps sounded on the polished, wide oak planks as he approached. A tightening in her gut told her that while she knew she had to accept he might never touch her again, not after she'd told him the truth, it'd be a long time before she ever stopped wanting him.

"I wasn't comparing the two." It was inevitable, though, to think about the view outside her terraced apartment at The Chateau, with the aspens winding up the side of the mountain, as she stared out at what seemed like miles and miles of open blue sky over an undulating carpet of green. "The green and blue go on forever."

He grunted a chuckle, the vibration of his voice next to her making the hairs on her arm stand up. "The green will be gone as soon as the corn's harvested, and Dad has to cut back the stalks." The warmth of his hand on her skin startled her, and she turned from the view and faced him.

"Prescott." She breathed his name out like a prayer. Of desperation.

"We're both too sore to be making love the way I want to, Phoebe." He leaned in and claimed her lips, and she wasn't sure what to make of it. As she kissed him back—it was impossible not to—she wondered if this meant he was willing to at least try to forgive her.

She gently rested her hands on his chest, mindful of his arm, and pulled back. Losing the connection left her lips humming with awareness. "What's this about, Prescott?"

He lifted his good hand and traced her lips, his eyes

focused on her mouth. "I know I should never trust you again. Anyone else would see that you played along to get what you wanted."

"But I—"

His finger covered her mouth, and he shook his head once. "No. My turn. I'm not anyone else, Phoebe, and you're not, either. When I thought we might both be goners last night, all I thought was I was glad."

"Glad? That we were crashing?"

"No." His gaze moved to her eyes. "I was grateful we'd had the time we did, no matter the circumstances. And when I came to in the ambulance and you weren't there, the EMTs had to hold me down to keep from trying to get out the back door to go find you."

"I think they already had me at the hospital, in the fire station's unit." She'd been okay, never lost consciousness. When he'd lain so still under her, in those initial too-quiet moments after the crash, she'd feared the worst. "I was afraid you'd been hurt more seriously, or that…" Phoebe wasn't going to finish the sentence. No sense putting words to something she never wanted to happen.

"The point is, we've made it this far." He kissed her forehead before he moved away, back to the kitchenette area. "We're stuck here for the time being. I say we make the most of it. You tell me all you can about the real you, the Phoebe you didn't share last week."

"And you'll tell me how you spent your time here on the farm when you were growing up. And how you manage to live the lifestyle you do now, going from film set to film set, and keep your sanity."

He poured them both some of the fresh brewed iced tea Jeannie had carried over when they'd brought their few items in.

"I'll drink to that, Phoebe."

She'd lost track of them. They'd been taken to the hospital; she'd seen the emergency units arrive and speed off in turn. As much as she detested the bumpkin town Prescott had grown up in, she had to give it credit for the acres of cornfields. They made for great hiding in a pinch.

The beat-up motel was a far cry from the five-star resorts Prescott had taken her to, and nothing near the cleanliness she'd enjoyed in his Southern California bungalow. But it was a great hideaway for her to regroup in. A small dark thing darted across the floor and she drew her legs up onto the too-soft mattress. She'd noticed the cockroaches last night when she got up to use the bathroom. Instead of repulsing her, though, they'd inspired her.

Ariella needed to be like a cockroach. Strong, resourceful and fast. Adaptable. So she hadn't knocked out Prescott's distraction from her as easily as she'd hoped. The first, and first few dozen, parts she'd auditioned for hadn't panned out, either. She'd gotten her first big break, though, and that had led to more.

Until the breakup with Prescott got blown out of proportion by the media and she couldn't get a two-bit extra part for the life of her. It was Prescott's fault she wasn't working, but rather than be bitter about it, she was going to be like a cockroach and not take it personally. It didn't erase the fact that Prescott was the only one who could fix the mess her career had turned into, though. Even her longtime agent had dumped her, the idiot. No one but she knew that she was going to be a huge star once she was working again.

The stack of bills she'd withdrawn from several different ATMs last month had dwindled, and she had to use discretion with her resources. She'd need the motel for another few nights, until she found out where Skye Colton was staying. It'd be easy if she was in the Reynolds family's farmhouse, in that dinky little guest room where Prescott's boring mother had tried to stash her. She'd shown them, making sure both his parents knew that Prescott never slept alone when Ariella was around.

But she'd only been able to check out the farmhouse once since the accident, and there was no sign of anyone there. Of course Prescott and his whore could have been brought there by his parents when Ariella had been checking into this motel. Plus she'd had to drive two hours to a large city rental place and trade out her vehicle for a new, completely different model. When her credit card had been declined, she'd been lucky that her looks hadn't failed her—the attendant had allowed her to pay cash and agreed to let her go without a credit card hold.

Her credit cards were maxed, and she had limited cash. The car crash was meant to be her last-ditch effort, her plan B. Another insect skittered up the wall and fell on its back on the nightstand. She watched its little legs flail, but within seconds it was back on its feet and disappeared over the varnished surface's side. The cockroach's best weapon was its persistence.

Ariella had stick-to-it skills, but she needed an additional weapon in her arsenal. She fanned the stack of bills and pulled a local phone book out of the nightstand drawer. Another benefit of being in the middle of nowhere—they still relied on quaint things like printed phone lists.

The Yellow Pages yielded at least three places where she should be able to pick up the best weapon for her money. As soon as she found Skye Colton, the woman was history. And Prescott would be Ariella's forever.

Prescott moved to the futon that rested along the windowless wall of the living area and bent to pull its frame out. The sun had set, and he and Phoebe had played enough Scrabble to make his eyes cross.

"What are you doing?"

"Getting ready for bed." He grunted when the frame didn't slide out with one arm. No way was his sore shoulder going to let him use it yet.

"You can't sleep on a futon. I'll take care of it out here, and you take the bedroom."

He stood straight, and before he gave himself the time he should have, he blurted out what he really wanted.

"We can share the bed. It's a king size."

Her amber eyes regarded him with a sadness he didn't expect. "What? What did I say?"

"That's not fair to you, Prescott. You're still figuring out if you can trust me again, remember? And you're going to let me sleep with you?" She slowly shook her head. "Sounds to me like your injuries are catching up to you. Why don't you get a long shower so that you can relax before bed? Then you take the bedroom. I've got it out here."

"No."

Her brow arched. "No?"

"No. We're both being stalked, and there's no way I'm letting you sleep out here, closest to the exit."

"You sound like a real cop."

"I'm not, but I've played them plenty of times," he informed her. "Besides, Tom told me that we should stay together at all times, no wandering off on our own."

"Being in a room not more than twelve, fifteen feet away isn't what I'd call 'wandering off.'"

He couldn't ignore the feeling in his gut. It was more than his attraction to her, which was considerable, something he'd never felt so strongly before. But it was different. A sense of protection that he knew he could give her, even with his shoulder messed up like it was.

"We'll share the bed. But I'm not going to take advantage of it, Phoebe." He never wanted her to think he'd use her like that. If he made love to her, it was for keeps, not to figure out if he trusted her.

You've already figured it out.

"Uh, I think you're the one who needs to be worried about being taken advantage of, Prescott. I'm the one who lied to you, remember?"

"You had your reasons." He met her gaze and saw

a flicker of the same emotion he was fighting, the one that had let him down too many times before.

Hope.

He'd agreed to her idea of a shower but made her go in first while he kept an eye on things around the perimeter of the barn. The loft stretched the entire length of the building, with windows at strategic points that allowed him to see the surrounding land and, more strategically, the drive that led back to the farmhouse.

What was most important, though, was the security system he'd had installed last Christmas. After the unsettling breakup with Ariella, he'd wanted to know he had a safe space to retreat to. The barn had been in the Reynoldses' lineage for at least a hundred years, and he had the best memories of when he'd played here for hours on end with his grandparents. The loft had been part of his restoration of the building, as his father had been faced with tearing it down. It was being able to keep things like family legacy going that made his earnings more significant than a number on a carefully negotiated movie contract.

The computer screen switched from camera to camera with precision, and so far he'd seen nothing but the occasional rabbit and a groundhog or two. No sign of Ariella.

She'd almost killed them both. Prescott didn't want to die, but the thought of living after something had happened to Phoebe tore him up. More than it should after knowing her for as short a time as he had, and for thinking she was her twin during most of that time.

"What's that?" Phoebe had come back, her hair wet around her shoulders, dressed in short pajama bottoms and silky top with tiny straps. Her eyes had recovered much of their luster after last night's rest and now the shower's restorative powers. He wished he'd been up to taking the shower with her—no. Not yet.

"It's the security system. Come here, I'll show you how to use it." He pulled the app up so she could see the options. "It's idiot-proof, really. There's a camera on each corner, and in the middle of each side. They're fifteen feet above the ground, so they're not going to be taken out without effort."

"Unless someone shoots them out."

"We'll hear that, and if any of the units are suddenly damaged, a siren goes off." He pressed a sequence of keys and the loft was filled with a loud alarm. After a few seconds, he shut it down. "If you hear that, call the police."

"It's not connected with the local station?"

"It is, but they'll respond even quicker if they get a backup call."

"Okay." She blew out a breath, and one of her red tendrils fell across her forehead. He reached out and moved it with his hand, the silky strand tugging his heart closer, nearer to the woman whom he couldn't dismiss as just another star chaser.

Phoebe was different.

Phoebe's skin thrilled to Prescott's touch, no matter how brief. Her forehead still felt the imprint of his fingers.

"It's your turn to use the shower."

He stood from the desk, and she noticed he didn't seem as stiff as he had earlier in the day. She turned to get a glass of water in the kitchen, but his hand stopped her, warm on her shoulder as he turned her to face him. Even with his chest, she looked up past the buttoned shirt to his throat, his chin that boasted a dark shadow, to the aquamarine eyes that made her feel like she was the only woman on the planet whenever he looked at her.

Phoebe swallowed. "Um…"

"I appreciate all you've put up with since we've gotten to know one another. It's not easy when my ex is after you." Regret tinged his tone, but his gaze held a warmth that she was coming to depend upon. As if his eyes were the portal to his heart and she could tell that maybe, just maybe, he'd find a way to forgive her for betraying him.

"I'm really sorry about the Skye ruse, Prescott. But to be fair, if I had to do it again, I still would. I'd have told you sooner, though, once I figured out I could trust you." His fingers were working along her neck, stroking and massaging the exact spots that ached the most. She groaned in sheer delight as the tension eased. "I wish I could do the same for your shoulder."

"It'll be fine in another day or two. I've had this before, many times, when I wrestled." His fingers paused, and she opened her eyes.

"I don't blame you for pretending to be Skye. Since last night, and hearing Tom and Daria talk about the need to keep you here, I'm realizing that you really didn't have a choice. You have that gut instinct with your twin, right? You told me about it." When she nodded, he went on to say, "And if it's been going off all week, you shouldn't have told me or anyone that you weren't Skye. Tom said that stalkers like the attention, the drama of getting people stirred up."

Her gut tightened at the mention of Skye's predicament, and she broke their embrace, hugged her arms around herself. "You mean that they'll keep Skye alive, if she's been abducted."

"Yes. Come here." He hugged her to him with his good arm, and she wrapped her arms around his waist, resting her forehead on his chest. "I'm sorry, Phoebe. We don't know if anyone has taken Skye. I was shooting my mouth off." His mouth moved on her hair as he spoke.

"You're being realistic. Even I can't pretend that Skye's okay. Something's wrong, because she thrives on being with people as much as I relish my alone time. At first it made perfect sense that she needed time by herself because of the horrible breakup, and how it was so public." Skye was all about her public persona and wouldn't have wanted any chance that a photo of her would be taken while she wasn't feeling one hundred percent.

"People change, sometimes. This could be a turning point for her, and she's taking more time to regroup." His words were meant to be a comfort, and while his very presence soothed her, Phoebe's twin radar was pinging.

"I hope you're right." She looked up at him and

smiled. "Thank you, Prescott. For understanding why I had to be undercover as Skye last week, and why I'm still so stressed."

"Phoebe, if you don't know it by now, the next few days are going to show you that this isn't about me being understanding, or polite." The meaning in his gaze struck through to her core, and desire exploded into a deep, needy thrum between her legs. Heat rose up her chest, made her nipples hard under the silk chemise and filled her cheeks. His gaze widened then narrowed in on her lips. Her mouth tingled in anticipation of his kiss.

"Hold that thought, Phoebe." He gently pushed away and strode toward the bathroom.

Phoebe used the time he was in the shower to dry her hair, using the blow-dryer she found in the bedroom vanity. Her eyes were bright despite the shadows under her eyes and the way her mouth wanted to frown. The sad parts were due to her worry over Skye.

But the light in her eyes, the strength of her heartbeat, the want that had settled in her most private parts—they were all for Prescott.

"Hey." He caught her attention with one word. He stood in the bedroom doorway, a towel wrapped around his waist. He'd left the sling off, still carrying his arm against his chest. "I don't want to be presumptuous, Phoebe. It's your call, always will be. My intention is to take you to bed. If you'll have me."

"If I'll—" She didn't finish as she was already across the room and had wrapped her arms around his neck, gently tugging his face to hers. "I don't want to hurt your shoulder."

"Screw my shoulder." He kissed her, and she thought she'd melt onto the floor as the desire that had simmered since the B&B spilled over the walls she'd tried to constrain it with. His tongue stroked, probed, titillating her with the promise of what they were about to share. Total electric connection.

"Prescott." She breathed his name as she gulped for air, then kissed him back with all the pent-up sexual frustration of the last week, of the constant need to be with him and holding back while she was Skye. Save for the B&B, she'd managed to somehow keep her desire for him in check, but all bets were off as she gave herself fully to the moment.

To Prescott.

"You are so damn beautiful." He shoved a satin strap aside and placed an openmouthed kiss on her shoulder, trailing his teeth gently across to the base of her throat, where his tongue pressed in teasing prods against her skin.

She gasped and clung to his good shoulder with one hand, the other reaching for the towel—which he'd already dropped. His erection revealed the same desire that pooled wetness between her legs. Before Prescott, she'd thought that being turned on was a simple binary fact. She either was or wasn't. But with him, it was all about the degrees. What she'd thought was a turn-on before she'd met Prescott had only been her baseline.

Prescott taught her a whole new appreciation of sexual desire, for certain, but so much more than her body's physical response to him. Each kiss, the way he was currently kissing his way to her breast, was all the more precious because her responses were attached to her soul-deep feelings for him.

When his tongue circled her areola and he nipped at the tight peak, his even white teeth in sharp contrast to the rosy skin, she began to stroke his length. He covered her hand with his and lightly bit her ear.

"Phoebe. The bed. Now." His breath was hot, and she felt the tingles all the way to her toes.

"Sure." She took a step back and shimmied out of the chemise, then pulled off the matching bottoms. Prescott's pupils dilated, and his sharp intake of breath sounded like a hiss as he looked at her.

Phoebe had never wanted to be with man so much in her life. This went beyond hormones and sexual need— this was the culmination of what she'd known since the first time Prescott had spoken to her in the ballroom.

They were meant to be together.

Prescott adored women, and he enjoyed sex like any other man his age. But what he wanted from Phoebe was inexplicable. As much as he desired her and found her the most attractive woman, ever, it was just as important, no, *more* important, for him to please her.

She lay on the quilted coverlet with one leg bent, on her elbows, exposed completely for his enjoyment.

"I could look at you all day, babe." He watched her gaze take him in, too, from his sorry shoulder down to his abs, which made him grateful he made it to the gym. When she went farther south and rested her gaze on his erection, her soft smile and heavy-lidded eyes confirmed that she was as turned on as he.

"Do you have protection?" She met his gaze, her query fair, expected. "Please, please tell me you do."

Laughter rumbled out of his chest, and even though his ribs were sore it felt good to be enjoying the moment, ignoring the constant tension that being a stalker's target dealt. "Are you kidding?" He quickly walked to the closet where he'd dropped his duffel. With only one usable hand, it took him longer than he wanted, but he managed to unzip the side pocket and withdraw the box of condoms he'd purchased while still in Roaring Springs.

"I bought these at the Roaring Springs Drug and Sundries last week."

She laughed, dramatically rolling her eyes. "Let me guess, the cashier knew who you were and tried not to giggle when she rang you up?"

"Actually, I think it was a male teenager, and he looked as embarrassed as I'd have been at that age." He tore off a packet.

"No, let me, Prescott."

"I'm afraid I don't have a choice, with one operating hand. But we're not ready for that yet." He placed the foil packet on the nightstand and climbed onto the bed, lying next to her. He gave himself the time he needed to look at her, get lost in her gorgeous brown eyes.

Phoebe wasn't just another lover who'd become a good friend. It had only been a little over a week, but he could safely say she was his best friend who also was the most incredible intimate partner he'd ever been with. And they hadn't been able to fully make love the other night because of her concussion. He'd be damned if he'd let his shoulder get in the way now.

Leaning on his good arm, he took her mouth and kissed her passionately. The heat between them didn't take long to combust, flooding his mind with nothing but the end goal of being inside Phoebe.

He slowly got to his knees and made to move between her legs, the scent of her arousal beckoning him to take another taste of her sex as he had at the B&B.

Her hand on his wrist stopped him, and he looked at her.

"I can't wait that long, Prescott. We have to be together now."

Her words underscored the urgency of his need, too, and he gave her one short nod, all he could manage without plunging into her on the spot. "Can you reach over for the condom, babe?"

She sat up, grabbed the packet, tore it open and placed it on him.

He closed his eyes, the feel of her fingers and hands working on him threatening to send him over the edge too soon. Prescott wasn't going unless he brought Phoebe with him.

"I think you're ready, Prescott." Her voice was shaky with her desire, and it turned him on even more.

"Babe, I've been ready for you my entire life."

She lay back, and he followed her, inch for inch, back down onto the mattress. As soon as he knew she was lying flat, he grasped her knee with one hand and nodded to the other. "Raise your leg for me."

Phoebe bent the other leg and Prescott took one last look at her sweet sex before he plunged into her, unable to stop himself at this point. Her tightness wrapped around him, and he groaned at the warmth that surrounded him. She bucked her hips for him and he thrust back, once, twice, and then all bets were off as he pounded into her, needing to hear her release.

"This is so hot, babe." He tried to keep his focus so that she'd come before he did. Phoebe's pleasure was his sole focus, and when she cried out in gasping release, he didn't have a chance to regroup and go after his climax. It was already upon him, slamming him from hotter-than-ever sex to a new definition of satisfaction.

Prescott had found the woman for him.

Phoebe listened to Prescott's breathing to make sure he was asleep. She'd had to switch sides with him after they made love, so that she was lying on his uninjured shoulder. His muscles were firm and warm under her cheek, his abs and pecs taut with pure male strength as she absently stroked her fingers across them. Contentment she'd never experienced swathed her in pure comfort, and she watched the fireflies as they flitted above the pastures from the full-length master bedroom window. Belatedly she hoped that the windows were privacy tinted. Otherwise they'd given the farm animals a good show.

She stilled her hand. If their stalker was out there, they'd seen her and Prescott in a most intimate act.

Careful to not wake him, she slowly rose and

grabbed her pajamas on her way out of the room. Phoebe dressed as she moved across the large great room, toward Prescott's computer. The frozen screen image came to life when she moved the mouse, and she saw that nothing of interest appeared to be going on around the barn. Even in the dark, the floodlights lit up whenever an animal the size of a rabbit or larger was on the premises. She made out two rabbits, a possible fox and three rats. The rats made her shudder, as they always had.

But there was no sign of an intruder, for which she was grateful. Grabbing her phone that she'd left on the desk, she checked for a message from Skye, to no avail. Her twin had to be in deep trouble, wherever she was. Phoebe sent up a silent prayer for Skye's safe return to The Chateau.

Her thirst reminded her that she'd never gotten that drink of water, and she smiled in the dim light. One of her thirsts had definitely been quenched with Prescott just now. Her fantasies of being with him had raged all last week and yet the reality was not only far more enjoyable, it was significant.

It wasn't as if she hadn't had sex before, or hadn't extensively dated, because she had. But what she and Prescott had just shared in this converted barn wasn't only sex. It was a heart commitment. At least it was on her part, and she thought she knew Prescott well enough to believe it was special for him, too.

Pulling a glass from the cupboard, she filled it with water from the refrigerator door and watched the liquid catch the light of the dispenser. She allowed herself a wide grin as she recounted the events of the past half hour or so. Her body was positively singing, the after-effects of the falls and automobile crash mere whispers.

Which was why she never heard the footsteps, never saw even a shadow. Only the cold hard flat surface against her throat told her she wasn't alone.

"Make a sound and I'll slit you from ear to ear."

Chapter 17

Phoebe involuntarily jerked, and the motion hit the glass upside the refrigerator before it dropped to the wooden floor and shattered into pieces. The sound reverberated in the large open room. The exact opposite of what the female intruder had demanded.

"Ariella?"

"What did I tell you?" Ariella's voice snarled like a rabid dog, and Phoebe closed her eyes, tried to brace for the inevitable. She'd only met her once but hadn't forgotten the woman's deep, angry voice. With a knife to her throat she wanted to scream, or sob, anything to let the pain out. Phoebe wanted more, she wanted a lifetime with Prescott. But instead she was going to end up the murder victim of a stalking ex.

No. Think.

She was bigger than the slight actress, and running had given her stamina. Phoebe had never expected to use her physicality in this way, but she'd do anything to fight Ariella. The woman couldn't be mentally stable, not if she was doing this. Once she killed Phoebe, she'd go after Prescott.

Prescott.

Phoebe's opened her eyes and looked around the small kitchen area, assessing her options.

"Stop moving, bitch!" Ariella dug the blade in deeper, and Phoebe knew at that point that she had no choice but to fight. Otherwise she'd end up with a slit throat, her future with Prescott over before it began.

Phoebe drew on the self-defense classes Russ had insisted she and Skye take as teenagers. In one deft move she shoved her elbow into the woman's gut and slammed down her bare heel on her instep.

A sharp howl of pain loosened Ariella's grip around Phoebe's neck, and she took her one chance. Grabbing the woman's forearm from around her neck, Phoebe tugged, hard. Ariella stared at her in surprise, holding the knife out and pointed at Phoebe's heart.

Phoebe faced death in the face. Ariella's mouth curved up into an evil grin and her eyes sparkled with hate.

"You're mine, you stupid bitch." Ariella moved the knife closer to Phoebe's heart.

Prescott woke the minute Phoebe left his side and got up, awkwardly shoving himself into shorts with one hand. Their coming together had been a long time in the works, as far as he was concerned. They'd only met less than two weeks ago, but Phoebe was the woman he'd waited his life for. And he intended to tell her, now. He grabbed a couple of condoms from the box and put them in his front pocket. It'd be fun to explore each nook and cranny of her body on the futon, the living room floor, up against the kitchen counter—

Prescott heard the glass break and had the hunting rifle he'd stowed under the bed in his good hand in a second. He'd loaded it just in case. Tiptoeing to the doorway, he listened.

And heard Ariella's voice. He hit the panic button that was in the nightstand and turned to go after the woman who threatened the love he'd only just found. The local police would be here in minutes, but that could prove too long.

No one was going to take Phoebe away from him.

As much as he trusted the local police force, he knew that somehow Ariella had gotten around the security system and was in the barn. That meant she was here for one reason—to hurt Phoebe.

He walked into the great room, the rifle pointing in front of him. The sight of Phoebe backed up against the kitchen counter shook him. The glint off the six-inch blade in Ariella's hand galvanized his anger into laser-focused determination.

Phoebe was not going to be hurt again.

Prescott moved farther into the room, not wanting to give Ariella any reason to move in closer on Phoebe.

He saw the fear on her face, but he also witnessed the sheer strength that she'd been revealing to him, layer by layer, all week. This was the woman he wanted to spend the rest of his life with.

He saw her eyes land on him, briefly, before she put her total focus back on Ariella. He wanted her to know he was here, ready to back her up. A wave of powerlessness reminded him that he wasn't in a position to do anything for Phoebe. If he shot Ariella now, he'd risk taking Phoebe out, too. Not an option.

"You'll never have him. If you'd have paid attention to the message I left you back at that stupid Chateau, it wouldn't have had to come down to this."

"It doesn't have to come down to anything, Ariella. We can talk this over. I understand what it's like to be the one that no one hears. Let's sit down at the table and have an adult conversation about this." Phoebe had to be scared out of her mind, yet she maintained steady eye contact with Ariella, and her voice didn't waver. He could still see only her face, and the flash of the blade as Ariella wielded it under her nose, but always brought it back to rest near Phoebe's heart.

"You're not too smart for a Colton, do you know that? The time for talking is over. I'm going to kill you and then pick up the pieces for Prescott."

"Prescott's not here. He left to go back to the farmhouse." Phoebe's lie hit him in the gut. She was trying to protect him.

Ariella's head tilted back as she laughed maniacally at the ceiling. Phoebe still couldn't make a break for it, as the knife was now up against her chest. But Ariella's head had moved enough for Prescott to see Phoebe's throat—and the blood that oozed from a knife wound.

It ends here.

Phoebe felt Prescott's strength from across the room and saw that he was holding the rifle, ready to shoot. She wanted to look at him but couldn't. Ariella was behaving too erratically, and there was the small problem of the knife blade that the woman kept pressed against her sternum. If Phoebe moved the wrong way, or Ariella leaned in any closer, it'd all be over. And not in a good way.

Phoebe had just found her heart match, and she'd be damned if Ariella would put a knife through it all now.

"Listen to me, Ariella, this isn't worth it. I'm not worth it."

"You stupid bitch, it's time for you to shut—"

"Put the knife down, Ariella, or I'm going to shoot you from here till tomorrow." Prescott's timbre cut through Ariella's words as it boomed across the narrow space, bringing a point of light into what had become Phoebe's worst nightmare. If she died now, she'd be of no use to Skye, and she'd miss out on the great life she'd only just caught a glimpse of.

She'd lose the love of her life before she had a chance to tell him how she felt.

"Forget it, Prescott, forget her." Ariella managed to stay facing Phoebe and answer Prescott over her shoulder as she wielded the knife like a magic wand, eager for Prescott to see she had the power to kill Phoebe. His eyes narrowed, but he never wavered with his aim.

Prescott didn't spare Phoebe a glance as he pointed the hunting rifle at Ariella. He stood bare-chested with only a pair of shorts on, without his sling. He had the butt nestled in his bad shoulder, but he showed no sign of being in pain. Only the paleness of his face revealed his discomfort.

Phoebe followed suit and returned her gaze to the delusional woman.

"Ariella." She prayed she'd get through to her. Or that the hunting rifle would.

"Shut up! This is about me and Prescott. That's what you've never understood." Ariella looked at her and still didn't move the knife.

"Drop the knife, Ariella." Prescott stepped closer.

"You'll never shoot me, baby. I'm the only one for you."

Ariella turned around and waved the knife at Prescott. She knew that he'd never shoot her, not with Phoebe behind her.

"Put the knife down." Prescott's face was like granite as he issued the command. "You're not going to get out of this alive otherwise, Ariella. The police are on their way."

Phoebe wondered if he was bluffing. She'd had no clue Ariella was on the property much less already in the barn. And Prescott had been sleeping when she'd slipped out of bed.

"No! You listen to me." Ariella backed up until her back was pressed against Phoebe's front. With the counter at her backside, Phoebe had nowhere to go but forward. Phoebe watched Ariella's arm wave the knife about. Her stomach sank. It was going to be up to her to neutralize Ariella—Prescott would kill both of them if he shot at her. Even though Prescott had a firearm, Ariella could take him out with one strategic throw of the lethal blade, and she knew it. Phoebe had to act. She waited for the moment to grab the woman and take her down, out of reach of Prescott.

"Whoa, calm down." Prescott lowered the rifle but still held the end of the barrel in his good hand.

"*You* calm down, Prescott." Ariella's voice was a feral growl, and Phoebe knew her eyes probably reflected how disturbed she was. The woman was past reasoning, but Prescott had a calming effect on her nonetheless. At least she still hadn't stabbed either one of them. Yet.

"I'm listening, Ariella. Tell me what you want." Prescott appeared to genuinely care about what the woman had to say. Phoebe knew it had to be his award-winning acting skills, because she saw how he held the butt of the rifle, ready to whip it up and fire if needed.

"This can be fixed, Prescott." Ariella wheedled with him. "I'll forgive you for taking up with this bitch, but you have to make the decision to come with me now. We'll go off the radar for a month or two, until all of this dies down. Then we can go back to work, both of us, and be bigger than ever." Ariella kept the knife moving but never gave Phoebe an inch to get past her. Phoebe had to act quickly, but a stupid move could prove deadly.

Go for it.

Prescott stood facing down their stalker, with only a pair of shorts on and a rifle against his leg, risking his life for her. Their gazes connected, and she knew in that nanosecond that Prescott felt the same as she did. They had so much to live for. Whatever the cost, it was worth the attempt to win it all.

Phoebe inched her hand onto the counter and infinitesimally reached her fingers to grasp the hem of one of the custom fabric appliance covers she'd admired when they'd walked into the barn apartment. It covered the large coffeemaker, and she'd have to move in one motion to make her plan work.

Never breaking eye contact with Prescott, she got the cover off the machine. One last look at Prescott and she saw his almost imperceptible nod—her go signal.

"Aaaaaah!" Phoebe ignored Ariella's protests as she covered the woman's head with the cloth sack, ducking from the knife's blade that Ariella tried to blindly stab her with.

"That's enough!" Prescott moved the moment Phoebe covered Ariella's head and had her wrists captured with both hands—Phoebe knew he had to be in excruciating pain—and forced the knife to drop out of her grip. The blade fell vertically and landed handle up, the blade tip solidly planted in the hardwood floor.

Phoebe didn't let her mind go to the images of what that blade would have done to Prescott's bare chest. Ariella still struggled between them, kicking out and behind. The sound of heavy footsteps up the back stairs, followed by a solid *thwack* as the door was forced open, was music to Phoebe's ears.

"We have her." Prescott shouted and then nodded at someone. A man wearing a helmet and full body armor raised his visor, and Phoebe recognized Tom Briscoe. He led a team of four uniformed SWAT officers. A female officer stepped forward and cuffed Ariella as she read her Miranda rights. Prescott handed Tom his hunting rifle and gathered Phoebe close. She wrapped her arms around him and clung to him for several minutes as the police scoured the apartment for any other intruders and then escorted Ariella outside. The steady beat of his heart under her ear was all Phoebe needed.

"I'm going to need a statement from each of you." Tom had returned and motioned for them to take a seat at the small table.

Prescott looked at her. "You up for this, babe?"

"I'm up for anything as long as it's with you."

Prescott's parents arrived once the police had lifted the order for them to stay hunkered down in the farmhouse. Both Phoebe and Prescott reassured them they were okay and urged them to go back to bed, which they did but only after Prescott promised they'd come up for breakfast in the morning.

After his parents left the barn, they sat with Tom for at least an hour as he and another police officer entered data into their laptops. Phoebe had been taken to the bedroom to give her statement separately, as did Prescott in the kitchen.

Once they'd finished, Phoebe made coffee for all of

them and brought out more of the strawberry shortcake that Jeannie had stocked the fridge with.

"You got here faster than I imagined you would." Prescott reached for Phoebe's hand as he spoke to Tom. He'd put a shirt on, and she thought she'd never be able to leave his side again.

"We were already on-site. When one of the officers saw that the cameras had been shot out and then your call came in, I made the decision to go." Tom looked at Prescott, then Phoebe. "You two okay?"

"I'm fine, but Prescott's shoulder can't feel that great." Phoebe had to stop herself from touching Prescott all over—she didn't want to embarrass him in front of his lifelong friend.

Prescott shrugged with his uninjured side. "It's fine. Trust me, it's a helluva lot better than having a knife put through it. If she'd hurt you, Phoebe—" The anguish in his eyes was bottomless. Phoebe knew, because she felt the same about losing him.

"No one got hurt, save for the scrape on your neck. And the nightmares you might have for a bit. The bottom line is that you both kept cool heads and got through it." Tom must have seen Prescott's tortured expression. "You're free to leave Iowa now, Phoebe. But I have to warn you that we weren't certain it was only Ariella stalking you until tonight. Daria Bloom has kept me informed that they're still on the lookout for the Avalanche Killer. With your sister missing, it's logical to think he'd come after you, too."

Shudders racked her and Prescott's arm was around her, pulling her close up against his side.

"I have to go back and help my family out. We have to find my sister."

Prescott and Tom exchanged a glance she couldn't completely decipher, but she thought it had something to with the way Prescott was acting in front of his best friend.

"You're not going anywhere alone, Phoebe. I'll take you back home."

"It's your time off—you stay here." Even as she said it, she knew what she wanted.

He grasped her chin, not seeming to mind that Tom sat right across from them. "You go nowhere without me, Phoebe Colton." And then he kissed her. The gentle caress started as a comfort but turned into a heated expression of their mutual need.

"I'll show myself out, and fill your parents in on what's happened before I leave the farm."

They broke apart at Tom's proclamation, but he'd already cleared the door and shut it behind him.

"That was rude of us." Phoebe smiled up at Prescott.

"No, it would have been rude if we'd done what we're about to do in front of him."

Chapter 18

Two days later Prescott drove the rental SUV up to The Chatcau's majestic, sweeping drive. Security cleared the way for them, past the large crowd of press gathered for their announcement.

The Coltons were making Skye's disappearance public. Because she and Phoebe were identical, Phoebe had to be present to give viewers the best idea of what Skye looked like.

He stopped the car and grabbed her hand. "Wait, babe."

"I wish I didn't have to get out of this car. That Skye was here to meet us, too."

He leaned over and kissed her tenderly. The heat between them simmered, and he couldn't wait to be alone in her Chateau apartment once they'd made their press statement. "She'll be back soon. We have to keep the faith."

"I can handle anything with you by my side." Phoebe gave him a quicker kiss and put her hand on the car door. "I've got to go out now." Her father, Russ, stood just outside her door, waiting to let her out.

"Go. I'm coming around." He slipped out of his door and walked in front of the SUV. Prescott watched as Phoebe's family embraced her. One by one, from Mara, Russ, each of her siblings. The three older brothers he hadn't met, Wyatt, Decker and Blaine. The adopted brother and sister, Fox and Sloane, who were also her biological cousins. The kids who'd been running around The Chateau all last week, Josh and Chloe, were adorable as they hugged their auntie Phoebe. Even the security man and some other hotel workers Prescott didn't know took their time to embrace Phoebe. Skye's absence was sorrowfully palpable.

"Thanks for coming." Phoebe spoke to her entire family. "We didn't need everyone here for the press conference, but it's so great to see everyone." She scanned the group. "Where's Molly?" Prescott knew that Molly was her cousin and Sabrina's sister. Molly had had a big scare during the avalanche last spring when she and the father of her unborn baby had been trapped in a gondola for six hours.

"She and Max are on an extended holiday." Mara spoke up and Prescott made a mental note to ask Phoebe later if Molly was in hiding from the Avalanche Killer.

"Prescott." Russ approached him, hand out. They

shook. "Thank you for taking such good care of my little girl. And I'm sorry about the cover-up regarding Skye."

"I won't ever let anything happen to her, Russ. I'd like your permission to make it official." He met the older man's gaze and waited to receive what he needed. A nod.

An angular man with features similar to Phoebe's walked up to him. "Hey Prescott. I'm Blaine, Phoebe's older brother." A woman was with him, and she smiled.

"I'm Tilda."

"Nice to meet you both. Phoebe tells me you're engaged?"

Blaine smiled. "Yeah, we are. It's a tough time, but we figure the family needs something happy to look forward to. We're going to get married at the Lodge."

"Congratulations." Prescott hoped Phoebe's family didn't mind more than one wedding in the near future.

"Prescott, can you please join Phoebe with Daria at the podium?" Members of the security team shook his hand and motioned to the wooden stand that had microphones from at least a half dozen media outlets. A uniformed Daria stood next to a tall man in a sheriff's uniform, whom Prescott knew had to be Trey Colton. Phoebe had filled him in that Trey and Daria were working around the clock to identify the victims from the bodies discovered at the base of the mountain after the avalanche last spring. Trey was running for reelection and his reputation had taken a beating, which according to Phoebe wasn't deserved.

"Sure thing."

Phoebe's eyes were sad, but when he reached her side, she looked at him and he saw what he'd hoped—trust. She trusted him to stay by her side through this awful nightmare.

He placed his arm around her waist. "You ready, babe?"

She nodded. "I am."

The sheriff kicked off the press conference, stating that the Avalanche Killer was still at large and they were working with RSPD and the FBI to nab the criminal. Daria stepped in and explained that Skye Colton was suspected to have been abducted by the Avalanche Killer, and they needed all citizens to be on the lookout for her, the identical twin of Phoebe. Russ took the mic and explained that Phoebe had posed as Skye last week, to keep the festival going and to stop any panic about another missing young woman. Mara spoke up and pleaded for whoever had taken her daughter to let her go.

Prescott hated watching Phoebe suffer, but he had a hope in his heart that the Coltons were far stronger than any criminal. They'd find Skye and apprehend the serial killer.

"Prescott, what's your status with Skye Colton?"

A noted reporter from a major network asked the question, and Prescott looked at Phoebe. They'd anticipated this. But Phoebe didn't know what he was about to do, along with answering the question.

"Good afternoon. As you've already figured out, Skye Colton wasn't here all last week. Phoebe and I were the couple that you all took such great photos of."

Some chuckles erupted from the press as they knew that he hadn't wanted all the attention on his private life. But it had been public, during the festival.

"Are you two dating, then?"

"Absolutely." He looked into Phoebe's eyes. Tears shimmered, and while he knew they were for her sister's sake, he also saw what he'd known was in his heart. Pure love. He turned back to the reporters for a final statement. "We're more than dating. With Phoebe's agreement, we're going to make this official sometime soon."

The reporters broke into a melee of questions, but he heard none of it. All he saw was Phoebe and the tremulous smile through her tears. Shielding her from the cameras with his body, he embraced her.

"I can't ask you properly, not now, and not here. The fact is that I'm in love with you. I love you, Phoebe Colton. Are you okay with spending the rest of your life with me?"

She didn't speak but reached up and kissed him, then pressed her finger to his lips as if afraid he'd retract his proposal. "Yes, Prescott. I love you, too. Forever."

* * * * *

Get 4 FREE REWARDS!

We'll send you 2 FREE Books plus 2 FREE Mystery Gifts.

Harlequin® Romantic Suspense books feature heart-racing sensuality and the promise of a sweeping romance set against the backdrop of suspense.

FREE Value Over $20

Remo took a very slow, very careful look up and down
the alley. The side closest to them was clear. But the
other? Not so much. Just outside Remo's mom's place,
the man Celia had so cleverly distracted was engaged in
a visibly heated discussion with another guy, presumably
the one from the car his mother had noted.

Remo drew his head back into the yard and hazarded
a whisper. "Company's still out there. We can wait and
see what happens, or we can slip out and make a run for
it. Move low and quick along the outside of the fence."

Celia met his eyes, and he expected her to pick the
former. Instead, she said, "On the count of three?"

He couldn't keep the surprise from his voice. "Really?"

She answered in a quick, sure voice. "I know it's
risky, but it's not like staying here is totally safe, either. A
neighbor will eventually notice us and give us away. Or
call the police and give Teller a legitimate reason to chase
us. And at least this way, those guys out there don't know

that we know they're here. Right now, they're trying to flush us out quietly."

"As long as you're sure."

"I'm sure."

He put a hand on Xavier's back. "You want to ride with me, buddy?"

The kid turned and stretched out his arms, and Remo took him from his mom and settled him against his hip, then reached for Celia's hand.

"One," he said softly.

"Two," she replied.

"Three," piped up Xavier in his own little whisper.

And they went for it.

Don't miss
First Responder on Call *by Melinda Di Lorenzo,*
available August 2019 wherever
Harlequin® Romantic Suspense books
and ebooks are sold.

www.Harlequin.com